# TEN
# RULES
## FOR
### *Marrying* A
# DUKE

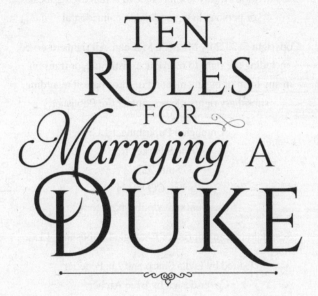

# TEN RULES FOR Marrying A DUKE

USA TODAY BESTSELLING AUTHOR
## MICHELLE McLEAN

Entangled Publishing, LLC
10940 S Parker Rd
Suite 327
Parker, CO 80134
rights@entangledpublishing.com

Scandalous is an imprint of Entangled Publishing, LLC.

Edited by Lydia Sharp and Liz Pelletier
Cover design by Bree Archer
Cover images from Period Images
Jeremy D. Smith/Getty Images

ISBN 978-1-64937-323-6

Manufactured in the United States of America

First Edition February 2022

*To all those who believe rules were made to be broken.*
*(Except for the ones I make for my kids…you two better follow those!)*

# Chapter One

"A respectable lady would never blackmail her way into matrimony."

The Honorable Miss Arabella Bromley glanced at Charlotte—The Right Honorable Lady Waterstack, if one wanted to be fussy about it— and rolled her eyes.

"Yes, my dear Charlotte, you are quite correct. However, what I am about to do is less blackmail and more bargaining, from my point of view. Besides, the question of my respectability is what created the necessity for this small deception in the first place."

Charlotte folded her arms and sat back against the carriage cushions. "You had, until recently I'll grant you, excellent marriage prospects. If you'd had any desire to take advantage of them."

"Which I did not," Arabella said, pushing her spectacles up her nose so she could keep her eyes glued to the window and the doorway beyond it, through which her salvation would hopefully be exiting. Any moment now. "And now it's too late. My family's reputation is in tatters, and I'll never get a husband who can help me fix this whole mess short of some sort of trickery. Well…trickery is the wrong word…"

"What would be the right word, then?" Charlotte smiled sweetly at her, but Arabella didn't buy it for a second. Charlotte at her sweetest was very dangerous indeed.

Arabella didn't answer her but went back to watching the door.

She wasn't any happier about her present course of action than Charlotte. Decidedly less so. But her choices were limited and her problems plentiful, and she would do what must be done.

The moment her eldest sister, Alice, had eloped with their groom, Arabella's desires ceased to matter. What mattered now was getting their younger sister Anne suitably wed. A prospect that seemed nearly impossible now that their family name was irreparably tarnished. No one wanted to marry the sister of a woman with so little regard for herself, her family, and her position in life that she would hastily marry someone so far beneath her. They looked at the pretty and vivacious Anne and assumed that she must be just as flighty and morally bankrupt as her sister. If not more so. She'd never find a suitable match. At least not one who would make her happy and give her the comfort and status in life she deserved.

As for Arabella…well, no one had ever looked

at or thought of her much. Which was how she preferred it. She would be quite content as a dried-up old spinster, alone in a quiet room with her books.

But this wasn't about what she wanted anymore. Anne had been inconsolable since Alice had eloped and the invitations began to dry up.

What they needed was a champion. A high-ranking champion no one would dare cross, who could ease them back into society's good graces and facilitate a suitable, and perhaps even advantageous, match for Anne.

And Arabella knew just the man. Silas Spencer, Duke of Whittsley. A distant cousin to the Queen, he was of a rank and status far above Arabella's own, despite her baronet father and relatively wealthy family. He was a bit rakish and too unserious for Arabella's tastes, but his background was impeccable, and his opinions carried great weight. If he accepted the Bromleys, society would follow. And no one would dare besmirch or shun his wife or in-laws.

"Ari," Charlotte said, leaning forward to get her attention. "If you insist on this absurdity, surely there are more suitable gentlemen to ask."

Arabella shook her head. "A more suitable gentleman wouldn't deign to listen to me, let alone go along with it."

"And you think he will?"

Arabella hesitated before answering. "I think I have a better chance of convincing him than I do anyone else. He's a bit eccentric, a prankster. A scheme like this might pique his interest, at least long enough to hear me out."

Charlotte sat back with a huff. "That may be so, but I still do not see why you think he will actually agree to your plans."

"Because, while there is certainly no shortage of women who would happily marry him—women who are, I'll admit, more suited to life as his duchess—he has made no secret of the fact that he has absolutely no interest in marriage. The last thing he wants is a wife as a permanent fixture on his arm."

"And this makes him perfect in your plot to get married, how exactly?"

Arabella smiled. "He still needs an heir. He is the last male descendant in his line. Unless he produces a son, his title will revert to the Crown. Even he can't shirk his familial duty forever. To get a legitimate heir, he'll have to wed."

"And unlike the throngs of women vying to be his wife, you want as little to do with him as he, presumably, wants to do with you?"

"Exactly."

Charlotte closed her eyes and rubbed her brow. "Your logic is making my head fit for cracking."

Arabella shoved her spectacles back up on her

nose and smiled. She did tend to have that effect on poor Charlotte.

"It's simple, Charlotte. Most women marrying someone of his stature will want to take advantage of their new position. They'll want to be seen, paraded around the country, soaking up the prestige and attention that comes with being the Duchess of Whittsley. And rightly so. But for a man who does not wish for a wife, this is surely a daunting prospect. I, however, would not only happily accept exile in the country, but I shall insist upon it. Once he helps my sister, of course."

"And once you conceive an heir."

Arabella grimaced. "Right." She took a deep breath, trying to calm the riot in her stomach at the thought of what she must to do uphold her end of the bargain. "In any case, I'll make no additional demands upon him. Once Anne is suitably wed, and…an heir is conceived…then we can go our separate ways. We'll both get what we need and then get back to our own lives."

Charlotte shook her head. "I still think this is recklessly ill-advised."

Arabella grinned. "Quite possibly. But that doesn't mean it won't work." She looked back out the window. "Assuming I can speak with him without causing another horrendous scandal."

Charlotte snorted delicately. "Good luck with that."

Before Arabella could say anything else, the door of the townhouse in front of which they waited opened, and she sat up with a gasp, her hand on the carriage door handle.

"There he is."

Her heart pounded in her throat. She had to time this perfectly. Alight too early and she might get a tip of the hat, but they could hardly converse in the street. Too late, and she'd miss her chance altogether. No, she had to time this…just…right…

Another few steps would bring the duke right in front of the carriage. All she needed to do was fake a tumble and fall gracefully at his feet. Shouldn't be too difficult.

Arabella closed her eyes, took a deep breath, and threw the carriage door open. Then she lurched forward as her dress caught on her boot heel, sending her careening out onto the street with a squeal of dismay.

• • •

Silas wasn't quite sure what happened. One moment, he'd been turning onto the sidewalk outside his townhouse, and the next, his arms were full of a squirming ball of feminine frippery.

"Hello, there," he said, trying to set her to rights as quickly as possible while she batted at her skirts like they were attacking her.

He set her back on her feet, straightening her hat and handing her the spectacles that had been hanging from one dainty ear. But the moment she put weight on her ankle, her face drained of color and her mouth opened in a soundless gasp.

"Op! Careful," he said, reaching for her again. He knew he was being terribly forward, but he couldn't exactly let her crumple to the street.

"Ari!" Another woman with bouncy blond ringlets stuck her head out from the carriage before quickly alighting. "Are you all right?"

"Fine," the woman in his arms said, though her voice was strained.

"I believe you might have injured yourself," he said. "I live just here. Perhaps it would be best…"

"That would be wonderful," the blond woman said, answering before the injured woman could say a word.

"Lady Waterstack," he said, finally recognizing her.

"Your Grace." She gave him a faint smile, though her eyes kept straying to her friend. "This is a dear friend of mine, Miss Arabella Bromley."

"Bromley," he asked, raising an eyebrow. "Lord Durborough's daughter?"

"Yes, I am Lord Durborough's daughter," the woman answered before Lady Waterstack could.

He gazed down into a pair of warm brown eyes, the gold flecks around the irises highlighted by the gold rims of the spectacles perched on the end of her rather blunt nose. She noticed him looking and quickly took them off, shoving them into the pocket of her skirts.

She needn't be self-conscious about them. Far from detracting from her looks, they added an interesting focal point to her face. Under normal circumstances, he'd point that out, but she seemed rattled enough as it was without him drawing attention to something that obviously caused her discomfort. At least at the moment.

Even without the spectacles lending some charm to her face, she had rather attractive features. When considered separately. Full pink lips. Cheekbones high enough to save her face from roundness but not so much as to appear sharp. Soft blond hair that seemed to have a tendency toward waviness, if the tendrils that had escaped from their pins were any indication.

And those eyes. Those velvety brown eyes that, upon closer inspection, also held hints of green, and more importantly, shone with intelligence and, at the moment, annoyance.

Yes, taken one at a time, they were very pleasing features indeed. Yet somehow, when observed as a whole, the picture became somewhat…muddled. Though perhaps that was more due to the red splotches on her otherwise pale face. Or the fact that her eyes had narrowed, and her lips pinched.

Distress did not agree with her.

He belatedly realized that the poor woman might be distressed because he still had his arms around her in full view of the entire street and had been scrutinizing her for the last several moments when she was obviously in pain from her injured ankle.

He hastily stepped back, allowing Lady Waterstack to take his place. "Please, I insist you come inside and rest your ankle for a moment."

"Very well," she said. "That is most kind of you, Your Grace."

He ushered them inside, his eyebrows rising again at the speed at which the ladies moved. It seemed Miss Bromley's injured ankle might not be as injured as he had thought. Interesting…

Once she was settled on a sofa in his drawing room with her ankle propped up, Silas sent a servant out for tea.

"Oh, look at the lovely plants. I think I'll just…"

Lady Waterstack gave her friend a hard look before quickly taking herself to the other end of the room where she wandered through the open doors and into the conservatory. She glanced back once before busying herself with a book she found on a table beside the door, giving them as much privacy as possible. She was still visible but decidedly out of earshot, leaving them, essentially, alone.

Intriguing, indeed.

Silas sat on the chair near Arabella. "Now, Miss Bromley, how may I be of service to you?"

She blinked at him, either confused or unsure how to proceed. He leaned forward slightly so he could speak quietly. "Your acting skills require a bit more polish before you can debut them on the London stage, I'm afraid."

Her mouth dropped open in shock and he rubbed a finger across his lips to keep from smiling before continuing. "As it is painfully obvious that you are not in true distress, physically at least, I can only deduce that you needed an audience with me for some reason. So, I ask again, how may I be of service?"

She hesitated for a moment, then nodded and dropped her foot back to the floor, smoothing down her skirts. Then she stood and took a deep breath. "You require an heir."

This time, he blinked up at her, momentarily flabbergasted. He tilted his head, looking her over. "That is true. Are you offering to bear me one?"

Her face flushed scarlet, but her head jerked in a quick nod. He sucked his lips between his teeth and bit down, trying to keep his face neutral. She could *not* be offering what she seemed to be. But since the cheeky little thing was in his parlor, offering to bear his children, and, he presumed, engaging in the activity that would bring that about, he didn't feel too poorly about playing with her. Just a bit.

He stood as well, smoothed his vest down, and gave her a small bow. "That is a very kind and, I must admit, intriguing offer, Miss Bromley. However, any child I may have must be legitimate, so I'm afraid I will not be able to accept."

Her eyes grew as round as saucers and her mouth dropped open again, all color leaching from her face. He allowed her a moment to recover from her shock, though it was physically painful to keep from laughing.

"N—n—no. That's not what I meant at all," she stammered. "Of course, you'll require a *wife* first." She spoke the word as though she were spitting out glass.

He raised an eyebrow. "Are you offering to find me a wife before providing me with an heir?" He tilted his head again, forehead creasing in mock confusion. "Again, kind of you, but I can't imagine any wife being happy about another woman bearing her husband's child."

Miss Bromley sputtered, and Silas felt just the slightest bit of guilt at goading her, but by the gods, it was the most entertainment he'd had in a fortnight.

"Or," he said, taking pity, "are you proposing marriage yourself, Miss Bromley?"

Her face flushed again, then drained of all color completely, and then turned a strange sort of mottled pink before she dropped to the sofa and put her head in her hands. She moaned.

"I'm making such a mess of this. You must think I am utterly preposterous," she muttered through her hands.

He chuckled and sat again, reaching forward to remove her hands from her face. "The thought has crossed my mind, yes. Why don't you start at the beginning, and we'll go from there?"

She took a deep breath and blew it out slowly. "Very well. I'm sure you're aware of my family's recent difficulties."

He hesitated and then decided to be completely forthright. "If you are referring to the unfortunate situation with your elder sister, then yes. I have heard a bit here and there." More than that actually, but he didn't wish to distress her with the sordid rumors that were floating about if she were not aware of them. Or remind her of them if she were.

She nodded sharply. "As you can imagine, this has harmed my family's position irreparably. For myself, I do not care. I am perfectly happy to live an obscure life in the country. But I have a younger sister... She was presented at court last year but came down with a dreadful illness that kept her from most of the festivities and cut her season short. She hoped to return this year and make a good match, but now...under the circumstances…"

Silas nodded. As unfair as it was, their elder sister's decision to run off with the family groom had certainly put her sisters' reputations in question. After all, if one sister behaved so injudiciously, the others would be presumed to follow her example.

"And you believe I can help with the situation?" he asked.

She nodded once but didn't elaborate.

His finger rubbed across his lips while he regarded her for a moment. "And how does my need of an heir play into all this?"

She dragged in another deep breath and closed her eyes, as if not being able to see him would make saying the words easier. "You need an heir. I need a husband for my sister. I thought we could help each other."

"So…you wish me to marry your sister?"

Her eyes flew open, and he hurried to dissuade her of any other foolish notions in her head. "I'm honored you deem me worthy of your sister, however, I have no wish for a wife, despite my apparent need of an heir, and—"

"Heavens no, that's not at all what I was proposing. You'd be the last person I'd want for her—"

He raised both eyebrows at that, and she blushed. "I only meant the thought *had* crossed my mind as it would settle your respective issues nicely. However, I do not believe it would be a good match."

"You flatter me," he said, drolly.

"I mean no offense, it is only…" An exasperated breath left her in a rush. "My sister is young, barely more than eighteen, and she craves excitement and all the advantages a husband could bring her. From what I have observed and know of you, you have even less desire to marry than I. So, becoming the husband of a woman who very much wishes to be a wife would be…disastrous."

Well, he couldn't fault that logic. It was, in fact, the reason he'd avoided matrimony for so long. Rather the way a ship would avoid a barnacle if it could. "Agreed," he said.

"I would like for my sister to find a husband, but I also want her to be happy. And…I do not think she would be so with you," she said slowly, as though she were afraid her words would insult him. And so they would, if he didn't wholeheartedly concur.

"Again, I agree. So then, where do you fit into all this?"

"Unlike my sister, I do not wish to be a wife."

"Ah. So, you think that makes you the perfect wife for me?" His lips twitched. He was simultaneously amused and horrified and yet unable to stop the current events from unfolding right before his eyes. He had to see how far she would carry this out. Frankly, he was surprised and a bit dismayed she hadn't already bolted. For all her blushes, the woman had a spine of steel, that much was evident.

She covered her face with her hands again. "This is all such a muddle."

He chuckled quietly and, again, reached forward to take her hands, only this time he kept them in his own. "Just say it quickly and get it over with."

Her eyes flashed to him and then she pulled herself together, firming her shoulders and sitting ramrod straight. "If you will marry me, help restore my family's honor and respectability, and find my sister a good match, I will provide you with the legitimate heir you need. After which, I wish nothing more than to quietly retire to your country estate and disappear from your life. You may do as you please."

It was much as he'd thought, though hearing it from her lips still made his head spin. And… "My country estate?"

She raised an eyebrow. "That is your only question?"

He shrugged and let go of her hands, sitting back in his chair to observe her. "For the moment."

Her cheeks pinkened again. "The library at Fallcreek Abbey is famed throughout the country."

He couldn't help the grin that broke out. "You wish to marry me for my library?"

Her eyes narrowed. "No. I require your help with my sister. The library is…a perk."

"Of course. And in exchange, you'll provide me with an heir and let me go on my merry way?"

She jerked her head in a quick nod.

He sat back, stunned. And intrigued. And… tempted.

His eyes unabashedly roamed over her from the top of the prim hat pinned to her simply coiffed hair to the tip of the surprisingly large foot that stuck out from beneath her dress. There were certainly far more beautiful women who vied for his hand. But none had ever caught his attention quite so completely. Miss Bromley was a walking contradiction full of surprises. What other secrets did those golden-brown eyes of hers hide?

Still…

He sighed and shook his head. "It's an intriguing offer, but one I must decline."

He stood and held out a hand to escort her to the door, but she remained seated, her forehead crinkled.

"Why?"

It was his turn to frown. "Why what?"

"Why are you declining?"

She couldn't be serious. "Because, aside from this being the most ludicrous scheme I've ever heard—and believe me, that is a compliment because I could tell you some tales—and despite the apparent advantages of said scheme, I have no wish to force matrimony on a woman who clearly does not want it. Especially since I do not want it myself."

She frowned harder. "It's not the marriage I object to, it's being a wife that isn't appealing."

"Yes, but you can't have one without the other."

"But that is exactly what I'm proposing. Think of it as a temporary marriage."

He dropped back to his chair and leaned forward, beginning to enjoy their battle. "Yes, but you are failing to acknowledge the fundamental flaw in your plan."

"Which is?" she asked, her eyes narrowing dangerously.

"You say now that you have no wish to be a wife and will neatly disappear once our bargain is concluded. But I have no guarantee that you will remain set in your resolve. Perhaps you'll find you enjoy your new status and will wish to continue to be my very public and present wife. And then I'm stuck with you."

Her eyes flashed. "Are you saying you're afraid I'll become so enamored with you that I will refuse to honor our agreement?"

He shrugged, pinning her with his most

roguish smile. "Stranger things have happened."

She raised a delicate brow. "I can assure you no such thing will happen with me."

"Oh? I'm rather a catch. And quite charming, so I'm told."

Her lips twitched. "Yes, I'm sure you're told rather a lot of things."

Ha! Saucy little thing. He ignored that. "And should you become so besotted—"

"I won't."

"But you might."

"But I won't."

"But you *might*."

Miss Bromley bit her lip, though whether it was to keep from laughing or screaming, he wasn't sure.

"Assuming anyone would wish to be stuck with you is a rather bold assumption, Your Grace."

He gave her a lopsided grin. That mousy exterior of hers hid a hint of a lioness. A scrawny, fragile, and probably toothless lioness, undoubtedly. But a feisty one, nonetheless.

"A bold assumption, yes," he said, "but my point stands."

Those golden eyes narrowed as they watched him. "Then you wish a guarantee?"

"Yes."

"Then I give you my word," she said with a nod, as if that decided it all.

"Which is trustworthy, I'm sure, but I'm afraid I require a bit more of a guarantee than just your word."

She tensed, her entire body going rigid at the implied insult. If she were a man, he'd expect to be called out after that remark. Judging from her expression, she might just do so anyway. Wouldn't that be entertaining?

Instead, she dragged in a deep breath through her nose and briefly closed her eyes before speaking again. "What if I could give you such a guarantee?"

"You can't."

"But if I could?"

"But you can't."

Her eyes narrowed again. "We could add a clause in our marriage contract."

He opened his mouth for another argument but paused. Hmm. "Go on."

Her eyes sparked, and she leaned slightly forward. "We will put it in writing that I will do my utmost to bear you a male heir and then will retire to the country."

"That seems—"

"But," she said, holding up a finger, "we also include that you will expend all your influence and resources to restore my family's reputation and make my sister a brilliant match."

He tapped his finger against his chin. "As part

of the marriage contract, hmm?"

She nodded and folded her hands in her lap, waiting for his answer.

He sat back and watched her while his mind spun. She was right about one thing. He *did* need an heir. Rather desperately. His grandfather had been harping on him to do his family duty for years now, and the older the man got, the worse the harping grew. And the lady was correct. Silas had no wish for a wife who would want his constant attention. He enjoyed his freedom and the way he lived his life. A wife would be a most unwelcome addition.

But…a wife who would provide him with the heir he needed and who was then obliged legally to remove herself? He'd have all the respectability and benefits of a married man without the hassle of actually dealing with a wife. He could trot her out when the occasion demanded it and not have to deal with a doting spouse begging for his attention when it didn't.

As an added bonus, his grandfather would *hate* that Silas had chosen his own wife. His grandfather didn't trust him to choose his own breakfast, let alone a suitable bride. Marrying a Bromley would give the old man indigestion for a year. Though he wouldn't say a word, because at this point, Silas was sure he'd accept anyone as long as it got Silas duly wed.

And it might be quite nice to have a strong, strapping son to carry on his name. So he'd been told. That bit was unavoidable no matter his feelings on it. Besides, he'd had more fun in the last half hour than he'd had in quite a long time. Their time together could be rather…diverting. For a multitude of reasons.

Very well…

He sat up and nodded. "I accept."

# Chapter Two

Arabella squinted at him, not certain she heard him correctly. "You do?"

He raised an eyebrow. "Did you wish for me to say no?"

Her mouth opened and closed for a minute, her mind grasping for an answer. Part of her certainly *had* wished he'd say no, though she was grateful he hadn't.

She sighed. "Of course not. However, if I'm honest, I didn't truly expect you to say yes. Now that you have…I confess I'm at a bit of a loss."

His lips twitched again, and her eyes narrowed further. She understood how ridiculous this must seem, but he didn't need to be so amused about it.

"What happens now?" she asked.

"Well, the marriage contracts, with our special clauses, must be drafted. I'll have to visit with your father to get those in line—"

She gasped, and he broke off and looked at her, eyes widening slightly. "Your father has no idea you are here, does he?"

Heat flooded her cheeks. "No. And I would

be much obliged if you didn't disclose to him the true nature of our...relationship." That eyebrow of his rose again, and she gritted her teeth to keep from rolling her eyes. "I mean, the nature of how it came to be. My father would not approve of my approaching you."

"I should think few fathers would. So, a bit of subterfuge is necessary, then."

She frowned. "I wouldn't put it quite like that."

He chuckled. "There is really no other way to put it as that is exactly what it is. You needn't worry," he said, waving her off before she could protest again. "I shall beg your hand in marriage, claiming I fell completely in love with you the moment you tumbled from that carriage into my arms and can't rest until we are wed."

Arabella pinched her lips together, ignoring the quick flash of longing his declaration inspired. How would it feel to have such a man truly love her so much? A Tristan to her Isolde. A Romeo to her Juliet. An Orpheus to her Eurydice.

Then again, perhaps she should look to less tragic lovers as aspirations for her own life.

"You needn't wax lyrical about it," she said, trying not to grumble. "My father will offer no objection if he believes it's what I truly wish."

"Have no fear, then. I shall keep my lyricism to a minimum."

She narrowed her eyes, unsure whether or not

he mocked her. Before she could decide, he moved on.

"Now, I assume that you want our...arrangement...to begin as soon as possible considering the season is already underway. If your main goal is to get a suitable match for your sister, then we have no time to spare. And to be frank, the sooner I am happily wed with an heir on the way, the less inconvenient my own life will be."

If the sudden icy tightness of her skin were any indication, her face had just drained of all color. How she could be in shock when she was the one who had set these events in motion was a true conundrum. But...everything was just moving so quickly! She glanced over the duke's shoulder to where Charlotte had disappeared. But her friend seemed to have found a kitten lurking in the conservatory and was busily occupied playing with it well out of earshot.

Arabella sucked in a bracing breath and met the duke's gaze, nodding. "Of course. There is no reason to delay."

He slapped his hands down on his knees. "Excellent. Well—"

"Pardon me, Your Grace," a footman said at the door. "But Lord Mosley is here to see you."

All good humor evaporated from the duke's face. "Tell him I'm not at home."

"Begging your pardon, Your Grace, but I tried

that and he's insisting he knows you are here and that—"

"Whittsley!" a voice boomed from the foyer, startling Arabella. "Where are you? I don't have all day."

The duke sighed and pushed up from his chair. "Please excuse me, Miss Bromley. I won't be a moment."

Despite his calm, though annoyed, manner, he hurried from the room, his slightly raised voice immediately joining that of the man beyond the doors.

Arabella leaned over in her seat and caught Charlotte's eye. Charlotte gestured to the door, motioning for Arabella to get closer.

She shouldn't. It was none of her business with whom the duke was speaking, and it certainly was none of her concern what they spoke about. She should keep to her seat and wait patiently for his return.

Her ear was pressed to the crack in the door before those thoughts had faded from her mind. As luck would have it, the footman had left the door slightly ajar, just enough that she could make out the graying hair of the visitor. Judging from the tone with which they spoke to each other, Arabella could only assume Lord Mosley, the duke's maternal grandfather, did not get along with his grandson.

"I'm sorry, Grandfather, but as I've told you, I'm busy just now, so if you'd be so kind as to return later—"

Lord Mosley scoffed. "You have never been busy in your life, my lad, and that is the problem."

"Under normal circumstances, I'd agree with you, but as fate would have it, I *am* actually quite busy at the moment…"

"It can wait. I need to speak with you."

"About what?"

"You married yet?"

A soft choking sound emanated from the duke, and Arabella snorted softly. At least she wasn't the only one on the receiving end of that exasperating line of questioning.

"You came here just to ask me that?"

"I was in the neighborhood."

"I dined with you just this Sunday."

"I'm aware."

"That was four days ago."

"What of it?"

"You think I might have gotten married in the last four days?"

"One can hope. I'd like to see a great-grand-child before I die."

"Well, you're still alive right now, so it appears we have some time."

"Not so much time as all that," Lord Mosley said, waving his walking stick at his grandson.

"You're already thirty years old—"

The duke mock-gasped. "I don't look a day over twenty-five."

Arabella slapped a hand over her mouth to keep from laughing.

"When I was your age, I was already running my father's estates and had produced three children."

"My condolences."

Lord Mosley must have been used to the duke's irreverence, because he patently ignored everything coming out of his mouth, grumbling like an old curmudgeon, though in a surprisingly affectionate way. "I want to see you settled before I die, my boy."

"Well, I don't think you'll die before I come to dinner *this* Sunday. Ask me again then."

He harumphed. "I'll die of impatience waiting for you to make a great-grandfather of me."

"Perish the thought."

"Don't be cheeky."

"I wouldn't dream of it."

"Hmm." Lord Mosley clapped his hat back onto his head. "I'll see you on Sunday."

"Goodbye, Grandfather."

Arabella spun and just managed to plop back in her chair before the duke walked back through the door.

She blinked up at him innocently, trying to strangle her overexerted breath into submission through sheer force of will.

The duke sat silently for a second and then glanced at her. "After we are wed, I'd be much obliged if you were to unabashedly sing my praises whenever we happen to meet the old man," he said, jerking his head toward the door. "If only to see the look on his face to hear someone with a decent opinion of me." He cocked his head. "Assuming you have a decent opinion of me, that is."

Arabella shrugged. "I'm a fair actress when necessary."

He barked out a laugh. "That will do." He took a deep breath and regarded her thoughtfully for a second. "Do you have any requests to make of me while we're on the topic?"

"Requests?" Begging him to marry her seemed like a big enough request to make. She hadn't considered anything else.

"Yes. I find I quite like your idea of having a rule or two in writing to ensure we each get what we want out of this arrangement."

"Well, I'd simply suggested the initial objectives be recorded..."

"Of course, of course. However, since we are putting things in writing anyway, we might as well include any other personal stipulations that we may want to have in place."

Her forehead creased as she thought that over, but she nodded after a moment. "Now that you mention it, I would appreciate having a few conditions more formally agreed upon."

He flashed a grin that had her breath catching in her throat. Saints alive. He was handsome, she'd give him that. Arrogant and a bit puerile, perhaps. But definitely handsome.

"Then let's begin." He rang a bell that she hadn't noticed sitting on the table near his hand.

"What are you doing?" she asked.

"I'm a bit peckish. I could do with a bit of something, couldn't you?"

"I…"

"Perhaps a lovely pot of hot chocolate."

"Hot chocolate?"

"Don't you care for it?"

She blinked at him, bemused into momentary speechlessness. "Of…of course. Though, I thought it more a…"

That eyebrow rose again, and she noticed a slight scar running through it. Probably from some exasperated former lover who'd finally gotten tired of it waggling at her and tried to shave it off.

Fine. If he wanted it straight. "I thought it more popular among the fairer sex, is all."

He flashed that grin at her again, and she returned it before she could stop herself. "I confess, I have a wicked sweet tooth," he said with a wink.

A maid arrived as he spoke. "Cook already has a pot brewing, Your Grace."

"Excellent."

"Would you like anything else?"

"Perhaps some of those biscuits from yesterday, if there are any left."

"Of course," she said with a small curtsy.

"And send in Thompson, will you?"

She nodded but Arabella said, "Wait." She turned to the duke. "Thompson?"

"My secretary. We did decide to immortalize our agreement in writing, did we not?"

Arabella's cheeks heated again. "We did. But…speaking of such things…in front of…"

She hated that she couldn't seem to get a thought out without stammering. However, in her defense, she had never spoken of intimate relations with anyone, let alone the man with whom she intended to have them, let alone in front of that man's employees.

"Ah," he said, thankfully seeming to understand her hesitancy. "Perhaps your friend…" he said, pointing toward the conservatory where Charlotte sat not so subtly trying to eavesdrop.

Arabella wasn't so sure having Charlotte record such a conversation was ideal, but she was certainly better than the alternative. And she'd probably like a cup of chocolate as well. She gave him a hesitant nod, and he turned back to the maid. "Forget Thompson. Chocolate and biscuits will be all."

She nodded again, and as soon as the door

closed behind her, the duke bellowed, "Lady Waterstack!"

Charlotte, eyes wide, popped her head out from behind a large fern and then hurried into the room. The duke waved a finger at a nearby table, and Charlotte reluctantly took a seat, looking at Arabella with raised brows. Arabella opened her mouth to explain, but then just waved her hand and shook her head, plopping back against her seat—proper decorum be damned—while the duke himself fetched paper, ink, and a pen from a desk near the window and placed them in front of a startled and confused Charlotte.

"We'd like you to take some notes, if you'd be so kind," he said.

"Notes?"

"Yes. We're getting married," Silas said with a huge grin. "Congratulations, you are the first to know and may spread the information about at your leisure."

Charlotte's eyes widened, a small frown creasing her brow. She looked at Arabella. "He actually agreed?"

The duke's eyebrow rose and Charlotte's followed suit. "It's wonderful, of course, but I'm sure you understand my surprise."

The duke pursed his lips and gave a lopsided shrug. "She needs a husband with the money and connections to make her family scandal disappear, and I need a wife who is able to tolerate me long enough to provide an heir and willing to disappear afterward. I think the arrangement suits us both rather nicely."

Charlotte glanced at Arabella, who also shrugged. Laying it out in such a way was perhaps a bit crude, but efficient.

"And the notes?" Charlotte asked.

"We have a few conditions we'd like to formalize."

"Of course you do." She prepared her writing supplies with a sigh. "Very well."

"Excellent." The duke took his seat.

Arabella's stomach spasmed and she pressed a hand to it, trying to calm her nerves. "Your Grace, perhaps we—"

"Silas."

She stopped and stared at him, completely dumbfounded for a moment. "Pardon?"

"We are engaged now, are we not? That certainly entitles you to use my Christian name. At least in private."

"I…" She had no earthly idea how to respond to such a suggestion. He was entirely correct, of course. Still, she couldn't quite bring herself to address him so intimately.

"You were saying?" he asked, his lips pulling into a slight smile while she gaped at him like an eel.

She blinked, her mind a complete blank. She had no idea what she'd been about to say to him. After a moment of mental scrambling, she finally waved her hand, dismissing it.

He nodded. "Very well." He turned to Charlotte. "Don't worry about getting everything down verbatim, Lady Waterstack. A few notes that we can expand upon in the final document will suffice."

She gave a hasty nod, and he turned his attention back to Arabella. "Now. Your main objective, as we have stated, is to get your sister suitably married."

Arabella gave him a quick nod, and Charlotte scribbled the note, the scratching of the pen grating on Arabella's frayed nerves.

"And mine is to gain a male heir. You are fertile, I presume?"

Arabella's mouth dropped open again, and Charlotte choked back a shocked breath, her pen skidding across the paper.

"I…" Arabella stammered.

Silas's eyebrow rose, his attempt at a passive expression belied by the slight upturn of his lips. He seemed to enjoy baiting her, uttering the most outrageous statements just to watch her squirm. Well, she wouldn't give him the satisfaction. Oh, she might be positively writhing with embarrassment on the inside, but she'd be damned if she let him see it.

She sat straighter, ignoring the heat burning her cheeks. "I, of course, have no proof of anything, as I have not yet given birth to any children. However, I have no reason to believe otherwise. My menses have always arrived punctually and regularly, I am young and healthy, and my mother successfully bore three healthy children before a fever took her from us."

His eyes widened in surprise, and, she thought, admiration. "All daughters, though," he said.

"Yes. All daughters," she said with a well-deserved glower. "Though I'm sure sons would have been forthcoming had she not been taken from us so young."

His arrogant amusement faded in the face of the pain she couldn't quite hide, and he solemnly nodded. "I am sorry you lost her. My own mother died when I was quite young."

Their eyes met, briefly uniting them in their shared pain before he looked away and nodded at Charlotte to resume her notetaking.

"Good. Well then, I assume we both want to achieve these goals as quickly as possible."

"Yes, of course. Perhaps we should agree upon a specific timeframe. After all, if you were to put forth a less than robust effort into my sister's situation, she could languish for years without finding a match."

He nodded. "Likewise, producing a child isn't something we can control as easily as producing a husband, and it's possible you might not be capable of providing me with an heir."

Arabella jerked a little, momentarily stunned and not a little offended by that observation. However, she did not argue, to his apparent surprise. After all, he wasn't wrong. Still...

"Likewise, as you have no children despite ample opportunity to have produced one, if rumors are true, it is equally possible *you* could be incapable of producing a child."

Far from being angry as she feared, Silas barked out a laugh. "Touché. And I suppose neither of us wishes to spend the next ten years trying."

"Agreed. Well then, as my ability, at least, to bear a child has not yet been tested, shall we say...one year? That should be sufficient time to accomplish both our goals, if they can indeed be accomplished."

He contemplated her for a moment, his eyes burning into hers until she was certain he could see all her darkest secrets and desires. And liked what he saw. His lips pulled into a slow smile that had her clenching her hands around the armrests of her chair to keep from squirming.

"One year," he agreed. "During which both parties will make *every* effort to...satisfy the other party as quickly as possible."

His slight pause before the word *satisfy* had her breath hitching in her throat, though she wasn't quite sure why. An innocent enough word under normal circumstances. But somehow on his lips—full, soft-looking lips that still smiled at her in a way that made her want to run for the door (though she couldn't decide whether it was to flee through it or lock it against interruption)— the word had her wriggling in her chair while a myriad of shockingly inappropriate images flashed through her mind.

Then those damn lips pulled into a smirk like he could read every thought in her head, and she scowled. Which only made him smile more.

His shockingly sapphire blue eyes traveled over her, leisurely perusing every inch of her body. She huffed loudly, hoping her obvious annoyance would bring him back to the topic at hand. Instead, those eyes flashed to hers, locking on her with a disturbing heat that had her wishing her corset had not been laced quite so tightly that morning. Until the amusement crinkling the corners of his eyes spiked a fresh wave of irritation. She would be seasick if her emotions didn't stop tossing her about. Her stomach couldn't seem to decide if it was ailing due to anxiety or imprudent desire.

Regardless of the cause, the result was the same, and she pressed a hand to her middle, trying to calm her riotous insides.

Silas rubbed a finger over his lips, utterly failing to hide his amusement. In fact, she'd be willing to bet he did it to draw attention to it, not hide it. Fine. She could play this game.

She tilted her head and indulged in a little perusal of her own, drinking him in from the top of his tousled, sandy-blond hair to the tip of his overly shined boots. Her lips pinched together as she regarded him. Not bad, actually. Broad shoulders, suit fitted perfectly to a slightly-too-lanky-but-nicely-muscular form, shapely legs encased in freshly pressed trousers.

Not bad at all. She nodded slightly before she realized what she was doing and stopped.

Whether or not she would enjoy this agreement hadn't really occurred to her. Nor did it matter. Her enjoyment wasn't required. She needed him to get her family comfortably settled, that was all. And she'd been quite ready to sacrifice her happiness to do it. But…

Perhaps it wouldn't be such a sacrifice after all.

# Chapter Three

Silas watched the emotions flitting across Arabella's face with interest. She seemed at times mortified to be having the conversation she'd initiated. He couldn't blame her there. He was damn near blushing like a virgin bride himself, and he was far from that. But she was a strongminded little thing, he'd give her that. Mortified or not, she seemed bound and determined to see this outrageous scheme through. And, judging by that flash of heat in her eyes as she'd looked him over just then, she might even be looking forward to it. Certain parts anyway. All for the better. If he had to have a wife, one who didn't revile his touch would be preferable.

The maid returned with their refreshments, and he took a bracing sip of hot chocolate, letting the rich, thick liquid slide down his throat as he waited for his new intended to gather herself, his last comment with all its innuendo lingering in the air like a tantalizing perfume.

Arabella finally cleared her throat, shaking her head a bit like she was trying to clear her thoughts as well. "Then we are in agreement," she said.

"One year to achieve mutual satisfaction."

He lifted his cup of chocolate to her in a salute. Touché again.

She subtly rolled her eyes, but her soft, inviting lips curved in a slight smile. "The sooner this is done between us, the better. However." She lifted a finger to stop him before he could speak. "I don't want you to find just anyone for my sister, nor will I allow you to foist her off on some derelict friend of yours."

He slapped a hand to his chest as though she'd wounded him. "Madam, I would never."

One side of her delectable mouth pulled up in a skeptical grimace. "Of course you wouldn't," she said, her tone heavily implying otherwise. He grinned, and she attempted a convincing scowl. "I wish for her to find a suitable match, but I also wish for her happiness. Not just anyone will do."

Silas nodded. "That's fair enough. To facilitate that, I'll obtain invitations to all the desirable social occasions, and I will ensure that my new sister-in-law will be properly presented and accepted by society. I know that is a particular concern of yours."

A small, relieved breath left her, and all her sharp angles seemed to soften a bit. A twinge of what might have been guilt lapped at him. Perhaps he shouldn't vex her quite so much. After all, she was in dire straits indeed to be offering what she was. If only it weren't so much fun…

"Thank you," she said. "That is most appreciated."

He nodded. "I'll also agree that you'll have final approval over your sister's intended and that I will continue my championing of their union for at least six months afterward to ensure her full acceptance."

"Also appreciated. Greatly." Her brow furrowed. "I suppose in return…I can offer, if you so wish, that is, a second attempt at a male heir should the first child prove female or sickly."

His mouth dropped open. Generous offer indeed.

"Although," she hurried to add, "I do reserve the right to open further negotiations should that prove the case."

Another smile tugged at his lips. This woman proved more and more intriguing by the minute. She might blush like the inexperienced maid she most certainly was, but she had a fiery intellect and more testicular fortitude than most of the men in his circle. "Agreed."

"I would also ask…"

Some of her bravado dissipated, and he leaned forward, curious. "Yes?"

She jutted her rather sharp chin in the air. "I would ask that any children that come of our union remain with me for as long as possible."

His eyes widened, but before he could

comment, she plowed on. "I'm aware that, as your heir, he'll need to be educated and you'll expect, I'm sure, to spend a great deal of time with him."

He hadn't actually given it much thought, though now that she mentioned it, he supposed he would have to take an interest in the boy's upbringing. The thought of a child, *his* child, at his side, learning his role as the future Duke of Whittsley as Silas had at his own father's knee, filled him with a rush of emotions he couldn't quite distinguish. Though there was certainly a healthy dose of fear in there.

"But I would ask, while he is young at least, that he remain in my care. Of course, I would expect—and hope," she said, her eyes flashing briefly to his, "that you'll be a regular part of his life. But as his mother…"

Silas held up a hand, wanting to erase the sudden uncertainty and hesitancy in her voice. He answered her as gently as he could. "I have no wish to take a child from his mother, Miss Bromley." Nor did he have any desire to deal with the headaches that surely accompanied young children. He was more than happy to leave the childrearing to her and step in once the child was old enough to begin learning the particulars of his birthright. "No matter our personal arrangements, I promise you, you may remain with our offspring for as long as you wish."

She released a long, slow breath, the smile slowly returning to her lips. "Thank you, Your Grace."

He fought the urge to squirm against the uncomfortable weight of responsibility. This child wasn't even here yet, and Silas was already making decisions that could ruin the poor creature's life. It wasn't a responsibility he was remotely ready for. Nor one he'd ever wanted. Not that it mattered much. Ready or not, the time was at hand.

He drained the dregs of chocolate from his cup, then put it down with a slight clatter and patted his mouth with his napkin, determined to move their conversation past mention of their future child and on to lighter fare.

"Well then, now that *that* is settled, do you have any other requests for your sister's mate other than 'suitable'?"

She tilted her head and scrunched her brow. "Such as?"

"Are you only aiming for the lowest bar, or would you prefer…I don't know, maybe an earl or a duke?"

She snorted softly. "No duke will wish to marry the sister of someone who upped and married her groom."

"I'm a duke and I'm marrying *you*."

"That's different. You have no interest in the social status of your wife. Although, you should,

I feel obligated to point out." He waved that off, and she shook her head and continued. "Or in obtaining a wife at all, in point of fact. You are only in it for the heir."

Silas laughed. "Most of us are only in it for the heir."

She narrowed her eyes, but Charlotte snickered and then shrugged when Arabella's gaze shot to her. "He's not wrong."

"Except in Lord Waterstack's case," Silas said. "He's embarrassingly besotted with his wife. Speaks of her incessantly."

Charlotte's cheeks pinkened, and she smiled before turning her attention back to the notes she was scribbling.

Arabella gave her friend an indulgent and pleased smile and then turned back to him, her smile fading. "Suitable will be just fine, thank you. As long as it is someone who will make her happy, as I stated before."

Silas rubbed his finger across his chin and regarded her for a few seconds. "And if I *can* get her an earl or a duke?"

She snorted again. "If you get her a duke, I will grant you any favor of your choosing, without objection."

He broke out in a grin. Damn, but he was enjoying himself. "Done. Write that down," he said to Lady Waterstack.

Her face flushed beet red and her eyes were as round as billiard balls, but she dutifully recorded everything they said. Excellent.

"Now," he said, leaning back in his chair, his steepled fingers resting on his chin. He looked forward to this next bit of negotiation with a great deal of anticipation. "When it comes to our…shall we call them heir-making attempts?"

He wanted to spare her sensibilities. Somewhat. But he couldn't resist a smirk when she blushed furiously. She scowled at his grin, and he made an effort to control his outward amusement. "I propose such attempts should occur a minimum of six times a month, at least twice a week, every week, save for when you may be…" He froze, trying to think of a delicate way to put it. "Indisposed." She scowled again but didn't object to his phrasing. "However, should one of those weeks be missed for any other reason, then a third day should be added to the following week."

She frowned, and he braced for her to argue against the frequency he suggested.

"I do not agree."

As he suspected.

"Six times a month won't be nearly sufficient."

His eyebrows hit his hairline, and her blush deepened so much he was surprised her eyes weren't watering. That…was *not* what he had expected her to say.

She took a deep breath. "I simply mean that only attempting twice a week will greatly reduce our odds and could make this drag on for months. As the objective is to accomplish this in as little time as possible, certainly within a year, I suggest, just for the sake of expediency, that we alter this to nightly relations. When possible. Until conception occurs. Upon which time I will immediately retire to the country, and you may do...whatever it is you wish to do."

"Nightly?" His eyes widened further, and his lips quirked up in a half grin he couldn't contain. "You must really want my...library."

Her mouth gaped open and closed a few times, and poor Lady Waterstack looked as though the vapors might overtake her at any moment. Or... perhaps she was trying to keep from pummeling him with the crystal paperweight her fingers kept caressing. He edged his chair a little farther from her, just in case, though not before plucking the paperweight from her grasp.

She glanced at him in surprise.

"Just in case you decided to put this to use in some misguided attempt to defend your friend's honor," he said, jiggling the paperweight in his hand before placing it on a shelf. Well out of their reach.

Lady Waterstack snorted. "It would serve you right, Your Grace."

He dropped back into his chair. "It would not. By all rights, it is *my* honor that should be defended."

"Yours?" Lady Waterstack said, incredulous.

"Yes!" He wagged a finger at Arabella. "*She* came to *my* door asking for *my* hand in marriage and *now* she's demanding nightly attentions from me. Not that I'm complaining, mind you," he said with a quick wink for Arabella, who sat stunned and gasping for outraged breath on the other side of the table. "But still."

He glanced back and forth at the women who were both doing admirable impersonations of suffocating codfish.

Arabella seemed to recover her sensibilities after a moment, though not her powers of speech. Very well, then, he'd continue. "Are there any stipulations you wish to place on our…attempts?" he asked her…with some trepidation, but also a great deal of curiosity. She had done nothing but surprise him from the moment she'd fallen out of her carriage and into his arms.

She blinked up at him, then straightened her spine and faced him full on. "Yes, actually, there are."

"I can't wait to hear them."

She gave him a skeptical look, but he meant every word. He was completely intrigued. And relieved, frankly. He'd thought he might have shocked her into permanent silence. He waited with bated breath.

"I would prefer these attempts to proceed as efficiently as possible and to only occur with the lamps lit throughout the process."

His eyes widened. The woman was a never-ending source of delight. He cleared his throat and ran a finger over his lips, trying to force the smile from them. "Lights on?"

She nodded. "I prefer to see what is occurring. I don't like surprises."

Charlotte choked on her chocolate and clapped her napkin to her lips. Silas's lips nearly screamed in agony from the effort to keep them in line. "If tha—" His voice came out in a croak, and he quickly cleared it. "If that's what you prefer."

She nodded again, and he moved on to her second stipulation. "And…efficiently?"

"Yes. No…dillydallying about," she said, waving her hand in the air. "Our touching should remain as limited as possible for as little time as possible."

Well now, that was just insulting. His brow creased. "You may need to explain further."

She sighed as though he were the biggest dolt on the planet. "I know some degree of touching is, of course, necessary."

"Oh good. I wasn't sure you understood that part."

She grimaced at him and continued. "However, *kissing* and other such activities are not things in which I am experienced, and I have no desire to be as I shall have no use for those particular skills once our contract is fulfilled."

He had no earthly idea how to respond to that. Which didn't seem to matter as she barreled on ahead without waiting for comment from him.

"From what I understand, such…activities aren't strictly necessary in order for…to…" She waved her hand limply again. "You know."

His frown deepened while he struggled for a diplomatic way to abjectly refuse her request. "I…cannot speak for other men. But for myself…I will find the act of procreation quite…difficult without being able to touch and kiss my partner."

She contemplated that for a moment and glanced at Lady Waterstack.

"I…" Lady Waterstack started before pausing to clear her throat. She darted a look at him before leaning closer to Arabella, her voice lowered, though Silas could still hear her. "Lord Waterstack also prefers such activities during…" Her words choked off and she flashed another glance at Silas, who had to pinch his thigh under the table to keep from laughing.

Arabella released a deep sigh. "Very well. If it is truly something you need, then I will agree to kissing and whatever other proclivities you deem necessary," she said, grimacing like she was describing some sort of disagreeable clinical examination.

She made him seem like such a deviant. He wasn't sure if he should be flattered or offended. Watching the heat climb in her cheeks and her chest shudder with the slight hitch in her breath, he decided he was flattered, because the lady was most definitely intrigued, despite her claims to the contrary. And suddenly he couldn't wait to get her alone. He was going to teach her that such *proclivities* could not only be tolerable but the most pleasurable experience of her life.

He gave her a slow smile as she continued.

"But only to facilitate procreation. I would like to limit those activities to our…heir-making attempts."

He nodded. "If that is what you desire."

She paused, frowning slightly at his word choice.

"However," he said, and her eyes narrowed to suspicious slits, "you should consider that we may need to show some sort of affection toward one another in public to make our union appear real."

She scoffed. "I hardly see why. The vast majority of couples I know who wed for money, power, or convenience never bother to pretend there is any affection between them. I don't see why our union needs to be any different."

"Under other circumstances, perhaps it wouldn't," he countered. "However, there will already be questions regarding both the haste and reasoning for our marriage. You are a lovely lady, but you will be a surprising choice for my duchess, especially considering the family issues you are currently facing. Displays of affection between us will go a long way toward cementing our union in the eyes of society at large and will give the gossips something to chew on other than your family's—forgive me—shortcomings. If I were destitute and you were an heiress, there would be no need for the subterfuge. As it stands, though…"

He shrugged. "A whirlwind romance is the least scandalous reason for our union. Provided, of course, our child arrives at least nine months afterward, which we know he will. I would prefer any children that result from this to not suffer from any further gossip than is necessary."

She seemed taken aback, but she didn't argue. "All right. That is understandable. And admirable."

"Thank you," he said. He turned to Lady Waterstack, who seemed to have stunned bemusement permanently etched on her face, though she had settled into her furious notetaking with a relish, judging by the amount of wording on the pages in front of her.

"Are you getting all this?"

She nodded. "Without going over all the

particulars, rule number one states that you will each endeavor to accomplish your goals as quickly as possible with a deadline of one year, after which the duchess will retire to the country and the duke may do as he wishes. Rule two," she blushed but continued along admirably, "heir-making attempts will occur nightly save for when the duchess is indisposed. With the stipulations that the lamps will remain burning during the course of…well…" She cleared her throat and plowed onward. "And… intimate touching will be grudgingly allowed."

Arabella scowled a bit at the *grudgingly* part, but she nodded. As did Silas.

"Splendid. And rule three, public displays of affection are allowed. And encouraged."

She rolled her eyes but again didn't object. Lady Waterstack continued her scribbling, and he clapped his hands together.

"Excellent. Anything else?"

# Chapter Four

Arabella raised her brow. Silas was having entirely too much fun considering the subject matter. She could only hope he actually meant to follow through on this whole scheme and wasn't simply having a lark at her expense.

"We've covered the most pressing concerns, I believe. What else did you have in mind?"

He shrugged. "Well, if we are to find your sister a suitable match, it will, of course, require her attendance at the most coveted parties and balls. Which she must attend with a chaperone. Now, I am always invited to these events, so there are no worries there. And I quite enjoy them for the most part, so I'm happy to attend. My one complaint is that it does get tedious fending off every vicious mama who has a marriageable daughter. However, you, my dear, will alleviate that concern nicely, assuming you'll consent to accompany me."

Those sweet endearments that seemed to drip so effortlessly from his eternally smiling lips were wreaking havoc on her equilibrium. Arabella flushed again and cursed her overly exuberant cheeks for their constant betrayal of her inner turmoil. She'd never grow accustomed to it.

He continued as though she weren't sitting there twitching with discomfort. "Appearing with my duchess on my arm will relieve me of having to dance attendance upon every other maid who wishes to throw herself at me."

"So, that is your suggestion for rule four? My presence at these affairs?"

"Yes. At every ball, party, and social occasion that I may wish to attend. And I will, of course, ensure your sister is invited as well."

She frowned. "As you may have deduced, I am not the most social of ladies. However, I do concede the necessity of my sister attending these events and her need for chaperones. If you are willing to both ensure she is invited and accompany her to these events as necessary, then yes, I will agree to attend whichever occasions you wish."

"Excellent."

"However," she said, raising a finger. "My father would allow me to put in an appearance and then find a quiet corner in which to read until the rest of our party was ready to depart. If you don't object—"

"I do," he said, and she huffed, which made him smile. "The purpose of attending these events is to be seen, not to hide away. It will be rather difficult to get society to accept you again if you aren't visible enough to *be* accepted."

She sighed. He had a point. "Then I would ask that you not abandon me the moment we arrive if I am not comfortable on my own. And on occasion, could we not stay for the entire duration of these events? Perhaps we may leave after putting in a suitable appearance if I so wish?"

His lips twisted for a second before he nodded. "I will agree as long as you at least attempt to have some fun at these affairs. They aren't meant to be torturous, after all."

She chuckled slightly. "Agreed."

"Excellent. Rule number five, then. You can't hide away, but I will stay by your side if you wish."

"And we can leave early."

"On occasion," he added.

"Agreed." She nodded. "This is going quite well, don't you think?" Arabella said, leaning forward with a smile before taking a biscuit off the tray and popping the whole thing in her mouth.

Charlotte shot her a disapproving look, but Arabella didn't care. Gorging herself on biscuits in front of a man was the least mortifying thing she'd done that day. Silas grinned and pushed the tray of biscuits closer to her. She found it slightly disturbing how much he seemed to want her to eat another one, his attention focused on her lips. But the slight catch in his breath when her tongue darted out to capture a stray crumb was oddly…

fascinating.

Before she could dwell on Silas and his capti-vation with her tongue too long, a commotion at the door of the library drew her attention. A small gray ball of fluff bounded through the door and tried to skid to a halt, though its soft paws had difficulty gaining traction on the polished hard-wood floors. After a second of seemingly running in place, it found some purchase and resumed its dead run straight to her.

"Watch out," Silas said, leaning forward in alarm as the kitten launched itself at her. "He can be quite dangerous when the mood is upon him." Silas tilted his head and frowned in confusion as the kitten landed in Arabella's lap, spun around twice, and promptly dropped into a contented ball of fur. "Or…maybe not." His frown deepened when a contented purr rose from the beast in response to Arabella's stroking.

"And who might this be?" she asked, scratching it under the chin. The adorable creature tilted its head up to give her better access.

"Beelzebub." Silas watched them with confused fascination and finally shook his head and sat back.

"You named him after the devil?" she asked in surprise.

Silas snorted. "He *is* the devil." He held up his hand where she could see a set of day-old scratches disappearing into his sleeve. "He has a few other names, but they aren't suitable for a lady's ears."

His tone had that undercurrent of amusement that it always held, but he seemed dead serious. Then he shrugged. "We call him Bub for short."

"Bub, huh?" She scratched the top of his head. "He seems like an absolute angel."

Silas raised a brow. "You'll think differently when you've gotten a chance to know him."

The kitten stood and stretched, lifting his adorably fluffed tail in the air before jumping from her lap to the nearest bookshelf, and she noticed for the first time that while the uppermost shelf contained a myriad of the normal knickknacks and small paintings often found in such places, the rest of the shelves were bare of anything but the books they were made to hold. Aside from a small wooden horse that had been left on the shelf nearest their table.

"I see you've noticed our unique way of displaying our trinkets," he said, nodding to them. "It's because he has a tendency—"

Silas's hand shot out to catch the figurine that Bub casually knocked from his path as he walked across the shelf toward Silas. "To knock stuff down."

Arabella laughed, watching the little ball of fur stalk toward the duke with the regal air of an absolute monarch while Silas watched his approach with amused resignation. He sighed just as the kitten stepped from the shelf onto his shoulder and settled down for another round of snuggling and purring.

Silas reached up to pet him. "But then he does this, so…" He carefully shrugged again. "I guess you need to like my cat also if you're to become part of my household."

Charlotte shook her head, her lips twitching. "Do you want that to be one of the rules?"

"That's not necessary," Arabella said. "I like him anyway."

"Yes, well, you want to marry me, so your judgment isn't exactly sound."

Arabella pursed her lips, and he grinned, his gaze holding hers until her stomach started its acrobatics again.

Charlotte cleared her throat. "Any more rules to add?"

"Oh, yes," Silas said. "One more."

• • •

"My grandfather," Silas said through gritted teeth.

"The gentleman who arrived earlier?" Arabella asked.

"Yes, actually." Silas raised a brow, wondering how much she'd overheard. Not that it mattered. If she were to spend any time at all in his company, she'd be hearing a lot from his grandfather. Then again, with her at his side, his grandfather would hopefully be mollified.

"And what rule would pertain to him?"

"We will be required to dine with my grandfather every Sunday. He may not be particularly welcoming at first, though I won't let him abuse you in any way."

"He won't approve of me?"

Silas frowned slightly, not wanting to offend her but also wanting to make sure she knew what she was getting into with his family. "He has always had a strong desire to keep any hint of scandal from his family name. And while I do not carry his name, I am his last remaining family, so…"

"Ah," she said, glancing down with a sad smile. "And my own family name is not quite as spotless as he'd prefer."

"Exactly." He took her hand and gave it a swift kiss, smiling when it trembled slightly in his own. "But don't worry about him. He'll get over it, and frankly, he might not mind all that much, as he's so desperate to get me married. I just wanted you to be aware of his…prejudices."

Arabella took her hand back. "Thank you for the warning." Her brow furrowed slightly. "What does that have to do with the rules?"

"As I mentioned earlier, I would be much obliged if you were to sing my praises to him at every available opportunity."

Arabella blinked at him, giving him the skeptical look his request deserved. "Anything in particular you'd like me to praise?"

He paused, a few juvenile and highly inappropriate responses invading his mind, but he kept his mouth shut and waved his hand. "Nothing too grand. The usual compliments will do. You find me witty, generous, responsible, dependable, mature, manly, impressive, respected, admired, trustworthy…things of that nature."

"Ah. So…you wish me to lie to your grandfather?"

He raised his other brow, though his lips twitched with amusement, even more so when he caught the mischievous twinkle in her eyes. "You wound me, madam. You needn't *lie* per se. Have you not found me exceedingly generous this morning?"

"You have been that," she admitted.

"And surely at least a bit witty? Charming, perhaps?"

"Hmm, I'm sure you find yourself so, yes."

He chuckled. "Well, whether you find me so or not, my grandfather has the unfortunate impression that I am a frivolous, immature, impulsive layabout with no real ambition." He scowled and then shrugged. "In fairness, I *am* all those things. Quite rude of him to constantly point it out, though."

Arabella laughed, a quiet, breathy sound that

she tried to keep captured behind her hand. "And you hope gaining a wife and heir will make him believe you've matured?"

"One may hope. So, anything you can do to facilitate that impression would be much appreciated."

She gave him an indulgent smile. "If you think it will help, then agreed. Rule six, lie to Grandfather."

He bowed his head in an appreciative salute, though he gave her a mock glare at her deliberate misstatement. "My thanks."

She nodded her head like a queen accepting the gratitude of her subject and he grinned. "Well then. We've done a good day's work already, haven't we? And we haven't even gotten to the formal contract with your father yet," he said with a chuckle. "Anything else you'd like to add?"

Arabella shook her head. "I think we've covered the important issues."

"Agreed. Let's have a look," he said, leaning over to take the paper from Charlotte and reading it quickly. "Works for me," he said, placing the paper back on the table. "Any objections?"

Arabella shook her head, a little dazedly perhaps, but definitely in the affirmative.

"Excellent." He took the pen from Lady Waterstack and scrawled his name along the bottom of the page before pushing it across the table to Arabella. She shyly glanced up at him from under her lashes before pulling her spectacles out of her pocket and slipping them on. She quickly read over the paper and signed it with more care but without hesitation, pulling off her glasses and sitting back afterward with what sounded like a sigh of relief.

He pushed the paper back in front of Lady Waterstack. "If you'd be so kind as to witness?"

She grimaced but also signed, though she glanced at Arabella first for confirmation.

"Well then, that's that," he said, clapping his hands once. "Now, I propose we announce our engagement immediately. Tomorrow will probably be best."

"Tomorrow?" Arabella's voice ended on a bit of a squeak.

"Yes. It will take at least a week, more likely two, to obtain the license. I would try to obtain a special license, but the Archbishop of Canterbury is a bit peeved with me at the moment and wouldn't be keen to do me any favors. So, a regular license it will have to be. I'm happy to pay the fees and whatever extra I can to expedite things, of course, but these things still take time. Besides, there will already be some talk about the haste of our marriage. We don't want to make matters worse by spending a fortune to hurry things along even faster. A quick engagement is one thing. A rushed marriage is quite another.

"We can meet, as far as society is concerned, at the Harthams' ball tonight, and you can charm me out of my set bachelor ways. I will call on you and your father tomorrow to formally propose. You'll be the belle of the season, having secured a match so quickly. And such an advantageous one at that! It will do wonders for you and your family's reputation."

Arabella blinked at him and nodded, though she looked a bit stunned with the speed at which things were moving. But she still hadn't made any objections to anything he'd said, so he wouldn't go looking for trouble where none was presented.

"A few weeks might not seem quick, but it will pass faster than you know. I believe it should be enough time to plan everything and of course visit the modiste for your trousseau and whatever else you may require. I, of course, am happy to pay for any expenses you incur." He glanced at her from top to bottom, biting his lip as he took in her appearance.

Arabella also glanced down, smoothing her hands over the voluminous skirts of what was probably her finest morning outfit.

"Is there something wrong with my clothes?" she asked.

"Nothing is wrong, necessarily, but…"

Her eyes narrowed. "We may not be as rich as

some, Your Grace," she said, her eyes raking over him. "But we are hardly paupers. My father has never scrimped when it comes to his daughters. We can cover our own expenses. And there is nothing wrong with my gowns. My Aunt Adelaide oversees our wardrobes."

"Of course, darling," Lady Waterstack said, and Silas turned to her with surprise at her interjection. "But you must admit, Aunt Adelaide can be a bit old-fashioned. And adorning yourself in the latest fashions has never been one of your passions. You are beautiful and perfectly presentable," she hurried to add. "But if you are to attend all the most fashionable events on the arm of His Grace…"

Arabella's tight, pinched expression softened a bit and finally she sighed. "You aren't wrong, I suppose." She glanced at him reluctantly. "If I must accompany you everywhere, perhaps a few new wardrobe items wouldn't come amiss."

"Goo—"

"However," she said, cutting him off. "I have no desire to be more in your debt than necessary. I am perfectly capable of obtaining and providing my own clothing, thank you."

"I'm sure you are," he said, hardly believing he had to badger a woman into accepting a fashionable new wardrobe at his expense. "But I am *more* capable and have the money and reputation to get it done quickly. And as my future wife, I have every right to bestow upon you whatever gifts I desire, and I intend to do so often. At least until you look the part of the new Duchess of Whittsley. I suggest you accustom yourself to the experience. I'll leave the particulars of the matter to you ladies, just send the bill to me."

He stood and strode out to the foyer, leaving the women to follow him, his steps lighter than they had been in months. Who knew becoming engaged could be such a liberating experience? If he'd known, he'd have sought it out sooner instead of actively avoiding it for much of his adult life. Then again, his happiness at his new circumstances probably had more to do with his intriguing new betrothed and their unusual arrangement than with his impending matrimony. All the benefits of a wife without any of the nuisances?

This was surely the best deal he'd ever brokered. As long as they stuck to their rules…

# Chapter Five

Arabella shoved her spectacles back into her pocket and hastily stood, gaping at Charlotte.

"I can't believe that worked," she said to her friend, whose exhale ended on a laugh.

"Neither can I. And I still don't trust it. Or him," she said, narrowing her eyes as she looked out the door to where Silas stood donning his hat, coat, and gloves.

"Well, I've got this at least," she said, holding up their list of rules before carefully folding it and slipping it into her pocket. "He was surprisingly amenable to my requests."

Charlotte delicately snorted. "Yes. And you to his."

Arabella opened her mouth to retort but couldn't really argue, so she just shook her head and hurried out to the foyer, Charlotte on her heels.

"Now," Silas said, "your sister will be requiring some new dresses as well, I'm assuming," he said, waiting while she stepped into the coat one of the servants held out for her.

"Yes, but again my family is perfectly able to…"

"Yes, I'm aware, we just hashed this out. You know, you are to be my wife and she will be my sister. Perhaps I am merely attempting to provide for my new family."

She hadn't thought of it that way. It was a thoughtful gesture, if that were the case, but she was already asking too much of him.

"That is very kind, but…"

Charlotte's elbow caught her in the ribs, and she sucked in a startled breath. He glanced at them, and Arabella gave him an overly bright smile, which only made his eyebrow rise higher.

"It is rather kind of me, is it not?" he finally said. "Now then, I have other matters to which I must attend this morning. So, I will bid you ladies adieu. Until this evening," he said, tipping his hat to them with a bow as his servant opened the front door.

Arabella dropped a small curtsy and hurried out the door with Charlotte before she could change her mind and call the whole thing off. The fact that her plan had succeeded, and relatively easily, unsettled her. Surely she would appear at the ball that night only to find the whole thing had been a fever dream brought on by the stress of their situation.

Except the moment they were ensconced in their carriage, Charlotte shook her head and laughed.

"Well, my girl, you are either the luckiest lady in England or the butt of the cruelest joke in history. Let's hope it's the former," she said, patting Arabella's knee.

Far too few hours later, Arabella pressed back against the cushions of the carriage, this time gowned and bejeweled, and firmly regretting the chocolate and biscuits she'd eaten that morning. With Silas. With her innards threatening a full revolt, she hadn't been able to eat another bite the rest of the day.

Her eyes closed as a fresh wave of nerves crashed about in her stomach. She tried to take a surreptitious deep breath and slowly blow it back out. Hyperventilating before they'd even arrived at the ball wouldn't do anyone any good.

Anne nearly bounced with excitement at her side, and Aunt Adelaide reached over and patted her hand affectionately. Lord and Lady Hartham's annual ball was one of the main events of the season, taking place just after the court presentations and setting the tone for the rest of the season. The impression a girl made there, if she were lucky enough to attend, could make or break her fortune.

Thankfully, Anne had been presented last year

and Arabella the year before that, so they wouldn't have to relive that nightmarish experience. She had put it off longer than most, avoiding it until she turned twenty. At which point Aunt Adelaide had insisted upon her court debut lest she tumbled headlong into spinsterhood without ever having been presented. Not that Arabella cared much about that.

Months of preparation all to march into the Queen's presence, drowning in fabric and feathers, and march back out again, only in reverse. Arabella had managed. Anne had been marvelous and had had numerous suitors…until she had fallen dreadfully ill. And then Alice had ruined all their prospects and the Bromley sisters had beaten a hasty retreat to Vinethorpe, their country estate. There had certainly been no invitations to the Hartham ball that year.

Arabella had never attended before. Nearly everyone was invited, and while Alice had enjoyed dancing the night away the year she'd come out, it had always seemed far too overwhelming for Ari. She hadn't been able to avoid balls and parties entirely, of course. But she did try to only attend the smaller affairs where she knew more people and could squirrel away somewhere when the burden of being social became too great.

And now here she was, their invitation having arrived late that afternoon, obviously arranged by the Duke of Whittsley. There would be no running off to hide in a secluded alcove this time. The whole purpose of attending this event was to sow the seeds of their romance so they could begin to undo some of the damage to her family's reputation. She couldn't do that if she didn't show her face.

"Oh, Ari, look how pretty!" Anne said, leaning over Arabella to peer out the window.

Arabella followed her sister's gaze and couldn't help but smile, despite her nerves. "It's very beautiful."

Hartham Hall, Lord and Lady Hartham's sprawling London residence, looked like a fairyland bedecked in flowers and whimsical paper lanterns. The tall trees that lined the drive to the house and the numerous bushes and plants surrounding the grand staircase were draped with flowers and bright ribbons. Music already filtered out through the open doors to entice the guests inside.

But Arabella's enjoyment of the sight immediately plummeted when their carriage got into line behind a vast row of others that were waiting to drop off their gowned and bejeweled passengers. Liveried servants scuttled to and fro, helping the upper echelon of society, dripping in all their finery, out of their carriages so they could be ushered into the house.

"So many people," she muttered.

"I'd be happy to accompany you back home

if you wish," her father said, giving her a sweet, understanding smile. He felt about the same way she did when it came to these affairs.

She wavered, the temptation to go back home and curl up in a chair with one of her books pulling at her. She sighed and closed her eyes to steady herself. This would be her last chance to turn back.

But Silas waited for her within. And Anne stared at her, silently pleading. She had been beside herself with excitement all afternoon, since the moment the invitation had arrived. How could Arabella destroy that look of happiness on her sister's face? Wasn't Anne's happiness the whole reason she was doing this?

She smiled and took her sister's hand, then turned to her father. "No thank you, Papa. I'll be quite all right."

When their carriage finally reached the front of the line, a liveried footman opened the door and they alighted. Arabella watched the wave of whispers precede them into the grand foyer of the home and spread throughout the throng of elegantly clad attendees while she waited with her family for their turn to be presented to their hosts in the receiving line.

Lady Hartham gave them a cool smile but didn't immediately demand their departure, so Arabella counted it a success. Lord Hartham gave them a distracted nod, and they moved past the foyer and into the main ballroom.

"Oh, isn't it beautiful," Anne said, holding on to Arabella's arm.

She nodded, but all her attention was riveted to the man across the room. Silas.

He'd come.

A large part of her had feared he wouldn't. Had been sure he would come to his senses and spend the rest of the season avoiding her. Instead, his eyes met hers, and that eternally amused smile of his slowly spread across his full mouth as he began to make his way over to her. Which wasn't difficult as the rest of the people at the ball had taken pains to stand removed from them, parting around them the way a brook flows past a rock.

Which meant when Silas finally did reach them, they were in full sight of every person at that ball.

He nodded to her father. "Lord Durborough, it's good to see you."

Her father squinted at him but nodded in return. "Thank you, Your Grace," he muttered.

Silas then bowed to Aunt Adelaide. "Miss Bromley, you are looking quite ravishing this evening."

Aunt Adelaide giggled like a twelve-year-old and swatted at him with her fan.

"Oh, go on with you, Your Grace."

He grinned. "Perhaps I could beg introduction to these lovely ladies."

She beamed. "My nieces. Miss Arabella Bromley, and Miss Anne Bromley."

He bowed to each of them in turn and then focused on Arabella.

"Miss Bromley, may I have this dance?"

Arabella swallowed hard and tried to drag a breath in past her suddenly tight lungs, but she managed to nod and offered him a trembling hand. "Of course," she said.

The moment his hand closed around hers, her stomach calmed. Oh, she was still terrified. She'd still rather run out the door than walk onto that huge, gleaming dance floor. But somehow, his presence steadied her. Or goaded her into refusing to give in, more like. But whatever got her through the rest of the night, she'd accept.

Eyes were already starting to swivel their way, and they hadn't even made it all the way onto the floor yet. She didn't miss the delighted gasp from her sister who clasped Aunt Adelaide's arm and immediately leaned over to whisper excitedly in her ear. Nor did she miss the expressions of the other women in the room who seemed too shocked to be dismayed. Eyes wide, mouths agape, staring at them like Silas was marching a twenty-one-year-old toothless broodmare around the room rather than a respectable young lady from a (previously, granted) good family.

The music swelled, and Silas took her in his arms to twirl her about the room. "Looks like we got their attention."

That startled a laugh out of her, and she relaxed a bit more.

"Changing your mind?" Silas asked, that irksome brow of his cocked in amused challenge.

"Of course not. There's just a few more people here than I anticipated, that's all."

He nodded, his lips twitching, and she stood even straighter, steeling her courage and her backbone, refusing to let him see her anxiety. The flash of approval in his eyes made her realize that's exactly what he'd intended to do all along. She hated to give him the satisfaction of knowing that his challenge had worked. But it was too late to back out now. Not that she would anyway. If he could go through with this, so could she. She raised her chin and concentrated on the dance steps.

He tilted his head, regarding her. "Are you cross with me?" he asked.

She glanced at him in surprise. "Of course not. Why do you ask such a thing?"

"Because you look cross."

"Well, I'm not. That's just the way my face looks."

His lips twitched again. "Well, try to control it."

"How am I supposed to control something I

don't even know I'm doing?"

"I don't know. Just…try. We're supposed to be besotted with each other. We need to make it seem real."

Arabella lightly snorted. "Then I think we're fine. Any woman would be constantly irritated in your presence."

He laughed, the sound startling her and apparently the dancers surrounding them, none of whom made any pretense of the fact that they were staring. Anyone who hadn't already been watching them certainly was now.

She took a deep breath and tried to relax. Her face felt frozen, every muscle going rigid under the sudden scrutiny of everyone in the room.

He gave her waist a subtle squeeze. "Remember, you're supposed to be having fun," he said. "Try it."

Her breath released in a whoosh, her waist tingling where he held her, and she grinned, unable to stop herself. "I shall try my best."

"Well, I can't ask for more than your best, can I?"

He spun her out and brought her back in, surprising a laugh out of her. "See?" he said. "It's not so hard."

And it wasn't. As long as she was with him.

When the music ended, they paused for a moment.

"Do you think that was enough to make everyone think you are smitten with me?" she asked, hardly believing her temerity.

He chuckled. "Best have another dance, just to be sure."

"But…it's not done…"

"Exactly. What better way to convince everyone we are besotted than to flout the rules of convention and spend more time in each other's arms?"

She sucked in a strangled breath.

"Perhaps I should let you recover from our first encounter for a moment, though, eh?" he said with a wink and a chuckle.

"If you insist, Your Grace," Arabella said, her heart racing. He was far too charming for his own good. She'd have to take care, or she might be in danger of falling for her own fiancé. And that was the last thing she wanted.

Silas smiled down at her and then led her back to her aunt. Arabella's heart swelled with happiness and excitement when she realized that her sister had been claimed for the dance as well and was slowly making her way back to them on the arm of a handsome young lord.

Aunt Adelaide was nearly beside herself with glee when Silas took Arabella's dance card to add his name to not one, but two more dances.

"The gossip mill is already at work, I see," Silas

said, leaning down to whisper in her ear. "Best give them enough to keep them going."

Arabella looked up at him and gave him a faint smile. To anyone watching, it probably appeared as though he were whispering sweet nothings in her ear. But then, that is what they intended.

"You may thank me at any time," Silas said, taking the hand she offered and bowing over it, lingering much longer than necessary. She bit her lip against the rush of heat that flooded her... unsure if it stemmed from embarrassment or the thrilling tingle that raced up her arm at the gentle squeeze of his fingers. Mostly likely it was both. If the gossips hadn't had enough to titter about before, they certainly did now.

"It was my idea, Your Grace. But you are carrying it out admirably, I'll grant you that."

He chuckled and took his leave. Arabella barely had time to release a breath of relief when several more gentlemen presented themselves to claim dances on her card. It took everything in her to smile gracefully and accept their invitations, but the sheer delight on Anne's face when she showed Arabella her full dance card buoyed her spirits. A few dances with strangers was a small price to pay for the happiness radiating from her sister.

She took her turn on the floor with each gentleman, but she could feel Silas's gaze all evening.

Every time she caught sight of him, he was nearby, watching her. Far from intimidating her, she found his attention…stimulating. Exhilarating even. She found herself looking for him. Meeting his eye over the shoulder of her dance partner. Locking onto his gaze as she sipped lemonade. She could not escape from those jewel-bright eyes.

Nor did she want to.

By the time he collected her for their second dance, she was nearly breathless, as though he'd been chasing her about the dance floor for real instead of just with his gaze.

He pulled her close, a bit closer than necessary. Just enough to send the gossip mavens into a titter, but not quite enough to cause a scandal. His good mood seemed to have dimmed a bit, though.

"Is something wrong, Your Grace?" she asked as he directed their steps.

"No. It is only…I seem to have belatedly realized that you will be obliged to dance with other men at these balls we've agreed to attend together."

She grimaced, which drew a smile back to his lips. "That is true, I suppose."

"Then I have another rule to propose."

She raised her brows in question, and he pulled her even closer. "You waltz only with me."

She cocked an eyebrow. "Even after we are wed? Married couples don't typically dance together, after all."

"Even after we are wed. You waltz with me, or you waltz with no one."

She narrowed her eyes at him. "We may cause quite the spectacle then."

His eyes twinkled with merriment. "So be it."

"Then you have no issue with me dancing with other men as long as it is not a waltz?"

"Correct."

She let out an exasperated sigh. "Might I inquire why?"

He gave her a slow smile that twisted her insides into an intricate knot and spun her again. "No."

She swallowed against the sudden dryness in her mouth and willed her heart back into a normal rhythm. How on earth did he do that to her with such a simple gesture?

"All right. That makes rule seven. I find it ridiculous and pointless, but I will agree without further caveats." She gripped his hand, relieved that her voice came out strong and steady.

"Excellen—"

"However," she said, grinning at his surprise. "I've been thinking upon it, and I'd also like to add another rule." He gestured for her to continue. "There are several non-season-related events that I would like to attend. I rarely have the opportunity to do so due to a lack of interested chaperone. So, I will go to the parties you wish to attend, and I will dance, saving the waltzes for you. But I would like you to accompany me to the events that I wish to attend."

"Such as?"

"The International Exhibition, for one. Also, several of my favorite authors do readings of their works. And Auguste Toulmouche has an exhibition next month that I would dearly love to attend."

The pained look he gave her almost made her waver, but she stood firm and, thankfully, he didn't argue. "To how many must I escort you?"

She pursed her lips and tilted her head to regard him. "Three."

He flinched. "I couldn't possibly manage more than one."

She rolled her eyes. "I'm sure your constitution is hardier than that, Your Grace."

"You'd be surprised."

She sighed. "Two."

"One," he insisted.

"A month."

He groaned. "Fine. Rule eight. I will accompany you to *one* non-season-related event of your choice." She cocked an eyebrow, and his lips twitched before he added, "A month."

"Good. Without complaint."

"Well, now you go too far."

She just smiled and waited, and finally he

grimaced. "Very well. Without *too* much complaint."

She giggled. "If I have to try and have fun at your parties without a book, you have to attempt the same at my events."

He snorted. "Better add that to the list, then, or I'm likely to try and weasel out of it."

That startled a laugh out of her loud enough that it drew the attention of those surrounding them. For once in her life, she paid them no mind. "Good of you to admit that. All right then. Rule nine. We shall endeavor to enjoy ourselves and each other's company at the events of the other's choosing."

"Agreed."

The music ended, and Silas brought her hand to his lips, pressing a kiss to its back.

Arabella gasped, both at the tingling sensation emanating from where his lips lingered on her gloved hand and at his sheer temerity.

"Your Grace!" she whispered, pulling her hand from his grasp.

"Just abiding by rule three," he said, stepping closer. "Public displays of affection were to be encouraged, I believe."

"*Appropriate* displays, Your Grace. We haven't even announced our engagement yet."

He sighed. "Very well."

He escorted her back to where Aunt Adelaide waited with her next partner.

"Until our next dance," Silas said, bowing as he took his leave.

Her eyes lingered on him as he melted back into the crowd, and she forced herself to pay attention to the next gentleman on her card.

She needed to snap out of whatever spell Silas was beginning to weave over her. If she wasn't careful, it wouldn't be the rest of society she had to worry about fooling with their sham relationship.

She might very well fall for it herself.

# Chapter Six

Silas squinted against the bright morning sun, trying, and failing, to ignore the chatter he'd now heard from two groups of gossiping mavens wandering around Hyde Park.

Another group consisting of two eager mamas and no less than five daughters between them passed close enough that he should have done the gentlemanly thing and nodded graciously. Instead, he turned to study a particularly interesting leaf hanging near his head, pretending he hadn't seen them.

"Did you see that dress she was wearing last night?" one of the women said, he assumed to her friend, as she made a half-hearted effort to keep her voice low. "It would have barely passed for high fashion last year and was certainly not near grand enough for the Harthams' ball."

"Hmm, no accounting for taste, I suppose," the other one replied, flicking her gaze toward him. He steadfastly looked at his leaf. "And throwing herself at the duke that way. The poor man must have been mortified. I'm sure he only danced with her out of pity."

"I don't know why they were even invited. After what happened with the oldest girl running off like that!"

"Hush, Agnes. We shouldn't speak of such things. After all…"

Their voices trailed off as they passed beyond his hearing, and Silas glared after them. Normally, he enjoyed a delicious bit of gossip. And if it involved a good fashion faux pas, all the better. Hearing the way the women derided Arabella, however, twisted something in his gut. The nerve! He knew fashion, and the Bromley sisters had been perfectly presentable. Their gowns may have been holdovers from the previous year, but they had been elegant and tasteful, nonetheless.

Old harpies.

"You're out early, Whittsley. And looking supremely displeased about it, I see."

Silas glanced over to see his friend Charles, Earl Grantson, strolling toward him.

"That I am. On both counts."

Charles stopped beside him and faced the paths that winded through the park, clogged with their bevy of riders, carriages, and elegantly dressed people enjoying the morning promenade.

"Looking for anyone in particular, are you?" Charles asked, his lips pulling into a sardonic grin as they surveyed the throng of eligible ladies and their chaperones, all flitting about like a flock of brightly colored birds.

"As a matter of fact, I am."

Charles's eyebrows hit his hairline so quickly Silas chuckled.

"You surprise me, Your Grace," Charles said.

"Do I?" He shrugged. "I do not see why. Even I must succumb to my destiny at some point."

"Well, now I know something is wrong. The last time you succumbed to anything it was that French dancer who kept you mesmerized before absconding with several hundred pounds of your money and a large chunk of your miserable heart. You were despondent for weeks."

Silas laughed again. "Ah, sweet Yolande." He sighed and looked back over the park. "Well, never fear. I shall not lose my head over a pretty face like that again."

Charles frowned. "Then what exactly are you out here looking for?"

"My soon-to-be wife."

Charles opened his mouth, completely flummoxed. "But…"

"Ah, there she is. I will see you later this evening," he said, tipping his hat to his friend and leaving him standing there with his mouth hanging open in the cool morning breeze.

Silas chuckled to himself as he made his way to Arabella and her party. So far this betrothal situation had proven itself to be great fun, if only for the element of surprise alone. Once it was time to follow through and he actually had to bind himself in the shackles of matrimony, it might lose some of its amusement. But for the moment, he was thoroughly enjoying shocking his friends. He couldn't wait to see his grandfather's face.

"Ah, Miss Bromley," he said, greeting Aunt Adelaide. "You are looking particularly well this morning."

Adelaide flushed and waved him off. "You are too charming for your own good, Your Grace."

He feigned confusion. "Is that possible?"

Adelaide merely giggled and pushed Arabella forward. "Why don't you two go enjoy yourselves. Anne and I will be just behind you."

Anne didn't look thrilled at being relegated to the roll of chaperone, but Silas had no doubt that several suitors would soon join them. She had already caught the eye of several gentlemen Silas thought would be a good match. His end of the bargain would be filled in no time. And Arabella's end...

He glanced down at her, his blood warming at the sight of her gazing up at him, a slight grimace on her face and challenge in her eyes. He grinned, and she rolled her eyes and turned to walk. Her aunt and sister followed at a polite distance behind them. Close enough that they weren't technically alone while still giving them enough privacy to speak freely.

"Last night seems to have gone rather well," he said. "My valet said the maids were all atwitter with the gossip this morning."

She nodded, though he couldn't tell if she was pleased at the news.

"Isn't this what we hoped for?"

"Of course," she said, giving him a faint smile. "I'm just not used to being so…interesting to the rest of the world." She nodded at the curious faces that all turned to them as they strolled past. "Before Alice left, no one noticed me much. And since then…well, it's a bit overwhelming at times, is all."

He nodded, thinking of the women he'd overheard earlier. "I understand. Though I hope it won't be too distressing for you. The interest is not likely to die down anytime soon. Nor do we want it to."

She sighed. "I know."

He allowed his arm to lightly brush hers as they moved down the path. "Take heart. With any luck, you could be comfortably ensconced at Fallcreek Abbey within the next month or two, awaiting the birth of our child. And avoiding all the best gossip."

Her face paled, but she turned a genuine smile to him. "Let us hope, Your Grace."

"Silas, please. We are soon to be affianced, remember?"

"How could I forget?" Her eyes twinkled with that teasing light he was growing to appreciate.

"Speaking of betrothals…I planned to pay a visit to your father directly after leaving here. Does that suit you?"

Her forehead creased. "Perhaps it would be best if I spoke with him first. To prepare him. This will come as rather a surprise."

Silas took her hand briefly to help her step over a small puddle on the walkway. "Having second thoughts?"

She grimaced. "No." She gathered her skirts, deftly stepped across the puddle, and released his hand. "I am not having second thoughts," she continued, "but I have never been one to consider marriage. To have a man suddenly appear, wanting to marry me, especially a man such as yourself…"

He shrugged. "I don't see why this should be so surprising. Regardless of your feelings on the matter, I'm sure some young man has expressed interest before now. Besides," he said, not waiting for her to answer, "asking for a woman's hand in marriage is hardly an unusual occurrence and surely one he must be expecting."

"Wished for, perhaps. But expecting, no. Especially as we have only just met. I just hope the shock doesn't kill him," she said in jest. At least, he assumed she jested. It was hard to tell for sure.

Silas chuckled. "I hope this will come as a

more pleasant surprise than that."

She frowned, brow creasing in thought. "I honestly cannot say," she said after a second. "He seems quite content to allow me to stay at home forever." A smile pulled at the corners of her lips. "Though my father has never wanted anything but my happiness. As long as he thinks this is what I want, I don't believe he will object."

"Excellent. Then we'll get this formality out of the way and my solicitors can draw up the formal contracts."

Her hand brushed across her pocket, crinkling a paper inside. "And what of…"

She carried it with her? Afraid someone might see the details, perhaps? Silas gave her that slow, deliberate smile that grew even wider when her cheeks flushed, and her pulse throbbed against the thin skin of her throat. That he could elicit such a response with so little effort delighted him. His would-be fiancée wasn't as indifferent to him as she'd like him to believe.

"Do not fret, my dear. They will have the utmost discretion for our personal addendum."

They passed Lady Waterstack, who sat on a bench beneath a tree with a lady whom Silas didn't know. The woman took in the appearance of Arabella walking so close beside the Duke of Whittsley and immediately began whispering to Charlotte, not even waiting until they had passed.

Charlotte looked back and forth between Silas and Arabella, and then sat back shaking her head with an exasperated sigh, though she gave Arabella a quick smile. She shrugged at whatever the other woman had said and then responded, spreading the word, Silas assumed, of the duke's newfound attraction.

"She's a good friend to you," Silas said, nodding toward Charlotte as they passed.

"Yes," she said with a warm smile. "I'm lucky to have a friend who will stand by my side no matter what outlandish scheme I get myself into. Not that I've ever tested that theory until yesterday." She chuckled softly. "I'm glad Charlotte was up for the task."

They had reached the line of carriages where the Bromleys' footman waited. Silas took his leave, bowing and once again kissing her hand. "I will be at your residence within the hour," he promised.

Arabella pressed a hand against her stomach, but she nodded. "I look forward to it, Your Grace."

"Silas," he commanded yet again.

She gave him a half smile. "I shall save that for *after* you've spoken with my father."

He chuckled and held her hand as she climbed into the carriage. "Until then," he said, tipping his hat.

He quickly took his leave of Aunt Adelaide and Anne before hurrying off to his own carriage.

The prospect of a wife still bothered him immensely. If she wasn't contractually obliged to quit his presence and leave him to his own devices, he'd be on the fastest ship to the Americas. But as it was…he found himself strangely looking forward to the prospect. At least some aspects of it.

As long as her father agreed. A circumstance of which Arabella did not seem sure. It was a new sensation, this possibility of not being approved. Oh, his grandfather disapproved of him daily, but this was different. That a lady's father might reject him…*him*, the Duke of Whittsley, as a suitor for his daughter was a situation in which he'd never dreamed to find himself.

And for one of the relatively few times in his life, Silas realized he was nervous.

What if Lord Durborough said no?

# Chapter Seven

Arabella, flanked by Charlotte, who'd graciously agreed to be present for moral support, met Silas in the foyer as he stepped inside the house. The footman who'd opened the door raised his eyebrows in surprise but otherwise said nothing. He bowed and left Arabella to her guest.

"Is there a problem?" Silas asked, his brow furrowed with concern.

"No. Just…I thought maybe I should give you some advice. To help with my father. I don't think he'll object, but it couldn't hurt…"

Silas grinned. "I'd be glad of some advice."

Arabella took a deep breath and released it quickly, along with a barrage of words she couldn't stop had she tried. "When we are talking to my father, don't mention my mother. It will only remind him of their marriage, which will not paint ours in a favorable light."

"All righ—"

"And it might be best to get straight to the point. No faffing about."

"If you thin—"

"I've never been one for theatrics, so if you wax too lyrical, it might not help matters…"

"I will keep my waxing to a minim—"

"Also, my father is soft-spoken, and he prefers to organize his thoughts before speaking, and some take that as a slight on his intelligence or think he is perhaps hard of hearing, but in truth he's quite brilliant and hears rather well, so if he pauses after you speak, just give him a few moments—"

"Arabella," Charlotte broke in, her voice level but stern. "I'm sure His Grace is perfectly capable of comporting himself with the utmost decorum and respect. There's no need to bark orders at the poor man."

Silas grinned. "It's all right. I was starting to like it."

Charlotte choked back a laugh, holding her hand to her mouth to cover the sound. But Arabella stood in frozen horror, belatedly realizing how she must have sounded.

"I'm so sorry. I just…in moments of extreme tension or in situations such as this—not that I've been in this particular situation, mind—I tend to…I just prefer if there is a set plan in place, and everyone knows what to expect or how to—"

She clamped her mouth shut on the stream of words. "I apologize, truly. I think…" She pressed a hand to the avalanche going on in her belly. "I think I am a bit nervous."

Silas smiled again and took her hand and kissed it, letting his lips linger long enough that Charlotte cleared her throat. Arabella yanked her hand from him; though, if she were truthful, she would have rather let him keep it. His touch somehow calmed part of her while intensifying the circus in her stomach.

"It is quite all right," he said. "Shall we go in?"

She nodded, and he wrapped her hand around his forearm to lead her inside.

"Life with you will never be boring, will it?" he asked, just as one of the footmen opened the door, leaving her no time for a response.

A mere heartbeat later, they were standing before her truly befuddled and flabbergasted father.

"I'm sorry, Your Grace," he said, looking between Arabella and Silas as if he'd never seen them before. "But…did you say you wish to marry my daughter?"

Silas beamed and nodded. "With all due haste."

"I'm…afraid I don't understand," he said, looking at Arabella, though it was Silas who answered.

"I've long admired your daughter."

"You have?" Lord Bromley asked, his bushy white eyebrows rising. He seemed to belatedly realize how that might sound, because he turned to Arabella with a crinkled frown.

She smiled gently at him, but Silas seemed

mildly affronted. "Who wouldn't? She's not only pleasant-looking but has also been blessed with a ready wit and intellect, not to mention a kind heart and genial spirit and a…a…wonderful sense of… of…hygiene."

Arabella glanced at him, eyes wide. Did he just say hygiene?

He gave her a quick lopsided shrug and turned back to her father.

"I'm aware of all that," Lord Bromley said drily. "I just hadn't realized you were acquainted enough with Arabella to know it as well."

Silas ignored that and surged ahead. "Arabella and I have discussed the matter at length and feel our union would be mutually beneficial—"

"Do you love her?" Lord Bromley said.

Silas gaped for a moment, and had the matter not been so serious, Arabella would have laughed at the stunned expression on his face.

"Father, this is what I want," she said, looping her arm through Silas's, though purposely touching him in such a way sent her stomach careening about her belly with the force of a violent storm.

He covered her hand where it lay upon his arm and smiled down at her. Which somehow seemed to calm her stomach but sent her heart crashing about in her chest. She took a deep breath and tried to keep her voice calm and steady.

"His Grace has been most kind to me and has

even promised to help secure Anne's future…"

She trailed off as understanding dawned on her father's face. Before he could object, she went to him and took his hands, drawing him aside. Silas, bless him, took the hint and joined Charlotte in studying the suddenly fascinating view out the window.

"You do not have to do this," her father said. "Anne will be just fine. The scandal will die down and she'll find a nice young man who will not care if there are a few whispers."

Arabella shook her head. "Whispers have a tendency to grow, not disappear. This last year has taught us that, if nothing else. What kind of sister would I be if there was something I could do to ensure her happiness for the rest of her life and yet I did nothing?"

"Hmm, and what of your happiness?"

"Father," Arabella said, her heart full to bursting with love for the man before her.

He shook his head. "It's too great a sacrifice."

"It is no sacrifice," she said. A quick glance at Silas set her cheeks burning, and she tried to calm them by sheer will. "The arrangement is one that suits me very well."

Her father glanced between them with new interest in his eyes. "Does it now?"

She couldn't help the embarrassed smile that peeked out. She finally shrugged. "I admit marriage is not something I had ever planned, but there are several benefits, not the least of which those that will help this family. Besides, I have always loved children. Having one of my own would be a blessing. Truly."

Her father wavered at the promise of grandchildren, and she pressed forward with more enthusiasm. "I'll admit the company of a husband isn't something I have ever sought out. But should it prove unwelcome, it's not something I will need to endure. The duke has promised that I can retire to Fallcreek Abbey whenever I wish. I can spend the rest of my days reading my way from one end of his library to the other. Can you imagine it, Papa?" she asked with a little laugh that brought a smile to his face. "So many books! Such a famed library! And if I choose, I could have a bed moved into it, have all my meals brought to me, and never leave it again. Believe me, such a life will not be a sacrifice."

"That would be wonderous indeed," he said, patting her hand. "But do you even like the man?" He shot Silas a skeptical look. "You will be required to spend quite a bit of time in his company. No estate, no matter how grand the library, is worth one moment of your unhappiness."

Arabella's heart clenched, and she squeezed her father's hands before risking a glance of her own at Silas. Their gazes met and held for a brief moment, but that was all it took to send a bolt of heat straight to her core and set her cheeks afire.

She looked down at her toes rather than meet her father's eyes. "I don't know him well, but I believe he is a good man. He seems amiable, kind even. He has been more than fair in our dealings so far. I do not believe he will make me unhappy."

Her father relaxed a little, but he still didn't give in. "Not being unhappy is not the same thing as happiness, my child. I'm glad that you will not be miserable by this arrangement, but I had hoped for something better for you. True love and happiness like I had with your mother."

She squeezed his hand again. "I think what you had with Mother was very rare. But please believe me when I tell you I am happy with my choice. It may be unorthodox and not what you had hoped for, but I am truly satisfied with everything."

Her father stared at her for a moment, as if trying to read the secrets of her soul. But whatever he saw in her face must have given him the answer for which he sought, because he nodded and turned to Silas.

"Very well. I'll give my blessing."

Silas put his hand over his heart and bowed with what looked like sincere respect and gratitude. She smiled, her heart warming. Whether he meant it or not, that he'd show her father such respect touched her deeply.

Silas made arrangements with her father for their solicitors to meet the next day in order to finalize the formal marriage contract, and then he stood to take his leave. She accompanied him to the foyer, where he surprised her yet again by taking her hand.

"Well, that went rather well."

"Hmm," she said, distracted by the way his thumb moved lazily across the back of her hand. "Now we just have to survive the rest of the marriage."

His laughter echoed through the entryway. "Oh, I don't think it'll be as bad as all that."

He brought her hand to his lips and pressed a lingering kiss to it, his mouth moving in a gentle caress across her skin. She sucked in a tremulous breath and pulled away, clenching her skirts to keep from cradling the tingling appendage against her chest. How did he do that?

"Um…" She cleared her throat and tried again. "Lady Waterstack has invited a poet to present some of his new work to a small group and has invited me to attend. Will you join me? Aunt Adelaide would be there to chaperone, of course, but I will count it toward your monthly obligation if you agree."

He smiled, though it quickly faded when she added, "It is on Wednesday at seven o'clock."

His brow briefly creased. "I regret I cannot.

In fact, I should have informed you that I will be unavailable for any activities on Wednesdays. Non-negotiable."

She glanced up at him with curious surprise. "Might I inquire why you need these days?"

"No." Unlike his usual responses, this one held no hint of humor. He seemed to realize that his response was harsher than he probably intended, because his stony expression softened.

"I apologize for my shortness. But on this particular matter I will not concede. Nor do I wish to discuss it."

Arabella wasn't sure what to think. His demeanor had changed completely from the perpetually jovial man she'd seen so far.

"There is nothing nefarious going on, I assure you," he said, giving her a reassuring smile that didn't quite reach his eyes. "I simply have a prior engagement I must see to and prefer to go about my private business with no questions asked."

She tried to push her misgivings aside and gave him a soft smile. After all, he truly hadn't asked for much considering what she'd asked of him. Most men wouldn't have let her in the front door let alone agreed to her preposterous scheme. One day to himself every week was a small enough request.

"I can't promise not to be curious about it, but I will agree to your terms."

"No questions asked," he repeated, firmly.

She nodded. "Rule number ten. Every Wednesday. No questions asked."

His smile radiated satisfaction and relief. "Thank you. You are indeed a kind and gracious lady."

He clapped his hat on his head, his customary mood restored. "Now. My carriage will arrive to collect you and your sister at ten tomorrow morning. Be sure you are ready."

She frowned and followed on his heels as he headed out the door.

"Ready for what?" she asked.

He stopped at the door's threshold and glanced back at her over his shoulder. And winked. Then he hurried down the rest of the steps to the gate.

"For what?" She followed him though she stopped just outside the door. "Your Grace!"

He didn't stop. "Until tomorrow!" he said, climbing into his carriage.

She crossed her arms and blew out an exasperated breath as she watched his carriage trundle down the lane. Until tomorrow indeed. He was insufferable.

But she couldn't stop the smile that spread across her lips as she stepped back inside to contemplate what the morrow would bring.

# Chapter Eight

Silas watched as the two Bromley sisters stood side by side with a team of seamstresses bustling about them. They could not be more different. Not in appearance...the sisters were much alike, though Anne's eyes were a nondescript shade, not the beautiful kaleidoscope of forest colors that made up Arabella's deep brown eyes. But in temperament, certainly.

Anne's smile lit the room, and she squealed with excitement as one of the seamstresses held up swaths of one gorgeous fabric after another for her to choose. In fact, she hadn't stopped radiating delight since they'd told her of their engagement, and she had been effusive in her welcome of him into their family.

Arabella, on the other hand, stood with pinched lips as Madame du Chard draped a deep green fabric about her. For a moment, it seemed as though she'd rip the cloth from her body. But he caught the slight softening of her eyes and faint smile as she rubbed the material between her fingers. Even she could not deny its beauty.

Or hers.

She met his eyes in the mirror and dropped the fabric, her lips returning to their pinched disapproval. He grinned, which only made her scowl more.

As soon as the seamstress finished taking her measurements, Arabella stepped down from the stool and joined him where he sprawled on a sofa.

"This is unnecessary," she said, for possibly the hundredth time.

He sighed and leaned his head back against the sofa. "So you've said."

"Yes, but you don't seem to be listening."

He snorted. "I could hardly do otherwise, my dear, as you never stop talking." He smiled at her to take the sting from his words.

She huffed. "Only because I'm trying to make you *hear* me."

"I'm more than just a pretty face," he said, reaching up to run his fingers along the edge of his ears. "These work quite nicely."

Her lips twitched, and she looked away, trying, and failing, to keep her amusement in check. He grinned. He tended to have that effect on people. "You will soon be the Duchess of Whittsley. I have an image to maintain. It will be decidedly more difficult to repair the reputation of your family if my own suffers because my wife doesn't look the part of her new station. Just think of it as a necessary evil, if you must."

She raised a brow. "So, you're worried that if I am not dripping in silks and diamonds, your peers will think less of you."

He flashed her another grin. "Precisely."

"And here I thought you were making some grand, selfless gesture to please your new bride. Or at least curry my favor. Instead, it's all to protect your ego," she said, though her eyes flashed with amusement.

He shrugged. "Perhaps it's all three. One dress can accomplish so much."

She shook her head but couldn't hide her amusement. "Whatever your motives, there was no need for you to drag these poor women to the house. We could have easily met them in the shop."

"Yes, but then I couldn't have been present to direct their efforts. Besides, this way I can make sure you actually order the dresses."

Her eyes widened, and she placed a hand on her impressive bosom with mock offense. At least he thought she was in jest. Difficult to tell sometimes.

"Do you think I would go against my word, Your Grace?"

He snorted. "Over this?" he said, waving his hand at the seamstresses pulling yet more fabric from their trunks. "In a second."

She tried to grimace at him, but her smile

peeked through, and she sat back with a sigh. "I simply find such frivolous expenditures... unseemly."

He shrugged with one shoulder and looked back over at where Adelaide and Anne were near shivering with delight at a basket of lace and trimmings.

"I do tend to be unseemly no matter what my expenditures. So why not be frivolous about it?"

Arabella scrunched her face with that adorably confused frown she often sported when conversing with him. "What sort of logic is that?"

He chuckled softly and then nodded toward her sister. "Look how happy she is. Do you really want to spoil her fun?"

Arabella watched her sister for a moment and then sighed in defeat. "No. Fine. I surrender. Do your worst. Drown me in frivolity. I shall complain no more."

He raised a brow. "Are you always this dramatic?"

Her lips twitched. "Not always, no."

"Ah, only when you're with me, then."

"So it seems."

He chuckled and raised her hand to his lips. "I am honored then to be the recipient of such special treatment."

"You're ridiculous," she muttered, pulling her hand from his grasp, though her cheeks flushed becomingly.

Arabella's Aunt Adelaide bustled over to them with an ecstatic Anne in tow.

"Oh, Your Grace, you have simply been too generous," Adelaide said.

Silas waved that off. "Nonsense. I'm happy to provide for my new family. Even though," he said before Arabella could object, "I know it isn't necessary. But Lord and Lady Linwood's ball should always be occasion for a new gown, and with time so short, I'm happy to facilitate the acquiring. Now then." He slapped his knees and stood, holding out a hand to help Arabella up. "I must away. I'll just have a quick word with Madame du Chard before I go."

Adelaide bustled her nieces out of eavesdropping range so he could conduct his business with the modiste, though Arabella pinned him with that soul-reading stare of hers. If he thought for one moment this union of theirs would be a conventional one in which he'd be obliged to enjoy her company for more than their agreed upon year, he'd be more than a little afraid of that stare. As it was, he seemed torn between constant amusement and abject terror whenever he was in her presence.

She saw far too much.

He worked very hard to make sure people only saw what he wanted them to see. Too long in Arabella Bromley's company and he feared she'd have him laid bare. A delightful and enticing prospect to be sure when talking of their impending physical relationship. But when it came to the inner workings of his mind and heart, he'd much prefer to keep his secrets to himself.

Something that seemed less and less possible with each moment he spent with his future wife. He would have to work harder to keep his distance from her until they could part for good. His life wouldn't be the only one affected if she got too close.

•••

True to his word, Silas had obtained invitations to all the most fashionable balls and parties for the season, and the gilded parchments had been arriving all day. While Arabella had no doubt their reception would still be chilly, at best, the fact that they would be let in the doors was a vast improvement to their lot a mere week prior. Their debut at the Harthams' ball had caused quite a stir. Silas's interest in her, in particular. For now, at least, the novelty of their association seemed to be keeping the more malicious gossip at bay. Hopefully, that would last long enough for Anne to make a good match.

Arabella didn't look forward to any of it. Well,

that wasn't strictly true. She smiled with gentle amusement at Anne fidgeting on the cushioned bench next to her. Even if she didn't find a match this season, the bargain Arabella had struck with Silas was well worth it if only for the joy on her sister's face in that moment.

Silas had promised to speed the procurement of their marriage license as much as he could, but it seemed they wouldn't be able to wed any sooner than a fortnight hence. A thought that should relieve her, considering she was about to become wife to a man she hardly knew. But as she had promised to marry him, and the contracts had been signed that morning, she'd rather get on with it. Get married. Hopefully conceive quickly. And then she could hide away in the country, buried in Silas's library, for the rest of her days.

She let a small sigh escape her. It sounded heavenly. She just needed to get through the next few weeks first.

Arabella didn't need to look for Silas when they arrived at the Linwoods' ball. He stood at the top of the stairs, waiting for her, much to the consternation of everyone who passed him. More than a few eager mothers were pushing their daughters at him with varying degrees of success. Arabella couldn't help but smile at the horror—or was it fear—that he seemed to barely keep in check as he tried to navigate the fine line between chivalry and self-preservation.

When she reached him, his relief was palpable.

"Ah! Miss Bromley. How lovely you look this evening," he said, gently extracting himself from the gaggle of giggling girls who surrounded him. "Miss Bromley," he said, giving Aunt Adelaide a gentlemanly bow. "And Miss Bromley," he said again for Anne. "Might I escort you lovely ladies inside?"

He held out his arm for Arabella to take, ignoring the audible gasps of several among his crowd of admirers.

Arabella was tempted to decline, just to see what would happen. But the relief in Silas's face and the pleading in his eyes won her over. Besides, doing so would undo everything they'd done so far to put their plans in motion. Definitely too steep a price to pay for a moment of amusement.

"Thank you, Your Grace," she said, taking his arm. "You are most kind."

"It's my great pleasure," he assured her. "Shall we?" he said, including Aunt Adelaide and Anne. They followed close behind Arabella and Silas into the house.

"You needn't have waited for me," Arabella said, leaning closer so only he would hear her. "We could have met inside."

"I thought perhaps it would be easier for you if I accompanied you."

"Easier for me?" she said, raising an eyebrow before casting a surreptitious glance over her shoulder at the bevy of eligible maidens who followed behind them.

Silas grinned, not at all repentant. "Yes. Though I'll admit it was for me as well. You do make an excellent shield."

Arabella laughed and Silas smiled again. "Besides," he said, "arriving together will cause a big stir and set those tongues immediately wagging. Much more effective than merely sharing a few dances. Though we shall do that too," he said with a wink.

Aunt Adelaide tittered behind him as they ascended the stairs. Anne stared speechless at their luxurious surroundings. And hoping to spy a favorite suitor or two from the previous evening, Arabella was sure.

When they reached Lord and Lady Linwood, Silas drew her closer. Despite her resolve to face everything bravely, she clung to his arm, though she hoped she exuded outward calm.

"Whittsley!" Lord Linwood said, clapping Silas on the shoulder. "I didn't expect to see you here tonight." He turned a curious eye on Arabella. "And escorting such a lovely young lady."

Silas smiled so proudly even Arabella almost believed that he was thrilled to be delivering his news. "I couldn't pass up your ball, Linwood," he said with a chuckle. "Lady Linwood, you have outdone yourself. Everything looks beautiful." He gestured to the rooms beyond them that seemed to be bursting with flowers, lights, food, and people.

"Thank you, Your Grace," she said, though her attention was focused on Arabella.

"And I'm very pleased to introduce Miss Arabella Bromley," he said, nodding down at her.

Arabella bit the inside of her cheek at the not-so-subtle jolt of recognition from Lady Linwood at the Bromley name.

"My fiancée," he added.

Arabella didn't know whether to laugh or find offense at the twin looks of utter shock on the faces of their hosts.

"That's…wonderful," Lady Linwood finally stammered out. "Congratulations, Your Grace. Miss Bromley." Arabella's name was said civilly but with considerably less warmth.

"And this is my soon-to-be aunt, Miss Adelaide Bromley, and sister-in-law, Miss Anne Bromley. This is her first season, for all intents and purposes," he added to Lady Linwood conspiratorially. "We expect her to make a brilliant match."

"But of course," she said, still obviously shaken but doing an admirable job trying to hide it. "In fact, there are a number of young men present tonight who I'm sure will be delighted to make her acquaintance."

Arabella very nearly applauded. In one swift interaction, Silas had announced their engagement, his support for their family, and ensured Anne would never be short of appropriate suitors. Indeed, she'd be sure to make a most advantageous match. Those who would not have considered her before would be eager to align themselves with the Duke of Whittsley. If she didn't have a proposal by the end of the month, Arabella would be surprised.

Lord Linwood had done little more than blink, apparently struck totally speechless at the previously inconceivable notion that the elusive duke might be ensnared. And by one such as herself, no less. His wife gave him a subtle but firm elbow in the ribs, and he snapped out of it.

"Wha—oh." He cleared his throat. "Congratulations, Whittsley. And Miss Bromley, of course. I… ah…" He frowned, squinting into the distance as if he were racking his brain for something to say. Then his face lightened.

"Oh, here's your grandfather. He must be delighted at the news."

Silas's head swiveled, quickly glancing over his shoulder. He muttered under his breath. "Oh, bloody hell."

Arabella's mouth fell open and she hastily looked to the Linwoods to see if they had overheard. But they were chatting with the next group in the receiving line. And telling them all about the duke's happy news, if the glances they were getting were any indication.

Silas quickly led them into the ballroom and set up camp in a corner that was a bit out of the way.

"Are we trying to avoid him, Your Grace?" she asked him.

"Yes," he muttered, his attention not on her but on where his grandfather could be seen peeking through the crowd at regular intervals, obviously trying to find his errant grandson.

"Wasn't part of the plan to tell him of our arrangement to improve relations between you?"

"Yes, but as I'm also not quite sure how he'll receive the news, I'd prefer to deliver it when we are not in the company of so many. I don't think the old man will cause a scene and publicly decry my choice of wife, but…let's just say I'd rather not tempt fate."

He took a step back, a move which placed him squarely behind a large potted plant.

Arabella watched him with growing amusement. "Why, Your Grace, if I didn't know better, I'd say you were hiding from Lord Mosley."

Silas peeked out from behind a particularly large leaf. "I fear no man."

Arabella raised a brow. "All evidence to the contrary, Your Grace."

His gaze flickered to her and then back to the leaf he held in front of his face. He dropped it with a snort.

"As I said, I fear no man. But Lord Mosley isn't a man. He's a demon. A fiend. A…a…a nincompoop."

"Did you just call me a *nincompoop*?" Lord Mosley said, appearing on Silas's other side. "How dare you, sir."

Silas yelped in surprise and spun around to face his grandfather. Arabella clapped a hand over her mouth to keep from all-out laughing.

Silas's face froze for half a second and then his eyebrow quirked up. "You take no issue with the demon or fiend description, though?"

Lord Mosley rolled his eyes. "I believe the word you are searching for is *grandfather*," he said. "Though why I claim to be that escapes me most days."

"Why didn't you tell me he was right behind me?" Silas muttered to Arabella under his breath as his grandfather greeted Aunt Adelaide.

She shrugged. "I wanted to see what would happen."

His eyes widened, flashing with surprise. And delight. "You diabolical creature. I'll have to—"

"I didn't expect you here tonight, Whittsley," Lord Mosley said, turning back to look his grandson over. "What a surprise to see you clean and upright."

Silas released a long-suffering breath and held up a finger to Arabella. "You and I will discuss this later." Then he turned to Lord Mosley. "Grandfather. I didn't see you there."

Arabella left them to their mumblings and glanced at Anne, a bit concerned they wouldn't be visible enough for suitors to see her.

"Don't worry," Charlotte said, making her way through the throng to stand beside Arabella. "After the duke's obvious interest at the Harthams' last night, Anne's prospects have been the talk of the town. Yours as well," she said with a significant look.

Arabella rolled her eyes, though she exhaled with relief at the sight of several dashing gentlemen already bearing down on Anne. Her dance card would be full in no time. Excellent.

"See," Charlotte said. "Her future is all but assured."

"Hardly assured, but definitely improved, I'll give you that," she said, smiling at her friend.

She took mental note of several of the young men so she could ask Silas and Aunt Adelaide about them later. It wouldn't do any good to encourage Anne toward a certain young man if he had dismal prospects.

"You what?" Lord Mosley said behind her.

Arabella and Charlotte turned back to the men,

leaving Aunt Adelaide to deal with supervising Anne's evening.

"Hmm. Apparently, the big news of the evening has been spilled," Charlotte said.

Arabella lightly snorted and glanced about the room. "Judging by the buzz happening behind the madly waving fans in this room, I'm surprised Lord Mosley hadn't heard anything before reaching us. We told Lord and Lady Linwood at the door, and I swear by the time we made it all the way into the ballroom, most of the people here had already heard about it."

"Good news does travel fast," Charlotte said with an amused smile. "And bad news travels even faster."

"Bad news?"

Charlotte raised a delicate blond brow. "For all the other dear mamas and hopeful misses in this room? Absolutely devastating."

Arabella wasn't sure whether to laugh or cry. She'd never been the object of envy before, and she was not enjoying the sensation.

Charlotte raised her fan and leaned over to whisper to Arabella. "How do you think old Lord Mosley is taking it?"

"I…" Arabella frowned. "I have no idea."

Whatever Silas had told him seemed to have struck his grandfather momentarily speechless. Silas regarded him, his head tilted slightly to the side the way her father's old bloodhound would whenever it heard someone riding up the lane to their house. She couldn't quite tell if Lord Mosley was happy, disappointed, or just in abject shock over the news his grandson would soon be wed. Happy news, she'd think, going by what Silas had told her. But marriage to a Bromley…well, she'd expect a man like Lord Mosley to object to that on some level.

Whatever the case, watching the range of emotions flit across Lord Mosley's face as he gaped at his grandson fascinated her. There was a good deal of dismay, as she expected, but the overriding emotion seemed to be surprise. Happy surprise. Well…perhaps *happy* was too bold a word. Relieved, maybe.

But since neither man had said a word since Lord Mosley's exclamation, Arabella just stood, watching the two men watch each other.

The stern Lord Mosley resembled Silas somewhat. Around the eyes. And something about the way they held their heads, as if they were both gearing up for battle.

That was where the resemblance ended. Where Lord Mosley was tall and wiry, bordering on thinness, his grandson was broad through the chest and shoulders, his torso tapering into a trim waist. Silas was flush with health and youth. Lord Mosley, on the other hand…there wasn't anything she could quite pin down, but she wondered if he had been ill lately.

He turned to her so suddenly that she jumped in surprise.

"My dear girl," he said, grasping her hands. "I have no idea what finally possessed my grandson to grow up and decide to settle down. But bless you. I'm truly sorry for the dire circumstance that must have induced you to accept my grandson's offer of marriage, as I'm sure nothing less would have persuaded even someone with a…well…let's say colorful background to accept his miserable hand. But while I might wish your family's recent troubles were not now aligned with my grandson, I must confess, I am still grateful to you for accepting him. Having said that, I've always believed in being honest and direct, so I'll admit you wouldn't be my first choice for him."

Arabella blinked up at the man, more than a little offended, though she had to admire his directness.

"However, I never thought I'd see the day the young pup finally did his duty, so if you are his choice, for whatever reason, you are truly most welcome to the family."

"I…" She wasn't quite sure how to respond to that extraordinary mixture of acceptance and derision. So she settled for a safe, "Thank you."

He released her and glanced at Silas—who

stood, mouth ajar, lips half quirked up in a smile…
or grimace of horror, it was hard to tell—and then
turned back to her.

"If he ever gives you a lick of trouble, don't
hesitate to call upon me, and I will set him to rights,
post haste. Have a pleasant evening, ladies," Lord
Mosley said, giving the Bromley women a gallant
bow before making his way back through the
crowd to the refreshment table, a spring in his step
that Arabella had never before observed in him.

"Well," Silas said, coming to stand beside her.
"That…went better than I expected."

Arabella could only nod wordlessly.

She'd known announcing their engagement
to the world would be overwhelming. Being the
center of anyone's attention was a bit much for
her. Being the center of *everyone's* attention? That
was a fraction more than she'd been prepared to
deal with. And Lord Mosley's surprised and very
vocal acceptance of her, despite the manner in
which it was phrased, was a good thing to be sure.
However, it also ensured any eyes that hadn't been
upon her after their arrival were now riveted to
her. Probably for the duration of the evening.

And suddenly she couldn't breathe.

# Chapter Nine

One minute his fiancée stood before him, a bit quieter than usual maybe, but that was understandable under the circumstances. And the next she'd gone. Bolted right through the clusters of fine ladies and gentlemen milling about the Linwoods' ballroom, skirts flying behind her.

Lady Waterstack and he stared at each other for a second. "I'll go after her," she said.

She didn't wait for Silas's response but turned on her heel and hurried after her friend. And Silas hurried after them both, not pausing to contemplate why he felt the need to do so.

"What are you doing?" Lady Waterstack asked when he caught her up moments later.

He shrugged, looking over the edge of the stone balustrade that surrounded the terrace leading to the gardens. "Call it curiosity."

He caught sight of Arabella sitting on a bench several yards down the path, luckily still within the well-lit glow of the house. He only made it down one step before Lady Waterstack stopped him.

She glared at him. "It's absolutely inappropriate

is what I'll call it. Engaged or not, if you two are caught alone her reputation will be in tatters. And it's already bad enough as it is."

"But we won't be alone, my dear Lady Waterstack. You'll be there to chaperone."

She opened her mouth, but he didn't wait to hear her argument. He had no doubt she'd be fast on his heels, especially since she feared so much for her friend's reputation. And she wasn't wrong. He should have given that sticky little issue more consideration before he'd gone running after her with half the aristocracy watching their every move. But she'd surprised him so much that he'd reacted without thinking. And since he was already there, with chaperone in tow, he might as well find out what sort of bee had gotten up his fiancée's bonnet.

Arabella glanced up with a gasp when he sat down beside her. She looked around, eyes wide, relaxing a bit when she saw Lady Waterstack take a seat on the bench across the path from them. She'd likely overhear everything they said, but it couldn't be helped. All three of them were within full and well-lit sight of the house, ensuring the safety of Arabella's reputation.

He didn't say anything for a moment. Truth be told, he wasn't exactly sure what he should say.

"You followed me," Arabella said, saving him from having to start the conversation.

He shrugged. "I've never had a woman run from me before. Quite a novel sensation."

Her lips twitched, and she looked down at her hands in her lap. "Sorry about that."

"Do you want to tell me why you felt the need to quit my company so quickly?"

Her eyes flashed to his, wide with surprise. "I wasn't running from you, Your Grace."

"Silas. Please."

"Silas." She flushed in the dim light. "It just… all seemed so overwhelming for a moment. I needed to get some air."

He nodded and stretched his legs out, crossing his arms over his chest. "I understand that."

She raised her eyebrows. "You do?"

"Certainly. I know I make it look easy but being the Duke of Whittsley can be a rather large pain some days."

The smile she flashed warmed him to his very soul. How did she do that?

"Is that why you spend so much time on frivolous pursuits?"

"I wouldn't call them all frivolous."

She raised a delicate eyebrow again, and he grinned. "Most, perhaps. But not all," he admitted.

She laughed quietly.

"I think if I hadn't learned how to have a little fun with my life, I'd have ended up a young version of my crusty old grandfather."

"He doesn't seem so bad," Arabella said, before her brow furrowed. "A little intense, perhaps."

He chuckled again. "Just a bit." He sighed and looked up at the stars. "When I was little, being the duke sounded like such a grand adventure. I'd be in charge of all I surveyed. I pictured myself like a general commanding my troops. Always dressed in fabulous uniforms and barking orders at everyone far and wide, and everyone always scrambling to do as I bid them."

Arabella smiled softly. "And has it not lived up to your expectations?"

"In some ways, I suppose," he said, returning her smile. "There is certainly no lack of people who will scramble to obey me. And that has its advantages."

"Such as ensuring a team of seamstresses work their fingers to the bone to finish two new ballgowns in a single afternoon."

He laughed. "Yes, as a matter of fact." Then he sobered, the weight of the true burden of being the Duke of Whittsley settling back on his shoulders. "But there's far more to it than I ever imagined."

"Is there?"

He nodded and looked at the ground. "My father caught me ordering the servants about one day. I was being a true tyrant, not to put too fine a point on it. Standing on the dais in the main hall and sending them scurrying in all directions just to see if they'd really do everything I commanded."

The familiar rush of shame he felt whenever he recalled that day hit him in the gut, and he paused to swallow against his tight throat. He shook his head slightly. "My father walked in, saw what I was doing, and boxed me about the ears before saying a word. Right there in front of everyone. I daresay it was a wonderful sight to them." His lips twitched, though there was no humor in it.

"You were just a boy," Arabella said, reaching over to take his hand.

He looked down at it, then up at her. She seemed almost surprised to have done it, but she didn't remove her hand, and he wrapped his own around hers, savoring the warmth of her that he could feel even through the barriers of their gloves.

"I may have been a boy, but I still knew better. I deserved what he gave me and more. He hauled me from the dais, my ears still ringing, and out to the stables. I thought for sure he meant to whip me."

She gasped. "Did he?"

"No. He had the groom saddle my horse, and he took me on his rounds with him to the village and farms. Every day after that, when I wasn't at my lessons, I was with him. Visiting with our tenants, haggling with the merchants who came to the estate, dealing with the disputes between farmers on our land. He even had me accompany my mother when she'd make her visits to the tenants' homes, bringing them baskets of herbs and bread from Fallcreek's kitchens."

Arabella smiled gently. "He was teaching you to be a duke."

Silas frowned slightly. "Not to be a duke, necessarily. But what it meant to care for the people who depended upon me. It was far more than just being in charge and shouting orders at those who couldn't refuse me. He made sure I understood that they were real people with real needs. In actuality, we depend upon them far more than they depend upon us. Without them, my estates would go to ruin. That's deserving of respect. He made sure I understood that before he passed."

She squeezed his hand lightly. "How old were you when he died?"

His heart stuttered painfully in his chest. He normally shied away from any mention of his parents. For many reasons. His throat grew thick with emotion, and he cleared it before trying to speak. "My mother died in childbirth a month before my thirteenth birthday. My father followed her a year later."

"Oh, Silas. I'm so sorry."

Arabella leaned against him slightly, not enough so he could feel her weight, but her presence soothed him nonetheless. A tendril of her hair fluttered against his neck, and he turned to her, just as she turned her face up to him. Her hand trembled in his and he tightened his hold, wishing there were no barriers between them so he could feel the heat of her skin. Their eyes met, and he stared down into those golden depths that drew him in until he saw nothing else. He brushed his thumb across her cheek, his hand lightly cupping her jaw as he leaned in—

"Ahem," Lady Waterstack said, the noise a strange cross between clearing her throat and a cough.

Arabella jerked back like a bucket of cold water had been tossed in her face, and Silas grimaced at Lady Waterstack, who smiled sweetly and raised her eyebrows as if daring him to challenge her.

He sat back with a sigh, reluctantly releasing her hand and putting a few inches of distance between himself and Arabella. Engaged or not, chaperone or not, if they were seen in a passionate embrace before walking down the aisle, no amount of subterfuge, goodwill, or downright bribery would restore her good name. Even if he still went on to wed her.

It was going to be a very long two weeks. Obtaining the license was taking rather longer than he'd hoped, but his agent had been assured it wouldn't be much longer. Thankfully. He might not want a wife, and he had no desire to be a husband.

But there were some advantages of matrimony that he could not wait to take frequent advantage of the moment the intriguing woman at his side said, "I do."

• • •

Arabella loved Charlotte. And she was grateful she was there as chaperone to ensure there would be no possibility of future scandal befalling her family.

But at the moment, it was really hard to remember all that.

When Silas had looked at her, his eyes boring into hers like she had captured him, and he couldn't escape. Didn't want to escape. His lips had been so close to hers. All she'd had to do was lean in…

She sucked in a deep breath of the cool night air, all remnants of his heat moving with him when he'd put distance between them. And rightly so. But…still…what would it be like when they could actually kiss? When he could take her in his arms and hold her close? Would her blood pound through her body the way it was doing now, until she was so lightheaded that she had to hold on to him or faint? Would she be daring enough to kiss him back?

She stole a glance at him and pressed a gloved

hand to her mouth to keep him from seeing her smile.

Yes, she absolutely would.

Though preferably not on a bench in full view of any who happened to look their way. And, as a quick peek at the terrace showed her, there were plenty who were trying not-so-subtly to watch them. No doubt waiting for the next Bromley sister to disgrace the family name and ruin the second chance they'd only begun to enjoy. No. She wouldn't give them the satisfaction. The duke would already be facing enough gossip from those who felt she wasn't good enough to be his duchess. There were certainly higher born and wealthier ladies available who came from families without a hint of scandal attached to their names. Many would question why he chose her. And she wouldn't give them any reason to question further.

She would just have to make sure such a moment never happened again. No matter how enticing the man tried to be. Not that he really tried. All he had to do was get within ten feet of her and her mind started thinking of things she'd only heard whispers of before. And seen once when she'd caught the kitchen maid Suzy behind the stables with Tim, the butcher's son. They had definitely seemed to be enjoying themselves. And she couldn't help but wonder if she'd enjoy it as much if Silas touched her the way Tim had been touching Suzy.

After this evening, she rather thought she might. A lot.

She choked down another strangled breath. Damn her corset. She'd had her maid lace it too tightly this evening. Though it hadn't bothered her previously. Still, sucking in enough air to satisfy her greedy lungs seemed an impossibility at the moment.

"I have something for you."

She blinked up at Silas, his voice startling her out of her naughty thoughts. Her face flushed hot, though she knew he couldn't possibly know what she'd been thinking. At least she hoped not. He always looked amused like he could see the innermost workings of her mind.

"I meant to give this to you earlier but got distracted by all the frippery that was fluttering about."

She narrowed her eyes. "Frippery insisted upon by you, I'll remind you."

"Yes, yes," he said, waving that off with a laugh. "Be that as it may, I forgot to give you this."

He pulled a small gold box from his pocket and placed it on her palm. Her heart pounded, already knowing what it contained. She hadn't expected an engagement ring from him. After all, their engagement wasn't what she'd call tradition-al. She could hardly expect him to follow the usual engagement traditions.

Then again, aside from the few love matches she'd seen, many marriages of those of her class were more for mutual benefit than actual love. So perhaps their marriage was more traditional than she'd thought after all.

Either way, she needed to open the box in her hand and found it curiously difficult to do so.

"Let me help," Silas said, taking it back from her.

She meant to protest but instead watched as he pressed the clasp that released the lid. Inside, nestled in the plush velvet, was a filigreed, gold-banded ring that held a large ruby surrounded by small pearls, creating the effect of a glittering flower.

"Oh, Silas," she breathed, so stunned his name slipped from her before she could think to feel uncomfortable about it. "It's beautiful."

He pulled the glove from her hand and slipped the ring on her finger. He didn't let go right away, but instead took her hand in his, holding it so they could both admire the ring. It *was* beautiful. But she was having a hard time concentrating on anything but the warmth of his hand enveloping hers. The glide of his thumb across her knuckles. Each brush sent a fresh bolt of heat sizzling through her veins. No man had ever touched her so. She hadn't anticipated that feeling his skin against hers would be so…decadent. Intoxicating.

The little circles he drew across her fingers were maddening. Deliciously so.

She took a tremulous breath and gently pulled her hand from his before she made an utter disgrace of herself.

"The jeweler said it's all the vogue to use the bride's birthstone in the ring but…" He gave her a sheepish grin.

She smiled. Of course, he didn't know her birthday. "It's an emerald."

"Ah. Well. I shall remember that for the future."

She glanced at the ring a final time and then pulled her glove back on. The material held the ring tight to her finger, pressing it into her skin. As if she needed a further reminder of the outrageous scheme that had somehow actually worked.

"Well," he said, "shall we return to the ballroom?" He stood and offered her his hand.

She sighed and grimaced in the direction of the brightly lit hall. "If we must."

He pulled her to her feet and tucked her hand into the crook of his elbow. "You needn't dance if you would prefer. We'll just tell any hapless gentleman that wanders by that you're feeling poorly or hurt your ankle."

"Heaven forbid I just tell them no."

Charlotte snorted as she followed them toward the steps, and Silas chuckled. "Perish the thought. You'd break their delicate hearts."

She rolled her eyes but couldn't help a quiet laugh.

"It won't be so bad," he tried to assure her. "It'll give us the opportunity to see how your sister is faring. I have a few particular gentlemen in mind."

"Do you now?"

"Hmm. In fact, there is one." He led her into the ballroom and found an empty seat along the wall to park her. He sat beside her, much closer than she probably should have permitted. But they were formally betrothed now, after all, and in full view of everyone in the ballroom. So she didn't say a word.

He leaned toward her. "See the gentleman just there, speaking with the Weatherby girl?"

Arabella followed his gaze to where a handsome young man stood talking to a rather pretty girl bedecked in an unfortunate arrangement of feathers and brilliants.

"That is Viscount Ashford. Soon to be sixth Earl of Isley if the gossips are correct about the state of his father's health. And the gossips are usually correct."

"An earl? Determined to get that extra favor?"

He gasped in mock horror. "Would I do anything so underhanded and selfish? I'm simply trying to find my dear sister-in-law a suitable husband."

"Hmm," Arabella said, watching him through narrowed eyes. "Well, then, what about him?" She nodded at the dance floor where a clumsy but earnest-looking young man was spinning her sister about.

"Him?" Silas scoffed. "Jasper Thornbrook? He has no talent, no grace, and no title. His family owns a shipping company."

"Yes, a very profitable shipping company. My sister would live in supreme comfort and wealth the rest of her days. And he's very good-looking as well."

Jasper tripped over his own feet and stumbled, nearly pulling Anne down with him. They managed to right themselves in a flurry of skirts and giggles and continued with the dance.

Silas raised his eyebrows with a look that clearly said he felt his point had been proven. Arabella laughed.

"Your sister would probably live in constant fear for her life, always wondering when her dear husband would trip over his own two feet and burn the house down or fall down the stairs."

"Oh, leave the poor boy alone. I think it's sweet. He's obviously so taken with her he's nervous."

"He's a menace. And not nearly good enough for my new little sister."

"Who would be, then?"

Silas scanned the room until his gaze alighted

on another gentleman. "How about Lord Chesterfield?"

Arabella looked him over and frowned. "He's a bit old, isn't he?"

"Only ten years older than me, my dear," Silas said with a wry smile.

"Well, he looks far more," she said. And she wasn't just trying to soothe his pride. Lord Chesterfield might only be forty or thereabouts, but his hair was liberally streaked with gray and the buttons on his vest were beginning to strain.

"He's still handsome enough and his bank account would make your sister a very merry widow when he did predecease her."

Arabella grimaced and Silas leaned in a bit closer. "He's also very kind, has a particular soft spot for kittens, and would spoil your sister rotten."

Arabella glanced at him in surprise, and he blinked innocently. "You really should give me more credit, my dear. I am still determined to make the most advantageous match possible for our dear Anne. But that doesn't mean I won't try to find someone who will be truly good to her."

Arabella ducked her head, touched that he did seem to have her sister's best interests at heart. Then she looked back up at him. "Kittens?"

Silas gave her that half smile that made her heart skip a few beats. "Where do you think I got Bub?"

She laughed, and he shrugged. "I had the misfortune of visiting him soon after one of his cats had queened, and he foisted the little beast off on me. It would serve him right if he got a wife as repayment."

Arabella cocked an eyebrow, and he grinned. "Not that a wife is a punishment, of course."

"I suppose that depends on the wife." He gave her a pointed look, and she narrowed her eyes, though she couldn't help but smile.

They spent the next couple hours watching Anne twirl around the floor with a variety of suitors while Silas pointed out the strengths and weaknesses of each one. He even introduced her to one or two he particularly liked. By the end of the evening, she had to admit his choices, for the most part, were sound. It was also the first time Arabella had ever made it through an entire ball without hiding in a corner to read or leaving within a few minutes of arriving. She was quite surprised to find she'd actually enjoyed herself… and spending the evening with Silas.

"Well?" he asked as they watched Anne dance with her last gentleman of the evening.

"I'll concede, you've chosen admirably. Each gentleman comes from a good family, has a sizable bank account, and seems, as far as I can tell, to have a good disposition. Most of them are even respectably aged and decent to look at as well."

"Why thank you, my dear."

"Although, I must put my foot down over your proposal of Lord Masterly."

"What is wrong with Lord Masterly?"

"You can't be serious."

Silas raised his brows. "I am. He's perfectly acceptable."

"Well, now I must question your faculties, Your Grace. The man is so old he must walk with the aid of a cane and an assistant."

Silas chuckled. "While that may be true, your sister won't have to put up with him for long. She'd be sure to be a widow near instantly, left with her freedom, a title, and an obscene amount of wealth."

"Yes. Well. Be that as it may, that is not what I want for Anne. She would prefer a happy marriage to lonely widowhood, no matter what she may gain from it."

He sighed. "Very well. No Lord Masterly."

She smiled at him gratefully. "Thank you, Your Grace. And I'll admit, for the most part, certain parties notwithstanding, your choices have been surprisingly thoughtful."

"Try not to sound so surprised, my dear Arabella. I do have rather excellent taste."

She laughed. "I'll endeavor to keep that in mind."

"Please do," he said with a coy wink before turning to ask Aunt Adelaide a question.

Ari tried to watch him when he wasn't looking. Watched the way his eyes would light up when he was trying to get her to smile. The way he'd hum along to the music during lulls in their conversation. The way he focused on every person he spoke to, sending most of them away with a smile.

Oh, her intended might be a bit less serious than she'd prefer. He might spend his days and nights in ways she didn't approve. But like it or not, she was pretty sure he was, at the heart of it, a good man. Not that he'd admit to it.

"A word, Whittsley," a voice said behind them, just as they'd stood to leave.

Silas sighed. "Grandfather, we were just on our way out. Perhaps we could speak on Sunday."

"I could be dead by Sunday, and you need to hear this now." His grandfather walked a couple paces away and waited none too patiently for him.

Silas sighed again and took Arabella's hand, kissing the back. "My apologies, my dear. It seems my grandfather will be shortly expiring and must make his grievances known immediately." He smiled, though the expression didn't quite reach his eyes. "I'll call on you tomorrow."

Arabella nodded and watched him walk off with a frown.

"What is it?" Charlotte asked.

"I'm just wondering what all that's about," she said, nodding toward the two men who seemed to be in argument over something.

"Well, then, let's find out."

Before Arabella could protest, Charlotte grabbed her hand and pulled her toward a columned walkway that would take them past where Silas and Lord Mosley spoke.

"You were there again last week, weren't you?" Lord Mosley said.

Ari couldn't see Silas's face, but his tone when he answered was one she'd never heard him use before, completely devoid of humor.

"It is none of your business how I spend my time, Grandfather."

"It is when it deals with *her*. I've warned you before. Let her alone. Continuing these visits is no good for either of you."

Arabella sucked in a gasp, though thankfully there was enough noise surrounding them to muffle the sound. She placed a hand over her mouth and glanced at Charlotte, who watched her with concern.

"And I've told you," Silas said, "that I won't just abandon her."

"And what will you tell your pretty new fiancée about her, then, hmm?"

There was silence for a second. "Arabella needn't ever know about her."

Her gut twisted and she could feel Charlotte staring at her, but she didn't want to see what might be on her friend's face.

"Secrets have a way of coming out," Lord Mosley grumbled.

"This one won't. It hasn't yet."

"We shall see."

"You are getting what you want, Grandfather. Me, married. An heir soon to follow, God willing. You even like my choice of wife, though I'm sure it kills you to admit it."

"I've never said a word one way or the other about your choice of wife."

"Oh, yes you have. I'm quite sure the Bromley women were on the top of your list of unacceptable virgins. But some part of that dark heart of yours must like her despite her family's reputation, because if you truly disapproved, my ears would still be bleeding from your barrage of opinions."

Lord Mosley snorted but didn't say anything else.

"I have chosen a wife, just as you wanted. The rest of my life is mine to live, and I will not change my mind about this," Silas said. "Let it be."

Lord Mosley made an incomprehensible noise and, by the sounds of it, marched off, followed shortly thereafter by Silas.

"What do you suppose all that meant?" Charlotte asked, her eyes filled with concern.

Arabella had an inkling. It must, of course, deal with his precious Wednesday activities that she wasn't allowed to ask about.

Her stomach sank and she took a few quick breaths. And then tried to shake it off.

"It doesn't matter," she said, giving her friend what she hoped was a bright smile. "This marriage is one of convenience. I'm doing it for Anne. He is doing it for an heir. After our goals are accomplished, we'll be quit of each other. It's none of my business what he does with his time. Something I agreed to in advance, in writing. His business is his own. So. That is that."

"Ari…" Charlotte said, but Arabella shook her head.

"I'm really all right," she said, though her churning insides said otherwise. "I need to find Anne and Aunt Adelaide and get home. I've already stayed later than I intended."

Charlotte didn't argue more but accompanied Arabella to her family, kissing her quietly on the cheek before she took her leave.

If Anne and their aunt found her overly quiet on their way home, they didn't mention it. Though they probably didn't notice in their excitement over Anne's prospects. She had met many lovely young gentlemen, several of whom were on Silas's approved list. They exclaimed with delight over her betrothal ring and barely noticed when she excused herself to bed as they made plans for all the callers who would be sure to show up the next day.

Ari climbed under her covers, the weight of the ring on her finger feeling more like a vise than the comforting band it had been earlier.

Why did she care so much? She barely knew Silas. She didn't want to be his wife any longer than absolutely necessary. She was already counting the days until she could seclude herself away in the country and they weren't even wed yet.

So why did the thought of this mysterious *her* wound her so much?

She took a deep breath and blew it out slowly. There was no point continuing to dwell on it. Especially when there were far more pressing things to contemplate. Such as her impending marriage, which would be upon her in a matter of days. Though it wasn't the wedding that sent shivers of anxiety and anticipation through her body. It was the wedding night.

Very soon, she wouldn't be climbing into a cold bed alone. She'd be climbing into *his* bed. *With* him.

She'd thought it would be so easy. That it would be a quick chore she could accomplish with little fuss at the end of each day and be done with it. But that had been before he'd touched her. Held her. Kissed her hand. Caressed her cheek.

That her body had responded with such… heat, such anticipation, with barely a brush of his skin, had been more of a shock than when he'd accepted her proposal. And she still wasn't sure how she felt about it.

Just that evening, when he'd slipped her ring upon her finger, she'd felt so alive. As if every ounce of her being yearned for…something. For more. For him. And his touch had been nothing more than a slight breeze, a whisper of his hand against hers. How would it feel when those hands roamed further? When they touched…*everything*?

She shuddered, her hand straying to her chest as if it could contain her wildly beating heart. When her scheme had succeeded, she'd thought herself so clever. Now, with their wedding looming too near, she was starting to wish she'd listened to Charlotte and come up with some other way to solve her family's problems.

But she hadn't, and now Silas was in her life and in her mind and very soon would own her body as well. And she wasn't remotely prepared. Though the fine tremor that ran through her wasn't entirely from fear. Part of her dreaded what was coming. But the rest of her, if she were honest, was waiting with bated and eager breath.

# Chapter Ten

The morning of the wedding found Silas sitting at his bedroom window, exhausted from a night of trying to sleep.

One would think he was a typical nervous bridegroom. And he was, though not in the way he imagined of most bridegrooms. He was about to marry a woman who had, for all intents and purposes, sold herself to him as a broodmare in order to save her family. Oh, he'd gone along with it well enough before, but now that the actual ceremony loomed, he wasn't sure he could go through with it.

He needed to speak to Arabella.

He dressed quickly, throwing on his wedding finery without waiting for his valet to assist him, and marched out the door while sleepy servants sputtered behind him. Except when he arrived at Bromley Hall, it was to discover that Arabella had also left in a hurry that morning. Only, she had been wearing her wedding dress, so he could at least have a hope that she still intended to marry him.

Though perhaps that wasn't a good thing.

He mounted his horse and rode to the quaint country chapel Arabella had chosen for their wedding. A surprising choice, considering her groom. They probably could have married at one of the palace chapels. But Arabella had wanted a small, intimate affair. Family and close friends only. Which left relatively few people sitting on his side of the church. His grandfather and Charles and his wife. There were others he could have perhaps invited, but those three were really the only ones he truly wished to be there. And his grandfather was a glaring *maybe* on the best of days. But if he was present at the actual ceremony, the old man couldn't very well accuse him of lying about being wed, so there was that.

There was one other he'd have liked to have been there, though she wouldn't have been welcomed by anyone but him.

He tied his horse outside the church and entered, not sure if he hoped Arabella would be there or not. But the moment he stepped inside and saw her sitting on a pew, his shoulders sagged in relief. Huh. Apparently, he really did want to get married after all. Though he was still fairly sure he didn't want to be a husband. Couldn't be a husband. Not the type of husband a woman like Arabella deserved, at any rate.

And then there was the whole issue of her not wanting to be a wife. And if that was the case, what were they doing?

She turned, glancing up at him with an unreadable expression. But she didn't seem surprised to see him.

"Couldn't sleep either?" she asked, her voice soft in the quiet of the church.

He sat beside her. "No."

She nodded, turning back to the stained-glass window she'd been staring at.

"It's lovely, isn't it?"

He frowned a little and followed her gaze. "The window?"

She nodded again. "So peaceful."

The multicolored light streaming through the window touched her face, infusing it with color and turning her gown into yards of shimmering rainbow.

She took his breath away.

Wispy tendrils escaped from her elaborate, pearl-studded bun, and he clenched his hand to keep from brushing them back from her face. He longed to touch her but didn't wish to ruin her hair or veil. She'd dressed with care that morning, despite her early arrival. Had she done so for him?

"Arabella," he said, hating the way his voice shattered the silence. "Is this what you truly want?"

She turned to him with a slight frown. "Trying to break the rules so soon, Your Grace?"

"Not at all. I just have no wish to force a

woman into marriage for the sole purpose of carrying my child." He tried to keep his voice even, but her eerie calm was beginning to get to him.

"It's not our sole purpose for this marriage," she said, and he waved that off.

"I promised to help your sister find a suitable match, and I will do so, whether you marry me or not."

She turned to look at him then, not saying anything as she regarded him with a slight tilt to her head. "And how many men will want her when not one but two sisters have disgraced their family name?"

He frowned, and she continued before he could speak. "Alice ran away with our groom, an act for which I'll admit I condemned her. On many occasions. But…" She shrugged. "She was in love. Who am I to stand in the way of that? And with news of our engagement and your championship of my family, that scandal seems to have died down. At least enough that Anne might have a chance at a good life. But if you break our engagement, leaving me literally at the altar, there will be no recovering from that. For either Anne or myself. I'll be ruined."

He opened his mouth to speak, and she cut him off again. "It won't matter who calls off the engagement. It won't matter that nothing untoward has happened between us. It wouldn't matter if you were completely at fault. I could have walked into this chapel and seen you in the arms of another woman and I'd still be the one with the ruined reputation if the wedding is called off. So, I ask you, Your Grace, do you intend to break the rules we set? Or do you intend to keep your word?"

Silas sighed and ran his hands through his hair. "I would never do anything to bring shame or misfortune to you or your family. And you're right, I didn't think through the implications of what I was suggesting. But that doesn't change the fact that I do not wish to force you into a situation you abhor."

He took her chin between his fingers and turned her face up to his. "I will walk up this aisle with you the moment the clergyman arrives and will proudly leave here as your husband, if you'll have me. But that doesn't mean you need to do anything you do not wish to do. Do you understand what I'm saying?"

"We made a bargain…"

"And I will keep my end. I release you from yours."

She stared into his eyes, saying nothing, the silence of the church pressing in on him until all he could hear was the sound of his own heart pounding in his chest. Then she slowly reached up and cupped his cheek, drawing him down until his lips were a breath away from hers.

"I do not wish to be released," she whispered.

He hesitated only a heartbeat longer before closing the distance between them. With the first brush of her lips against his, he was lost.

His hand slipped behind her neck, and he dragged her to him, his mouth moving over hers until she opened beneath his lips. A slight whimper escaped her throat, completely unraveling him. He deepened the kiss with a low growl, shaking at the fire that streaked through him at the first taste of her. Just that one taste, and he knew it would never be enough. She intoxicated him. He held her close, and she clung to him, keeping him a willing captive in her arms.

He lifted his head once, his eyes searching her face, making sure she was there with him. Feeling what he was feeling. Yearning with him. For him.

She didn't give him a chance to worry. Her fingers threaded through his hair and dragged him back down, her thumbs caressing his jawline beneath his ears as she drew him back to her. He hauled her close with a groan, his mouth plundering hers as—

A slight breeze brushing his face was the only warning they had before someone cleared his throat.

Silas and Arabella froze, their lips still pressed together for half a heartbeat before they jerked apart and stared at each other for a brief second.

Then they turned their heads toward the door. And the dozen or so people who stood there watching them.

The clergyman pushed his way forward, his face red with shock, though his eyes twinkled with amusement.

"I think perhaps we ought to begin the ceremony. The sooner we get you two wed, the better."

Arabella gasped and pushed away from him, her hand over her mouth, though a nervous giggle emanated from beneath her gloved hand.

Charles clapped him on the shoulder and forcibly turned him to lead him up to the front of the church.

"You couldn't wait another fifteen minutes?" Charles muttered to him.

Silas laughed. "I'm in a church, standing before a man of the cloth. I think my good intentions are clear."

Charles snorted. "Just in case, I'm keeping my eye on you until the ceremony is over." He shook his head. "Only you would defile a church on your wedding day."

"Well, now that's a bit dramatic."

"Is it?" Charles asked with a laugh.

Silas opened his mouth to deliver a truly spectacular retort, but the organist struck up the first chords of that horrendous piece that had been in vogue since the Queen's eldest daughter had played it at her wedding, and he turned to face the aisle.

Arabella slowly walked toward him on the arm of her father. She glanced around her briefly, her cheeks still flushed, though whether it was from what they'd been doing or the fact that they'd gotten caught, he wasn't sure. But then she turned that gaze upon him. Their eyes locked, and a soft smile spread across her lips.

And for the second time that morning, she stole his breath away.

• • •

Arabella didn't know what had come over her. One moment she'd been sitting on the pew, staring at the window and praying she could make it through the day without disgracing herself, and the next she'd thrown it all to the wind and acted the fool anyway.

She had full control over her faculties. Most of the time. Until Silas looked at her in that way he had. And touched her. Like she was something soft and precious and utterly desirable. Before meeting him, she would have thought there was nothing that could overcome her strict code of behavior. But with Silas... She didn't know how he did it, but somehow, he made all her good intentions fly right out the window.

And now she was marrying him. Probably a good thing considering how many people had just seen her in his arms. In the middle of a church, no less. Her cheeks flamed and she glanced around her, trying to gauge what might be going on in the heads of their guests.

But the moment her eyes met his, her thoughts quieted. He smiled, his gaze taking her in from veiled head to slippered toe, and he beamed with approval. For the first time, she was glad Aunt Adelaide had ignored her when she'd said she'd never marry and had commissioned two bodices for her court presentation gown. One for the presentation, and one to be worn on her wedding day. Which, at the time, she had no intention of ever having. But Adelaide had ordered the second bodice anyway, either out of hope or just knowing better than Arabella did that she would need it someday.

She would have to thank her later. Arabella had been too nervous that morning to say much of anything.

She kept her eyes on Silas as she reached him at the altar. Devilishly handsome, as always, if a bit rumpled from their little indiscretion. Still, his suit fit him to perfection, the coat, vest, and trousers hugging every line of him as he took her hand from her father's and turned with her to face the clergyman.

She hoped their marriage would prove quickly fruitful so she could make her escape. Because for the first time in her life, she could see herself becoming one of those women who were so besotted with their husbands that nothing else in their lives mattered. Look at the state of her mind after a couple short weeks in his company. And one mind-shattering kiss. She scarcely recognized herself. And that frightened her more than anything else so far.

She hardly heard the words of the clergyman as he had them repeat their vows. And she knew her fingers were ice-cold when Silas slid her glove off to place a simple gold band next to the beautiful engagement ring he'd given her. He frowned slightly, squeezing her hand as his eyes searched hers. She smiled, trying to ease his concern. She hadn't changed her mind. It would have been too late, anyway, as the clergyman pronounced them man and wife.

Her heart leaped in her chest, and she sucked in as deep a breath as she could manage.

It was done. She was now Arabella Spencer, the Duchess of Whittsley. God help her.

Silas placed a chaste kiss upon her lips and turned with her to face their audience of beaming family members and friends.

"I don't believe I've ever looked forward to following a rule so much in my life," Silas said, leaning down to speak in her ear so only she could hear. She glanced up at him, eyebrows raised. "To rule number two," he said, kissing her hand with a grin before leading her back up the aisle to the raucous congratulations of their guests.

She swallowed hard. Rule number two. Heir-making attempts. Nightly. Insisted upon by her. *What had she been thinking?*

Her stomach flipped, even her tightly laced corset unable to keep it under control. Though, whether it was in fear or anticipation, Arabella wasn't sure. Perhaps it was both.

Either way, they had a party to get through first. The reception would be held at Bromley Hall and would be much grander than their ceremony. It would not be a full-fledged ball, thankfully. Which meant Arabella wouldn't have to worry about dancing with all eyes in the room on her. But she would have to greet everyone who came through their door at the side of her new husband. And the notoriety of their pairing, combined with the fact that the duke was…well, the duke, and had been the most popular and coveted bachelor at that, meant they could be sure of a splendid turnout.

Arabella was thrilled for Aunt Adelaide, who was in her element being able to orchestrate such a huge undertaking. And for Anne, who would surely be even more sought after now that she was officially the sister of a duchess. The Bromleys' fortunes and reputation had vastly changed, thanks to Silas. Oh, there might still be whispers here and there. But that's all they'd be. And with any luck, Anne's wedding would be the next one that would be celebrated.

In the meantime, Arabella had to get through a few more hours without passing out or fleeing to the quiet safety of her room.

Silas gave her hand another squeeze and helped her into his carriage for the short ride to Bromley Hall.

"Don't worry," he said as soon as the carriage had lurched into motion. "It will be over with quickly and I'll be by your side the whole time."

She smiled up at him. "Are my nerves that obvious?"

He chuckled. "If they are, I'm sure people understand. It is your wedding day, after all."

She let out a long breath. "Yes, it is." As unbelievable as that felt.

"Just a few hours," he said, leaning closer to cup her chin. "And then it will be just the two of us."

If he'd meant to make her feel better, he'd failed. But before she could say anything, his lips descended and she was right back where she'd been that morning, no fear, no hesitation, and no thought in her head but him and the sensations that coursed through her. She kissed him back, her lips moving beneath his with a sudden urgency she couldn't explain.

He groaned against her mouth and her heart pounded, thrilled that she was the one causing him to make those sounds. He pulled away from her far too soon and rested his forehead against hers, dragging in a ragged breath.

"I have half a mind to tell this carriage to keep driving," he said, pulling back just enough to look into her eyes. "Think anyone would miss us?"

That startled a laugh out of her, and she sat back. "Possibly."

He sighed and ran a hand through his hair before replacing his hat. "Very well. I suppose we must attend to our guests, then."

She put a nervous hand to her hair, wondering if it had become disheveled.

"You look perfect," he said. "Beautiful."

She gave him a relieved smile, and he stepped through the door the footman had just opened, turning back to hold out a hand to her.

As she alighted, he whispered in her ear, "I'll be counting the minutes until we are alone again, wife." And then he tucked her hand into the crook of his arm and led her up the steps into her childhood home, as if he hadn't just sent her heart careening about her chest.

Tonight. They'd be alone. And they'd begin

trying to make an heir.

And it suddenly occurred to her she wasn't sure exactly what that entailed.

She needed to find out. Quick.

# Chapter Eleven

"There he is," Silas said, leaning down to get Arabella's attention.

"Who?" she asked, nodding at the party guest who'd just given her their congratulations.

Silas noted, gratefully, that there was no one else waiting just then to be greeted, and he pulled his new wife to a small alcove where they could talk undisturbed for a moment.

"Your sister's soon-to-be betrothed," he said, nodding over his shoulder to the crowd of people milling about the Bromleys' salon.

"What? Has someone proposed already?" she said, looking up at him in surprise.

"Not yet. But D'Auvergne is perfect for her. Once she meets him, she'll want no other suitor. See? He's there, over by the lemonade."

Arabella craned her neck, trying to spot him, and frowned slightly. "D'Auvergne? He's French?"

"Yes, but don't hold that against him," he said with a chuckle. "He spends most of his time here. He has extensive estates near Herefordshire. He comes from an illustrious family, very wealthy, very well connected. And very titled."

She raised a brow. "Oh really?"

He nodded solemnly. "He is actually Jean-Pierre Henri Louis Clermont-Allier, Duc D'Auvergne. He's a distant Bourbon cousin, though of course the title doesn't give him much claim to the throne now. Not that he had much of a claim before. His family had the foresight to get out of France with the bulk of their wealth in time to keep their holdings, and their heads, intact. The current republic has so far left him and others in his position alone as long as they don't go getting delusions of grandeur. But his ancestry still carries weight. Just think, your sister would be a duchesse. And a wealthy one at that."

Arabella pursed her lips. "I'm less concerned with his wealth and ancestry and more concerned with his nature."

"You'd be hard-pressed to find anyone who would say an ill word of him. He's honest to the point that I spend as little time in his company as possible. Boring old sod, for the likes of someone such as myself. But he's jovial enough that I have found myself enjoying his company whenever it is forced upon me."

"Too boring and honest for you but jovial enough to entertain you when called upon? High praise indeed," she said wryly.

"It is," Silas insisted. "I tried to teach him how

to bluff while playing cards once. He was dreadful at it. Found trying to trick his opponent distasteful. And preferred not to gamble away his money on games of chance, if you can believe it."

"Perish the thought," Arabella said, pressing her hand to her chest with a mock gasp. His new wife was a right comedienne, it seemed. He ignored that comment and nodded at Jean-Pierre again. "And if that isn't enough to persuade you, just look at him."

She sighed. "His appearance is hardly releva— Oh…"

Silas glanced down at her to find her staring open-mouthed at the Frenchman. He scowled, though it was more at the unfamiliar jolt of jealousy that was blossoming in his chest at the sight of his wife's clear admiration for another man. "All right, all right. There's no need to lose your wits over the man."

"I might have to disagree with you," she said, still staring.

"Is that so?"

"Well…I mean…" She gestured at Jean-Pierre and then looked back at Silas, eyebrows raised in a *what do you expect* expression.

It was his own fault. He was the one who'd pointed the man out to her. And frankly, that chiseled, angelic face of his was one of the reasons Silas found it so tedious to be around the man. He had a habit of striking any woman in the vicinity speechless with admiration. He just hadn't expected his own wife to fall prey to the Frenchman's pretty face.

He leaned down until his mouth brushed against her ear, smiling when she shivered at the contact. "I'd like to remind you that you wed *me* not two hours ago. So unfortunately you are not an available candidate for D'Auvergne's hand."

A small sigh escaped her. "I suppose that's true."

He reared back, jaw dropped, and Arabella laughed, her cheeks flushing red and her eyes watering with the force of her mirth.

"Oh," she wheezed, her hand pressing to her middle as she tried to catch her breath. "You should see your face."

"No, thank you," he said, infusing his tone with an offense he didn't truly feel. "I wouldn't want to frighten myself with my hideousness. I'll just keep staring at D'Auvergne."

She nodded. "Good idea. I'll join you."

His jaw dropped again, but before he could say anything else, she sucked in a breath. "Oh, look."

He followed her gaze to where Jean-Pierre stood, bowing to Anne while Aunt Adelaide flushed with excitement and even his new father-in-law looked on with interest. Anne bobbed a small curtesy in return and followed Jean-Pierre to the refreshment table where he handed her a cup, and they began to talk over cake and punch.

Silas and Arabella glanced at each other, and Silas grinned. "Looks like I might fulfill my part of the bargain first."

She raised an eyebrow. "I didn't realize it was a competition."

"It's not. Exactly. I suppose I did have an unfair advantage, since we cannot begin trying to fulfill the second half of the bargain for at least another two hours." He took her hand and brought it to his lips, watching her carefully as he pressed his mouth to her skin.

Her pulse visibly jumped in her delicate throat, and her breath hitched. Even that tiny reaction was enough to make his blood sing. Maybe they could slip out after another hour and a half.

Her tongue darted out to moisten her lips, and his own pulse leaped. Make that an hour. Tops.

"Definitely an unfair advantage," she said, her voice squeaking out in a ragged whisper. She flushed and cleared her throat. "Then again, Anne has still not made a match, despite your confidence over your selection of suitors, so perhaps I will win after all."

He didn't wish to point out that he had every intention of spending his every waking moment devoted to not only making sure she won, but also ensuring she enjoyed every second of the pursuit. No need to divulge his strategy.

"You seem very confident," he said, turning to face her and effectively blocking out the sight of everyone else. The handsome Jean-Pierre in particular. Though Arabella didn't seem to notice as her attention was firmly pinned on him.

"Do I?" she asked in that breathy half whisper that seemed to seep into his skin and set fire to his blood.

"Yes." He kissed her jaw. "Very." His mouth moved to her cheek, and she leaned into him ever so slightly. "You are the picture of utter confidence."

He kissed her lips, his arm going about her waist to pull her closer. She sank against him, her mouth moving under his, drinking him in. Her hands slid up his torso to his chest, resting over where his heart pounded furiously for her.

She tensed beneath him, giving him only a split-second warning before she gasped and pushed him away.

"What's wrong?" he asked, frowning, reaching out to brush a thumb across her cheek.

"We shouldn't," she said, her eyes wide.

"Rule number three says we can. Encourages it, even," he said, kissing her again. "I'm publicly displaying my affection."

She pulled away with a laugh. "Yes, we are definitely public. But the rule specified *appropriate* displays of affection, I believe."

He gave her a gentle smile. "We're married now. What could be more appropriate than that? Your reputation will hardly be ruined if you are found alone with your own husband."

She relaxed a little, her breath leaving her in a rush. "Perhaps. That might depend on what I'm doing with my husband at the time."

He chuckled and kissed her again, unable to keep his lips from seeking hers out. "What do you want to be doing with him?" he whispered in her ear, smiling when she shivered against him.

"I… I…" She looked up at him, the desire blazing in her eyes turning to what he swore was panic. Her eyes shifted from his, her gaze darting about, anxious enough that he frowned in concern.

"Arabella?"

She took a step away from him, and his frown deepened. "I'm fine. I just…" She caught sight of someone and some of the tension went out of her. "I need to speak with Charlotte. I won't be long."

She left him standing there watching as she hurried to Lady Waterstack's side, whispered furiously in her ear, and bustled off with her, arm in arm.

"Scared her away already?" Charles said, appearing at his elbow.

Silas scowled at him but then snorted. "Apparently. Not sure how, though."

Charles chuckled. "It was probably just your winning personality." He clapped him on the shoulder. "Don't worry, my friend. You are now bound together by law and church in holy matrimony. There's no escape for either of you."

Silas blinked and looked back to where his wife and her friend had disappeared up the stairs.

Now why didn't that sound as horrible as it had two weeks ago?

• • •

"What is it?" Charlotte asked when Arabella hauled her up to her bedroom and plopped down on a chaise in a poof of skirts and tulle.

"I need to know what happens."

"What happens when?" Charlotte said, sitting beside her.

Arabella took a deep breath, her stomach flopping. But better to be embarrassed in front of Charlotte than in front of Silas.

"Tonight…"

Understanding dawned on Charlotte's face. "Has Adelaide…ah, no, I suppose not."

Arabella shook her head. Her spinster aunt was no help with this particular problem.

"Do you…know anything at all?"

Arabella frowned. "Well, I'm not completely in the dark. We have animals on the farm. I assume the concept is the same."

Charlotte flushed and blinked a few times. "Oh…well, yes, I suppose, when you come right down to it… There is a bit more to it than that, of course."

"Right. That's where I was hoping you could help."

"There are some things that the two of you will figure out as you go along, of course."

"Yes. But just in general." She took a deep breath. "I would just prefer not to go into my wedding night completely in the dark."

Charlotte nodded. "I do understand that. My mother, bless her heart, told me nothing. She was too embarrassed to even tell me that I'd need to remove my clothing, so you can imagine my surprise when Jasper—" She blushed bright red. "Well. You can imagine. Or…perhaps you can't." She let out an embarrassed laugh.

"So…no clothing? You mean, he'll want to see…everything?"

"Well, I can't speak for most men, but if he's anything like Jasper, then yes."

"Oh," Arabella said, finally understanding Silas's enthusiasm for her insistence on keeping the lights on at all times. That little devil. Not that he could have told her, she supposed, but still.

She sucked in a deep breath and let it out slowly. "Tell me everything."

Charlotte nodded, took a deep breath of her own, and did, indeed, tell her everything.

And by the time she was done, Arabella's head spun. She wasn't actually sure if she believed everything Charlotte had said, though her friend certainly had no reason to lie. But some of it seemed…fantastical.

When someone knocked at the door, Arabella and Charlotte both jumped and then looked at each other and giggled as they used to when they were young.

"Arabella dear," Aunt Adelaide called. "May I come in?"

Charlotte patted Arabella's hand. "Don't worry about tonight. You two will find your way."

Arabella wasn't as confident about that, but at least she wouldn't be going into her wedding night wholly ignorant.

"Arabella?" her aunt called again.

"Sorry, Aunt Adelaide. Come in, please."

Her aunt bustled in. "I believe the duke is ready to depart, my dear. We need to get you changed."

Arabella smiled at Charlotte and then nodded, standing. Time to get on with it, then.

She would be moving into Whittsley House, the duke's London residence in a prime section of Grosvenor Square. Her aunt had prepared her to run a grand house, so she didn't doubt her ability to do so. Both with his London residence and with the palatial Fallcreek Abbey in the country. Though, everything would certainly be on a much grander scale than she was used to.

Of course, with any luck, she'd be able to stay at Fallcreek soon and leave the London residence, and all the duke's other properties, to him. In fact, the only thing she really wanted at Fallcreek was the library. Perhaps Silas would be amenable to creating a library just for her in another location. Then they wouldn't need to be involved with each other at all. Except, of course, when dealing with their child. Should one arrive.

And one must. It was her duty to provide the duke with an heir. Rule number one.

And to get that heir, she would need to walk out her door and climb into that carriage with Silas. And then do…all manner of other things that made her blood rush to her cheeks…and a smile tug at her lips.

Part of her wanted to run to the attic and hide until Silas gave up looking for her and left. But the part that remembered the feel of his lips against her skin, the way her heart pounded at the mere touch of his hand…that part was beginning to overtake her nerves. When she thought of what Charlotte had told her…well, she was even somewhat eager to discover what really went on between husband and wife.

Unfortunately, by the time she got changed, said her goodbyes, and climbed into the carriage with Silas, he didn't seem nearly as eager as he had been in the alcove. She'd had a lot of expectations when it came to her wedding night. Dealing with a reluctant groom hadn't been one of them.

Well. She was just going to have to find out what had dampened his mood. And do what she could to remedy the situation. Which would be much easier if she had any clue what she was doing.

# Chapter Twelve

Silas sat across from his bride, silent for probably the first time in his life.

He hadn't known what to make of her sudden disappearance after their interlude in the alcove. She had certainly seemed to enjoy his attentions. Right up until the moment she'd pushed him away and run off, that is.

Perhaps it was nerves. After all, she was a young, newly married woman. She thankfully didn't seem averse to his advances, and a few nerves were to be expected, he supposed. He actually had no experience with virgins whatsoever, and he found himself suffering a few nerves himself.

It only took a few minutes to arrive at Whittsley House. He stepped down from the carriage and took Arabella's steady hand in his own to help her down. She smiled up at him, no hint of whatever worries might be roiling about inside her.

In fact, she seemed the picture of poise, greeting the staff with a confident smile and following his housekeeper, Mrs. Stewart, to his mother's old suite. Her chambers now. Separated from his by a common sitting room.

She inspected everything with a serene smile that told him nothing of what she might be thinking or feeling. By the time Mrs. Stewart left them in their sitting room with a bottle of wine and a plate of bread, fruit, and cheese in case they were hungry, Silas was about to pull his hair out.

The moment the door closed behind Mrs. Stewart, Silas rounded on Arabella.

"What are you thinking?"

She blinked up at him. "About what?"

"Everything. You've hardly said a word to me since you left me in that alcove, and since you've never been short of words, I'm in a bit of a quandary as to what is going on in that mind of yours. Are you happy? Tired? Hungry? Do you like your chambers?"

She glanced over her shoulder toward her new room. "Everything is lovely, Silas, thank you."

"That, right there," he said, waving a finger at her. "You're being too polite. Stop it."

She raised a brow. "You would prefer I was less polite?"

"Yes! At least then I'd know what you were truly thinking."

She shook her head with a short laugh. "I'm not thinking anything, Silas. It's been a very long day. A bit overwhelming at times. I'm simply trying to…take it all in, I suppose."

He watched her warily. "Are you sure that's it?"

"Of course. What else would it be?"

He shrugged. "You could be changing your mind about our arrangement."

She laughed. "A bit late for that, isn't it?"

"No." He took her hands and drew her down to sit beside him on the sofa. "No, it's not."

He ran an agitated hand through his hair and tried to calm the riot of emotions rushing through him. A few weeks ago, the only thought in his mind had been what he could get out of this arrangement. Now…that just didn't seem like enough. He didn't want her to be there because she signed some contract. Agreed to some rules. He wanted her to be…happy. Willing. As eager for him as he was for her. Charles was never going to let him live this down.

"I meant what I said in the church. I know we made an arrangement, and we can't do much about the marriage part, since that's already said and done. But we don't have to go any further. If you've changed your mind about your side of our bargain, or even if you'd like to…postpone things for a while, until we know each other better or you're more comfortable, all you have to do is tell me. I'll still hold up my end. Your sister will have the best husband I can find her, I promise you. In fact, Jean-Pierre was quite taken with her, and she seems equally taken with him. I have it on good authority he will be calling on her first thing tomorrow. So, you needn't worry about your sister or the rest of your family. I will ensure everyone is taken care of."

Arabella reached over and took one of his hands. "Thank you, Silas. I appreciate that, more than you know."

His stomach dropped, and he waited for her to tell him that she had, indeed, changed her mind.

"Why did you give me my own chambers?" she asked, and he blinked at her in surprise.

"Do you not approve after all?"

"It's not that. The room is lovely. I just…" She flushed and looked down at her lap with a small smile. "I assumed that we would share a room. If we are to follow rule number two, at least. It seems nightly heir-making attempts will be more easily performed if we are in the same room."

"Ah," he said, grinning at her. "My parents always had their own rooms, though they obviously spent time with each other occasionally, or I would not be here. I thought perhaps you would prefer to have your own space in which to hide away when I got to be too much."

She smiled. "You are already planning on driving me into hiding?"

He chuckled. "I do seem to have a knack for getting under your skin."

"That you do, Your Grace. However, while I greatly appreciate the kind gesture, I think our goals might be better served if we were to share a room at night."

"Arabella," he said, wanting to make sure she knew he would not hold her to their agreement if she didn't wish it, "despite our agreement, we needn't rush into anything. We don't know each other well yet. If you prefer to wait, just know you don't have to—"

Her finger pressed against his lips, stopping further words. "We have gone over this. Repeatedly. I am your wife. I intend to be your wife in every way. And with any luck, I'll soon be the mother of your heir. Now, it's been a very long day. I've spent a great deal of it working up my nerve to meet tonight head-on, and changing my mind now seems a waste of all that effort. I didn't anticipate having to talk my groom into consummating the marriage," she said with an amused half smile. "I'm afraid I have no idea how to go about doing that, so you're going to have to help me."

He blinked at her, feeling rather like a shy virgin himself, though he was no such thing.

"Silas." She placed a soft hand on his cheek and leaned into him. "Kiss me the way you did before," she whispered.

And his heart nearly stopped on the spot.

...

Arabella watched emotions flitting across Silas's face with growing amusement. He seemed torn between desire, enjoyment, and confusion. And if she wasn't mistaken, there was a bit of trepidation in there as well.

She was with him on that point. No matter what she'd just said, she was so nervous her heart was jumping about in her chest like a jackrabbit whose tail had been caught in a trap. But there was no turning back now. She'd meant what she said. And while she didn't quite have the courage to tell her newly shy husband this, she was actually looking forward to continuing what they'd started in the church that morning, and in the alcove afterward. The sensations he caused when he touched her were something she had never imagined. And she wanted more.

For a moment, she wasn't sure he'd obey her request. But before she had to ask again, he reached over and cupped her face. Even that small touch had her rubbing her cheek against his palm like an overgrown kitten.

He drew her to him, pressing a kiss to her lips so gently her heart ached. Then he took her hand and led her into his bedroom. As soon as they were past the threshold, he spun on his heel, wrapping an arm about her waist while his other hand caressed her jaw. His thumb trailed along her lower lip until it quivered under his touch.

She leaned against him, going up on her toes to bring her mouth closer to his, though she couldn't quite get up the nerve to close the last little bit of distance between them. The anticipation building in her had her clutching at his arms. If he didn't kiss her soon, nerves or not, she might have to resort to climbing him like a maypole and doing the job herself.

The tip of his nose brushed across hers, and her mouth opened with a little gasp.

"If at any time you wish to stop, tell me," he said, with a voice gone rough and gravelly.

She nodded, touched that he still thought of what she may wish. And impatient that they were still discussing it.

His lips closed over hers, and she melted against him, clinging to his waist when he wrapped his arms about her and held her close.

He broke their kiss and drew in a ragged breath. "Did anyone explain to you…"

She smiled up at him. "Charlotte told me what to expect, though she didn't go into great detail."

He laughed with evident relief and then resumed kissing her. His fingers trailed to the long row of pearl buttons on the bodice of her silver-gray gown, making much nimbler work of them than she expected. With each layer he divested, the ball of nerves in her gut grew until it burst into a thousand butterflies that cascaded in her stomach. But his hands and lips never stopped moving, exploring each new bit of skin that he uncovered, stoking that burning desire within her with every brush, lick, and caress. The cavalcade of sensations he wrought within her warred with her jangled nerves and sent her head spinning.

Or perhaps it was just him. His lips. His hands. His touch. Even his easy smile, those intensely blue eyes that gazed at her as if she were a goddess to be worshipped, his sweet murmured words that somehow meant nothing and everything all at once. He was everywhere, every second, until she stood trembling in his arms.

Somewhere between her flounced petticoat and corset she decided it was unquestionably unfair that he was still fully clothed, and she pushed his jacket from his shoulders. From then on it was a game to see who could remove the most clothing from whom without ever breaking their kiss, which grew more passionate and all-consuming by the second.

When they were down to her chemise and his linen drawers, he stopped and stood back enough that he could look at her. His smile grew as his eyes traveled over her.

"What?" she asked, resisting the urge to cover herself with a herculean feat of willpower.

"I had a feeling rule two, especially the caveat about leaving the lights on, would be my favorite."

She tried to scowl at him but couldn't stop smiling. "Funny, I was just thinking what a mistake that particular point had been."

He chuckled. "Remember, that knife cuts both ways." He cocked an eyebrow and stepped back so she could watch as he undid the few buttons holding his drawers up before letting them drop in a pool at his feet.

She sucked in a breath. So, this was what a naked man looked like. Some parts of him—his broad chest, muscled arms, lean waist—she'd enjoyed observing for weeks and weren't any particular mystery. She'd seen shirtless men before. Though none who would have tempted her from her books. Her imagination had always been better than the real thing. Until him.

It was the other bits she was really curious about. And those... Her eyes traveled down until she took in her new husband in all his manly glory.

He tilted his head, brow still raised, and waited for a response.

She smiled and put her hand up to cover her mouth.

His lips twitched. "Is the view not to your liking, Your Grace?"

Oh, she liked it. Very much. And now that she'd had a good look, she couldn't help but wonder, with a great deal of anticipation (and a good bit of anxiety), how everything was going to feel.

"It's…not quite as I'd imagined."

His lips pulled into a full grin at that. "Do I want to know what you were imagining?"

"Probably not."

"Hmmm. Do I at least rate your approval?"

"Oh yes," she breathed. Then her brow furrowed in a slight frown. "Only…"

"Yes?" he asked, his tone both amused and curious.

"You're…quite a bit larger than I'd expected."

He broke into a wide grin. "I've been told that's a good thing."

Was it? She hoped so. Because if what Charlotte had described actually happened, Arabella wasn't entirely sure how he was going to…fit. *There*.

He'd been watching her watching him, his expression growing more heated the longer she looked, and she realized her breathing had gone shallow again. Probably from imagining all the wonderful naked maleness in front of her actually touching her.

Except she didn't have to imagine it anymore.

She met his gaze, held it, while she slipped her chemise from her shoulders and removed the last bits of linen that covered her until she stood completely bare before him.

A nervous laugh escaped her. "Definitely

thinking I've made a mistake with rule number two."

"Oh no," he said, his tone one she'd never heard from him before. Soft. Almost reverent.

He shook his head and took her hands to pull her closer to him. "I didn't truly appreciate until this moment what a gift you were giving me."

Her heart skipped a beat, but she couldn't have responded even if she'd been able to make her brain work through the haze of desire that burned through her with ever-growing intensity as his hands and lips began to show her just how much he approved of what he saw.

He walked her backward until her legs hit the edge of the bed. She sat down, scooting back. He followed, looming over her, his mouth and hands keeping up their worship of her body until she whimpered. His lips captured the sound, drank it down. And then his finger slipped inside her and she gasped, rocking against him before she knew what she was doing.

Charlotte hadn't told her about *this*.

A second finger joined the first, stretching her, filling her, sending a riot of sensations building low in her core until it suddenly reached a fever pitch and broke over her. Her body shuddered and pulsed around his fingers. Before she could question what had just happened, Silas moved over her, kissing her again and again until she clutched at him, wanting, needing more.

"This will probably hurt for a minute," he warned.

She nodded and braced herself. Charlotte had told her about this part.

His lips moved over hers, distracting her. Relaxing her. Stoking that flame of desire that burned through her hotter and fiercer until she moved beneath him, struggling for something she wasn't sure of yet.

Silas thrust his hips, and she gasped at the sudden burning pain that tore through her.

He didn't move. Just held on to her, letting his lips and hands soothe her while she grew accustomed to him. After a moment, he began to move again. The pain ebbed. It was still uncomfortable, but that pressure was building inside her again beneath the skilled movements of mouth and fingers. When his tongue flicked across her nipple, her hips lifted of their own volition, bringing him deeper. They fell into a rhythm, their bodies moving together as if they'd been created to do nothing else.

This had been a mistake. Her thinking that she could do this every night and have it not affect her. How could it not? She'd known, of course, it would be intimate. But that word had meant something else before. She'd thought she could do this and keep her mind separate, keep herself separate. But she should have known that would be impossible with him. He drew her in, drank her down, and sent her crashing, yet somehow remained her anchor. This was more than just two bodies coming together. So much more.

She clung to him, her heart pounding so hard she could hardly draw a breath. Until once more that wave sent her hurtling over the edge. She threw her head back with a cry that was nearly a sob and with a final thrust, he followed her.

He held her close until their breathing slowed, murmuring sweet nonsense to her while her mind spun. When he finally disentangled himself from her, she kept in her sigh of disappointment. After all, there was nothing in the rules that said he had to stay with her each night after their...attempts. Of course he'd wish to sleep separately.

But before she could move, he'd returned with a damp cloth, and a lump rose in her throat at his thoughtfulness. He helped her clean up a bit and then climbed back into bed, spooning up behind her.

"Are you all right?" he asked, pressing a kiss to her temple.

She nodded, snuggling back against him. "I think rule number two is my new favorite. Though I'm still rethinking the lights."

His chest rumbled with a quiet laugh, and he drew her closer, wrapping his body around her. "Mine too, wife. Mine too." He kissed her again.

"And the lights stay on."

She smiled. She'd always been a rule follower, but she'd never expected to enjoy it quite so much.

# Chapter Thirteen

Silas stood beside Charles, sipping his champagne while they both stared at a painting of a trio of ballerinas. Though neither man was particularly interested in the exhibition. Silas was there because of rule number eight. His new bride had chosen this exhibit as her non-party event for the month. And Charles was there because of rule number nine. If Silas had to pretend to enjoy himself during an evening of staring at what looked like slightly blurry artwork by a Frenchman he had no interest in, he needed Charles there to entertain him.

"You know, most men would be happily on their honeymoons right now," Charles said, taking another sip of champagne.

"I disagree with the happily part."

Charles snorted. "If you aren't happy on your honeymoon, then you are doing something wrong."

Silas chuckled. "I am doing *nothing* wrong; you needn't worry. We simply decided we were more needed at home while Anne navigates her first season. A honeymoon can wait. And that's not what

I meant in any case. I was referring to the event leading to the honeymoon. How many men do you know who went willingly into matrimony?"

"I did," Charles said, shrugging. "Mary is the best thing that ever happened to me."

Silas looked around. "Better not let her hear you say that."

Charles laughed this time. "She's very well aware that she is the better half of our couple. And correct me if I'm wrong, but you seemed pleased enough going into your own wedding a scant few weeks ago. Has something happened to change that?"

"Not at all. The arrangement suits me wonderfully." Though he couldn't tell his friend exactly what that arrangement was and why he'd been so eager to enter into it. So, he settled for saying, "So far, marriage seems to be agreeing with me rather nicely."

"Hmm, I thought I detected a happy glow about you this evening."

Silas ignored his friend's sniggering and turned back to the painting, though his mind was on his wife. Marriage not only agreed with him, he was downright giddy. A state which was not only unusual, and therefore troubling, but would also be fleeting, and was therefore undesirable. From the moment his darling wife had thrown herself at him to suggest her ludicrous scheme, she had made no secret of the fact that the moment she found out she was with child, she would be off to the country. And his presence would not only not be required but would also be unwanted. Something he'd been very happy to agree to at the time. But now…he wasn't sure how he felt about it. That had been before the marriage had actually taken place. And every day since had been spent in absolute wedded bliss.

Rule number two explicitly stated that heir-making attempts would occur nightly. However, not only did they occur nightly, but multiple times during the night. And the following morning. And several times throughout the day. Including on the carriage ride to this very exhibition. And just thinking about it made him want to find her and drag her off to an unused closet for another attempt or two.

Yet, despite their obvious enjoyment of each other's company, Arabella had made no mention of altering the state of their agreement. At least rule number one, which would see her hidden away in the country and see him alone. Again. To be fair, he hadn't mentioned changing anything either. Perhaps it wasn't something he should be thinking of trying to alter when they were in the first flush of their marriage. Surely, after a time, the delights of the marriage bed would wane, and they'd grow tired of each other. At which point, he'd be glad that she preferred exile in the country to his company in town.

But he hadn't reached that point yet. And the more time he spent with his surprisingly enthusiastic wife, the less he was sure he ever would.

Speaking of his wife…

Arabella rounded the corner, talking animatedly with Lady Waterstack and Charles's wife, Mary, and his heart leaped in his chest at the sight of her. He rubbed it absentmindedly. Quite embarrassing, really. Good thing no one could see his reaction. Though the way Charles watched him with that amused grin made him think his old friend was able to see more than he'd like.

"Oh, Silas," Arabella said, coming to stand beside him. "Aren't they lovely?"

She gestured to the paintings, beaming with delight.

He raised a brow at Lady Waterstack, who merely shrugged. "I don't see in them what she does, but to each their own."

Arabella's jaw dropped, and she turned to him. "Don't tell me you feel the same way?"

Was there a good way to answer that? "It's not a style I'm used to. I'm afraid I prefer the more traditionalist painters. But I do find this artist's use of color interesting. And the way you can see all the brush strokes up close, but from far off the painting becomes clearer, is an intriguing technique."

"Isn't he brilliant?" she said, clasping her hands together in her delight. "We must go to Paris soon. There's to be an exhibition I've been told, one that will showcase all the masters of this… Impressionist technique, it's called. Wouldn't it be wonderful to be able to see them all?"

Wonderful to see the paintings? No. To see his wife's unabashed delight in them? Undoubtedly. Enough that he heard himself saying, "Whatever you'd like. We need a honeymoon after all, don't we? Who wouldn't want to spend it in Paris?"

He wouldn't, that's who. Though Paris was peaceful for the moment, the city, indeed the whole country, had been nothing but a hotbed of upheaval and trouble for decades. But with her happiness and excitement shining from her face, he could deny her nothing. He was becoming downright selfless. An alarming development, to be sure. But he just couldn't help himself.

"If you'll excuse me, I should round up my own husband before he disappears on me again," Lady Waterstack said.

Arabella waved goodbye to her with a promise to meet up the next day. Charles and Mary also took their leave, though Silas barely heard them go. His attention was all on his wife. And the fact that they were the only two in the room at the moment.

He put his arm about her waist and stood beside her while she gazed up at the row of paintings before them.

"Which is your favorite?" he asked, leaning down a little, though it wasn't necessary in order for her to hear him.

She looked up at him with a smile and then took his hand to lead him to one of the paintings on the far wall. "This one," she said, stopping in front of a painting of what looked like two drunk people sitting in a café.

"This is your favorite?" he asked with surprise.

"Yes. I'm not sure why…" She tilted her head and regarded the artwork, a small furrow forming between her brows.

He wasn't sure why either. The painting depicted a rather worn-down woman, with a glass of spirits before her, seated next to a man who looked decidedly worse for wear. The colors, unlike many of the other paintings, were more muted, without any bright pops of color. He actually found it rather depressing.

"I'm not sure why either," he said. "They both seem rather sad, do they not?"

She nodded. "Perhaps that's why I'm drawn to it."

"Are you sad, then, Arabella?" His heart clenched at the thought of her unhappiness, and he marveled again at how much he had grown attached to her in the few weeks since they'd met.

She gave him a soft smile that lightened the

ache in his chest. "Not at all." She took his hand, giving it a squeeze. "I am quite content, I promise. But I understand sadness," she said, looking back at the painting. "After my mother died, there were several years where I struggled to find happiness in anything. Except my books." She smiled wistfully, as if she were remembering a dear friend.

"When I was lost in the pages of a book, I could escape. I didn't have to be in the real world where my mother no longer existed. Where my father was too sad to laugh and play with us any longer. Where my older sister suddenly felt responsible for us all and was resentful because of it, and where my younger sister cried for our mother constantly." She took a shuddering breath, and he put his arm about her shoulders, drawing her against him. "I could just be a part of another world for a time."

He'd never thought of reading in that way before. To him, it was always a chore to get through. A lesson to learn and quickly abandon. He liked her view of it better.

"Then doesn't the painting make you sad?" he asked.

She looked at it again, quiet for a moment as she contemplated it. "In a way. But it also makes me hopeful. Because I've felt that soul-crushing sadness before. And then," she said, looking up at him, "I found happiness on the other side."

And the way her eyes were shining as she

gazed up at him made him believe he was a part of that happiness. It sent a wave of warmth through him. But there was trepidation as well. If he was her source of happiness, he could be the source of its destruction. And their relationship had been made to be broken. By their own agreement. Being the cause of her unhappiness would break something in him, and there were moments where he feared he wouldn't be able to stop it.

But for now, he would do what he could to chase the lingering sadness from her eyes. She came willingly into his arms when he gathered her to him, her face raised for his kiss.

Except one kiss wasn't enough. It would never be enough.

After a moment, she pushed away from him with a breathless chuckle. "Silas, you're breaking rule number three again."

"Some rules were made to be broken," he said, pulling her back to him so he could kiss her neck.

She giggled and squirmed when he nipped at a particularly sensitive spot. "I see I should have been clearer when defining what *appropriate* displays of affection constituted."

He sighed. "Appropriate is so boring, darling. Besides, rule number nine explicitly states that we are to try to enjoy each other's company at these events." He kissed along her jawline while his fingers brushed across her exposed collarbone. She looked beautiful in anything, but he did love her evening gowns that bared a little more skin than her day dresses. "And I am very much enjoying your company."

"Silas…" she breathed, her eyes fluttering closed as she swayed against him. But a second later she gave her head a little shake. "We must stop. Someone will see," she said, pushing away from him, her cheeks red as her eyes darted around, though the ragged breaths she struggled to draw in betrayed her response to him.

"Home, then. Now." He realized he was grunting single syllable words at her but suddenly seemed incapable of doing more than that.

Her eyes widened, and he released a deep breath, laughing. She had him under her spell and he was very happy to stay there. "My apologies. I find I cannot help myself around you, wife."

After a quick glance around to ensure they were still alone, she leaned her forehead against his neck, nuzzling him before placing a quick kiss right beneath his ear that sent his blood racing in his veins. "I want you too," she whispered.

He looked around, smiling when he spied a dark alcove half hidden behind an enormous potted fern.

"Come," he said, taking her hand to pull her into the shadows it offered. "No one can see us here." He spun her around so her back was pressed against the wall, his body blocking hers from view. His mouth trailed across the globes of her breasts that threatened to spill from the low bodice of her evening dress.

"Are you sure?" she asked, though her hands were already making hasty work of the buttons at the front of his trousers.

"We can be quick about it," he said, hiking up her skirts. "And quiet." He gave her a pointed look, and she nodded, her breath already coming in short pants. "Hook your leg around my hip," he directed, and she did as she was told without hesitation.

He entered her with one quick thrust, and she sucked in a sharp breath, already shuddering against him. He covered her mouth with his, his lips muffling any sound that threatened to escape while his tongue tangled with hers.

It didn't take long. A handful of strokes and she clutched his shoulders, pulsing around him and bringing him over the edge with her.

They stood locked together, their ragged breaths mingling. A quiet laugh escaped her, and she slapped a hand over her mouth. He grinned and pulled his handkerchief from his pocket, quickly cleaning them both up as much as possible before stepping back so they could right their clothing.

Voices carried to them, faintly at first, then growing stronger as a group of people slowly filed through the room, chatting while they viewed the paintings. Arabella stood, eyes wide and both hands clapped over her mouth until they left.

He quickly looked her over and, not seeing anything out of order, took her hand to lead her from the alcove. They returned to their spots in front of the painting of dancers that he and Charles had been looking at earlier.

Another laugh escaped her, and he glanced down, eyebrows raised.

"I can't believe we just did that," she said, eyes alight with merriment.

"Probably something we shouldn't make a habit of," he said with a wink, and she laughed again. Then shrugged.

"I don't know. I quite enjoyed it."

He turned to her, mouth open, too stunned to muster up a response, which only made her laugh harder. She rose up on her toes and pressed a quick kiss to his lips. But when she went to pull away, he wrapped his arms about her waist, drawing her close while his lips recaptured hers.

He'd meant to give her a passionate enough kiss that she'd be distracted for the rest of the evening, thinking only of him. Instead, the moment their lips touched, he was captivated, lost in the soft touch of her, the way she melted against him. His mouth tenderly explored hers, his hands cupping her face and neck. His thumbs brushed across her cheeks and jawline, and when she leaned into him with a soft whimper, his heart nearly exploded.

Her hands came up to cover his, and they slowly pulled away, just far enough that he could look into her eyes. They stayed that way for several moments. Staring at each other. He could drown in those deep amber eyes of hers and be happily lost forever.

That kiss wasn't a kiss. It was…different. Soul-searing. Terrifying and exhilarating and…could never happen again.

This wasn't what their relationship was about. He wasn't supposed to *feel* when they kissed. And judging by the wide-eyed look Arabella was giving him, he wasn't alone in experiencing whatever had just happened between them.

"Ari, there you are," Anne said, rounding the corner with Aunt Adelaide and Jean-Pierre in tow. "I've been looking everywhere for you. Where have you been?"

"I… We…" Arabella stopped, eyes wide, and then broke into a huge grin.

"We were enjoying a private exhibit," Silas said, coming to her rescue.

"Oh, how lucky," Anne said. "Is it something I'd enjoy?"

"Oh no, it was…" Silas's eyebrows rose, and Arabella stuttered. "I mean, I quite enjoyed it. Immensely, actually." He gave her a slow, heated grin that made her face grow redder, and she stammered again.

"That is, I enjoyed it, but I don't think it would be appropriate for you, just yet, that is, and…"

Anne narrowed her eyes, obviously noticing her sister was hiding something from her. His wife was not one for subterfuge, apparently. An admirable trait under normal circumstances, but in this particular instance, not very helpful.

"Have you shown your sister your gift, my dear?" he asked, hoping to steer the conversation in another direction.

"Oh, not yet," she said with a grateful smile before dutifully holding out her wrist to show her sister the gemstone-studded bracelet he'd given her before they'd left that evening.

"Oh, how lovely," Anne said, moving aside so Adelaide could also exclaim over it.

Arabella smiled politely, accepting their compliments, though without any real pleasure, he noticed. They moved off as they chatted, leaving the men to follow behind them.

"Is something wrong, my friend?" Jean-Pierre asked as they trailed behind the women.

Silas glanced at him in surprise. "No. Well, not wrong exactly."

Jean-Pierre waited for him to elaborate, and Silas chuckled, shaking his head. "My wife doesn't seem to enjoy her present as much as I thought she would, that's all."

"No? Most women enjoy pretty baubles."

"True. Which is why I assumed she'd enjoy the bracelet. And the necklace I gave her after our wedding. And the gold collar I gave her to put on Bub, since she and the beast get on so well. She didn't have much jewelry when we married, and as my wife, that was of course something I needed to remedy."

"And she does not enjoy these things?"

Silas frowned slightly. "I'm not sure. She thanks me for them and seems to like them. But…"

"There's no real pleasure behind the enjoyment?"

"Yes, that's it exactly."

Jean-Pierre shrugged. "Perhaps your wife is not like most women, then."

That statement stopped Silas in his tracks. "No. No, she's not."

His friend turned to look back at him. "Then perhaps you should try to find her something that *she* would enjoy, not something that just any woman would like."

Silas nodded slowly, a few ideas taking shape in his mind. "I think you might be right, my friend." He clapped Jean-Pierre on the shoulder, and they started walking again. "Now, tell me how things are going with Anne."

# Chapter Fourteen

Arabella made another circuit around the ballroom, just to be sure that everything was in place.

"I don't think anything has moved since the last time you checked," Silas said with a chuckle.

Arabella scowled at where he leaned against the doorframe, watching her. "It's our first ball. There's already enough talk due to our speedy marriage and your 'unfortunate choice of bride.' The last thing we need is to give the gossips more to cluck about with a poorly planned event."

He caught her arm as she walked by him and drew her close. "It will be fine. Everything will go off perfectly, and everyone will be utterly impressed by your talent and skill at party organizing," he said, chuckling when she slapped at his arm. "You worry too much."

"Hmm. Maybe you don't worry enough."

"But there are so many more worthwhile things with which to occupy myself," he said, pressing a soft kiss on her lips that had her sinking into him.

"Maybe we should cancel the ball altogether and spend the rest of the evening in our room," he murmured against her mouth. "We do have an heir to make, after all."

She grinned and pulled away.

"For someone who was so against being a responsible adult, you are certainly in a hurry to become a father."

He shrugged and leaned against the doorway to watch her again as she continued to fuss about the room. "I'm not in a hurry to reach the destination, as they say, but I *am* vastly enjoying the journey."

Arabella giggled and shook her head. The man was insatiable. Not that she had any complaints. What she'd thought would be an awkward chore had turned into her favorite part of the day. Just thinking of their escapades had her shivering with anticipation. Even more so because of the interruption of their nightly escapades due to her courses the prior week. Though thankfully they had been much lighter than normal and had only lasted a couple days. All the stress of their whirlwind wedding must have affected her, but for once, it had worked to her advantage.

She'd thought to feel disappointment at the proof she had not yet conceived, except, while there may have been a hint of regret, she instead found herself pleased at the prospect of enjoying her husband's attentions for a few more weeks. And since that went against everything their agreement stood for, she tried not to dwell on it too hard. Especially since there were so many more delightful things to dwell upon. Such as the sight of her husband, resplendent in his evening finery. And the even more resplendent sight of him out of it that she would get to enjoy once their guests departed.

"I know that look," he said from right behind her, and she jumped with a little squeak.

"Don't do that," she said with another playful slap at his chest. "You startled me."

He wrapped his arms around her waist and tried to pull her closer. "You were thinking about me, weren't you?" He leaned down to kiss her cheek. "You can admit it. I promise you, I won't hold it against you."

"I was not," she lied, wiggling away from him. "Now, can you please be serious? Guests will be arriving any minute and…"

She picked up another book from a chaise in the corner of the room. "What's this?"

"This," he said, plucking it from her hand, "is called a book. Some people like to read them, or so I'm told. I never quite understood the fascination."

"Hmm, you can imagine my surprise." She picked it up again from where he'd dropped it back on the chaise. "But what is it doing here? And what about those?" she said, pointing to the first stack she'd found. "Or…that one? Or those?"

she asked, pointing to other books she was now noticing scattered about the room in out-of-the-way corners.

She let out a little gasp. "Ohhh, you!" She rounded on her husband. "You're incorrigible."

"What?" he asked, putting on his best innocent face, though it didn't fool her for a second.

"Do you really think the lure of the page and a hidden corner will entice me so much?"

"Yes. Yes, I do." He grinned mischievously.

She narrowed her eyes. "You're trying to tempt me into breaking rule number five, aren't you?"

He slapped a hand to his chest. "Me? Whyever would I do that?"

"Why indeed? It will take more than a few strategically placed books to break me. I agreed not to hide away. I can follow the rules."

He gave her a slow nod. "Of course you can."

She let out a long, exasperated sigh and rolled her eyes. "Getting *you* to behave, on the other hand, is the bane of my existence."

He gave her his best angelic look and she pursed her lips together to keep from laughing. The man would be the death of her.

Carriages had been arriving for the last quarter hour or so, but of course no one wanted to be the first to enter. With more carriages arriving every minute, Arabella expected an influx of guests soon.

She took a deep breath and pressed a hand to her roiling stomach. Was it normal to vomit at one's first ball? Because she was in imminent danger of doing so.

"Arabella." Silas stepped into her line of vision and cupped her face in his hands. "You've somehow managed to turn five shades of white and green simultaneously. An impressive feat, to be sure, but concerning nonetheless. Are you ill?"

She shook her head and leaned her forehead against Silas's chest, taking several slow, deep breaths, drinking in the sharp, slightly minty scent of him. For once, he didn't speak or joke, but just held her. After a moment, the frantic pounding of her heart eased, and her stomach settled. She looked up and gave him a small smile.

His thumb brushed across her cheek. "Better?"

She nodded and took another deep breath. And then realized just how intimate a moment they were sharing. Standing so close together, staring into each other's eyes, where just anyone could come upon them.

She stepped back, flustered.

"I'm not sure if I should be flattered or offended that my scent is apparently more effective than smelling salts," he said with a wicked grin. He offered her the crook of his arm, and she took it so he could lead her over to greet their guests.

She laughed. "Knowing you, you'll be flattered.

You take everything as a compliment whether it's meant as one or not."

He shrugged. "Why go about feeling affronted by everything? It's so much more amusing to enjoy oneself, especially when someone is trying to lay an insult. Nothing upsets an offender more than for their chosen victim to laugh at their attempted slights."

"I'll have to keep that in mind."

He nodded and gazed down at her, his expression suddenly serious. "You should. The opinions of these people mean nothing. Don't let them affect you."

She stared at him for a moment and then gave him a hesitant smile. "I'll try."

Truly, she didn't think she'd care so much. Then again, it wasn't just her life that would be affected if the people about to walk through her door wouldn't accept her. Her sisters, her father, even her husband and future child…all of their reputations felt like they rested on her shoulders. She knew she was placing too much importance on this ball. It was one night. And Silas's reputation had certainly suffered through worse over the years than one party gone amuck. But she couldn't shake the dread pooling in the pit of her stomach.

The chattering noise of a bevy of descending guests filtered to them from the entry hall, and she pressed a hand to her stomach again.

"Here," Silas said, thrusting his arm beneath her nose. "Breathe in."

She laughed and pushed his arm away from her face. "I'm fine."

"Hmm," he said, watching her with suspicion.

"I would love to leave early, if at all possible, though, since I can't hide away with a book. No matter how you've tried to tempt me."

He raised a brow. "You wish to leave your own ball early?"

"Is that bad?" she asked, feigning ignorance.

Silas barked out a laugh and pulled her close for a quick kiss.

She melted into it for a moment, wishing they could leave right then and there. But she quickly pushed away, putting a hand to her hair to make sure all was in place.

"Silas, behave."

He shrugged, that wicked grin in place again. "I'm merely following the rules, my dear. And rule three distinctly states I should show my affection."

"Appropriate affection. You always forget the appropriate part."

He chuckled and turned to their first group of guests. "That I do, love. That I do."

• • •

Despite Arabella's constant worry for the last

several days, the ball had so far gone off without a hitch. Their ballroom was packed with everyone who was anyone, the gossipmongers were happily chattering about fairy-tale romances, drowning out the few who would focus on less pleasant possibilities for their hasty wedding, and Anne was in her element, fairly swarmed with eligible suitors. Silas couldn't have asked for a better outcome.

Well, he could wish that his wife would have a little more fun. She'd done her hostess duty, danced with all who asked, run about making introductions, ensured everyone was enjoying themselves, and even managed to look not completely miserable while doing it all. But he didn't miss her slightly pinched lips or the way her eyes stayed wide when she laughed instead of twinkling and crinkling in the corners like they did when she was genuinely amused.

It seemed the moment she was surrounded by people, the funny, surprisingly passionate little spitfire that he knew retreated back behind her mousy shell, and she looked like she'd rather be anywhere but there.

And that just wouldn't do.

Silas made his way through the crowd, nodding to people who greeted him but not stopping to chat. He did stop by the band director on his way to retrieve his bride and had a quick word. Then he politely plowed through the gaggle of giggling women surrounding Arabella and extracted her with as much tact as possible.

Arabella also nodded and apologized to her guests and then turned to him. "What is it? Is something wrong?"

"Yes. You haven't smiled in…" He pulled out his pocket watch and took a quick peek. "Nearly two hours. I'm afraid you'll forget how."

Her lips twitched, and he grinned. "There you go."

"Silas, our guests—"

"Can wait." He cocked his head as the notes to the next piece began to play.

Arabella immediately frowned and turned to head for the band. "That's not right. They should be playing a quadrille now. I spoke with—"

Silas caught her hand before she could get too far. "I spoke with them, too, and requested they play a waltz now."

She frowned. "Why?"

He took her hand and drew her close, pressing his hand to the small of her back. Much lower and tighter than was proper, not that he gave a damn.

"Because I want to dance with my wife," he said, twirling her onto the floor and into the crowd.

"Silas, this is highly irregular. What will people think?"

"I imagine they'll think I'm completely besotted with my beautiful wife and cannot bear to be apart from her any longer."

She scrunched her lips together and snorted softly. "Or they'll think you a spoiled popinjay who enjoys shocking people and always gets his way."

"That too," he said with a wink. And was rewarded by the first real laugh Arabella had had all night.

"There you are," he murmured to her.

She sighed and shook her head, though he was pleased to see her smile remained. "You're incorrigible."

"True. But that's part of my charm."

"I hate that you aren't wrong."

"You mean I'm right?"

"I wouldn't go that far."

His laugh rang out across the dance floor, drawing every eye. He didn't care, of course. Arabella, however, stepped a tiny bit closer to him.

"They are all watching us."

He leaned down and whispered in her ear. "Let them watch." Then he stole a quick kiss and spun her again. And kept spinning her until the haunted look left her eyes and she had relaxed into his arms.

"There now. Still wish to hide away with your books?" he asked.

She gave a quiet sigh. "Always."

He pursed his lips. She'd seemed to be having more fun, but... "If you truly wish to leave, I will make your excuses."

She raised her brows. "And what of rule number four?"

"What of it? You've made an appearance at the ball…though I would argue that as it is *your* ball, it doesn't truly fit the description of one which I, alone, wish to attend."

"A fair argument."

"But you have been the perfect hostess. And you haven't scurried off with one of your books once, even though you had ample opportunity."

"Hmm yes, thanks to you," she said, narrowing one eye.

"Guilty," he said with a wink. "So yes, you have been gracious enough to follow rule four. I will be gracious in return if you wish to invoke rule five."

She looked up at him with that twinkle in her eye that he loved so much. "Thank you, Your Grace. But I find I am rather enjoying myself, after all. I think I shall stay. A bit longer, at least."

"That is the best news I've heard all evening," he said.

She beamed up at him, and he was rather stunned to realize that he meant what he said. Seeing her smile, hearing her say that she wanted to stay, with him…holding her in his arms, breathing in that sweet, floral scent of hers. He could stay there swaying with her to the music for the rest of the night and consider it time extremely well spent.

She pressed a little closer to him, her hand tightening on his, and his heart thundered. She wouldn't be the only one counting the minutes until they could leave. He couldn't wait to—

He nearly stopped dancing in the middle of the floor. What was he thinking? Forget thinking. What was he feeling? He had no right to be feeling anything. She didn't want any of this. Neither did he, and he'd do well to remember it. He couldn't keep her. He didn't want to. Right?

Even if he did, she'd made no secret of the fact that she had never wanted any of this and she had never made any indication that she'd changed her mind and wished to stay. It was a necessity, for her sister, her family. This…all of this…the closeness, the smiles, the flirting…it was all for show. Wasn't it? Yes, they were getting on better than he ever expected, but even if she was feeling the same as he, not that he knew what these emotions flickering through him *were*, did he really want to be stuck with a wife forever?

The fact that he couldn't answer that question anymore sent a rush of fear through his gut. For possibly the first time in his life, he was up against something he couldn't joke or seduce his way out of. His feelings might not be the only ones at play here. Or maybe they were…and he wasn't sure if that was better or worse.

Either way, he needed to tread more carefully. They had a year. Less than a year now. And then this, whatever this was, would be over, for all intents and purposes. He needed to remember that if either of them had a hope of leaving this arrangement with their hearts intact.

The music ended, and Arabella stood, looking up at him, waiting…

He slowly pulled away, pretending he didn't see the flash of hurt in her eyes. He paused to press a kiss to her hand.

And then he let her go.

# Chapter Fifteen

Arabella sat on the edge of her bed, breathing through the queasiness rolling through her stomach. She didn't know what was going on lately. She pressed a hand to her brow and focused on taking one slow breath after another. Her gown would wrinkle if she stayed on the bed for too much longer. But perhaps just another minute or so.

A knock sounded at the door, and Charlotte poked her head in before Arabella could say anything.

"Are you not ready yet?" she asked, coming in and closing the door behind her. "I thought you didn't enjoy being fashionably late?"

Arabella just groaned at her and dragged herself off the bed to her vanity table to don her jewelry. Which, thanks to Silas, she had much from which to choose.

"Are you feeling all right? You look a bit peaked."

Arabella waved off her concern. "I'll be fine. It's just a bit of an upset stomach. It usually goes away after I eat something." She pulled a dry biscuit out of the drawer of her vanity where she'd stashed a few and nibbled on it.

Charlotte's smile lit up the room and she plopped down on the chair near Arabella. "And does this upset stomach of yours occur every day?"

"Lately, yes."

"Is it your courses, perhaps? I know there are some months where I can't stomach anything."

"Perhaps." She frowned. "I am a few days late I suppose, though last month they were so light I nearly missed them altogether so I'm not exactly sure when to expect them. In any case, they have never made me ill."

Charlotte nodded knowingly and Arabella frowned slightly, feeling like she was missing something.

"And it's been going on for…oh, I'd say the last week or so?"

"Yes! Is it that obvious? It's generally passed by the time we go out for the evening, but I know I'm a bit paler than usual. I thought perhaps I might be ill, but since it always passes… What?" she asked, because Charlotte was still grinning at her like a cat who'd lapped up all the cream.

"Ari, you're expecting."

Arabella stared at her, her words not quite sinking in. "Expecting?"

"A child. You're pregnant."

"No, I…" Oh. Well now.

Charlotte's smile faded. "Are you not pleased?"

Arabella blinked at Charlotte, her mind spinning. Pleased? She was shocked. Well, not completely shocked. This was what she'd agreed to, her entire role in the agreement she'd made. And while she was inexperienced, she of course knew that the…activities she and Silas had been engaging in with embarrassing frequency could, and apparently did, lead to a child.

She placed a hand on her stomach, the whole idea of a child still so abstract she couldn't quite get a handle on what she was feeling. But…

A slow smile spread across her lips as excitement began to course through her.

"Yes. Of course I'm pleased," she said, her smile growing wider when Charlotte grinned and rushed forward to hug her.

"It's probably best to wait a few months, just to be sure. Or send for the doctor to confirm, though they are fairly useless for a few more months yet. But I do believe congratulations are in order."

Arabella laughed and put her hand over her mouth. "I'll have to tell Silas. He'll be so excited. I think."

"Of course he'll be thrilled," Charlotte assured her. "Every man wants an heir."

She laughed again. "That's true. I just can't believe it's happened so quickly. I…"

Her smile faded and Charlotte leaned forward

and grasped her hands. "Are you all right? Do you need more biscuits?"

"What?" she asked, frowning in confusion. "Oh, no, it isn't that. It's just…"

"What?"

"Well…I know it's silly but…Silas and I, we've been having so much fun together. I know this is just an arrangement and it was only supposed to last for a year, whether I had a child or not. I guess I just didn't expect it to happen this quickly. And I didn't expect…"

She trailed off, not wanting to put into words the thoughts flying through her head. But Charlotte knew her too well.

"You didn't expect to enjoy your arrangement as much as you have?"

Arabella slumped back against her chair. "Yes. It's just all been so confusing lately. He's always been playful, and of course when we are in public, we pretend to be madly in love with each other. But lately, even when we're alone…it just feels like maybe it's not so pretend anymore. That although it might not be real, maybe it *could* be real."

"Do you want it to be?"

"I…I don't know."

And that was the problem. Did she want what was between them to be real? Did she want a real relationship with him? He was certainly not the type of man she'd thought she'd marry. Then again, she hadn't thought she'd *ever* marry, so she couldn't exactly hold that against him.

But if she did want this to be real, and if he did also, then this baby was the best possible news for them. If it wasn't real for him, though, if he was just biding his time until their agreement was fulfilled…then telling him about the baby would mean the end of whatever it was they had between them. She was excited for the baby. So very happy about it. But…she wasn't quite ready to say goodbye to Silas yet.

"I think it's something you need to figure out," Charlotte said. "And soon. Because you won't be able to keep this news to yourself for too much longer."

Arabella took a deep breath and blew it out slowly, nodding. Charlotte was right, of course. And maybe Silas would want her to stay as much as she was starting to want to stay. Then again, maybe he wouldn't.

But how would she know unless she told him? And then, if his answer wasn't what she hoped, it would be too late…

• • •

Silas sat beside Arabella, trying to behave himself and pay attention to the truly gifted string quartet that had been engaged to play for them that evening. Not an activity he would generally attempt. Attending the musical performance had actually been one of his events, not Arabella's. But he had wanted to attend less for the music and more for the social aspect. To see and be seen. Chat with Charles, chaperone Anne and Jean-Pierre, who were sitting close beside one another and quietly talking throughout the performance.

But instead of being his usual social self, Silas found he couldn't concentrate on anything or anyone but the woman at his side. Who was being unusually reserved. Which was saying something when it came to Arabella in a social situation. Still, this evening, though one of his events, was something that would normally pique her interest. However, she sat motionless, hands folded neatly in her lap and mind obviously very far away.

He leaned over to whisper to her, "It's lovely, isn't it?"

"Hmm?" She turned to him, eyes blank for a moment before pasting a vague smile on her lips and nodding. "Oh yes, quite."

She turned back to the small dais that had been erected in Lady Chisolm's drawing room, the faraway look in her eyes once more.

He was pleased to see her wearing the necklace and earrings he'd given her just after their wedding. Though lately he'd taken Jean-Pierre's advice to heart and had been selecting gifts for Arabella that he thought she, personally, would enjoy. She seemed pleased by his efforts. But he didn't know if she was truly happy. Or just exceptionally good at pretending.

Right. He might not be able to answer all his burning questions just then, but he could, at least, liven the evening up a bit and make sure he—and his wife, of course—had a little fun.

The quartet finished their piece and paused for the audience to politely clap before beginning the next. Silas leaned over to murmur a few words to Arabella, though they had nothing to do with the music they'd just heard.

"There's a nice potted palm over by that alcove," he murmured. "Meet me there in five minutes."

Arabella turned startled eyes to him. "What?"

He glanced over at the out-of-the-way corner he'd mentioned and then looked back at her, waggling his eyebrows. Her lips pursed. And then twitched. She tried to school her face with noticeable effort and turned back to the performance.

"You're terrible," she whispered back to him.

He leaned a little closer, reaching over to trail a finger across the back of her hand. She squirmed in her chair and moved her hand. He followed. She moved it again. He followed again, his fingers finding hers for a gentle caress every time. She looked up at him, eyes narrowed in a glare, but lips still pursed to keep from smiling, and he blinked at her innocently.

"Will you stop?" she whispered.

He shrugged. "Sorry. Can't help it." This time he captured her hand and entwined his fingers with hers. And then lifted her hand to his mouth, brushing his lips across the back of it.

A shiver visibly rippled through her, and she quietly cleared her throat, moving in her chair like she was trying to disguise the fact that she was trembling from just that small touch. He silently chuckled and let her go. Rule number three was his favorite rule to bend almost to the breaking point. He'd never been one to openly display affection. Then again, he'd never really felt any affection for someone of the fairer sex to warrant showing it at all.

But he was terribly fond of his wife. A surprising and puzzling turn of events, to be sure. Oh, he'd expected to enjoy their private time together. She was an attractive woman, and he was a healthy, young male after all. But it wasn't just their heir-making attempts that he looked forward to. He'd actually been anticipating this evening all day. Looking forward to sitting there listening to some rather dreadful music, if he were honest, just because it meant he could sit beside his wife and tease her throughout the performance.

He would really miss spending time with her

when she left. Would she feel the same? Or was she still counting the days until she could be free to scurry off to the country to hide away from everyone? From him?

Her large booted foot crept out from beneath her skirts and subtly kicked him in the shin. His mouth dropped open in surprise. And delight. Wicked woman.

She didn't look at him but leaned slightly over and murmured, "Stop staring at me and pay attention."

He chuckled again. He hadn't noticed that he'd been staring at her while his mind spun with intriguing possibilities. Not for the first time, he wondered if she were feeling even a bit of what he had lately. There was one definitive way to find out, of course. He could simply ask her.

But if her answer wasn't what he wanted, that would be the end of their fun. And truly, he wasn't completely sure what he wanted her answer to be. All he knew for sure was that this…whatever it was between them…was the best time he'd ever had, and he wasn't ready for it to end.

"Palm tree, five minutes," he whispered to her again, the moment the next song was over. And then he stood and headed for the secluded alcove, ignoring her startled sputtering.

He waited behind the palm with an anticipation he hadn't felt since he was a small child waiting for his gifts on Boxing Day. Would she come? What did it mean if she didn't? Not that it would really mean anything other than her desire to exhibit the proper decorum and behavior expected of someone in her position. Making love behind an overgrown plant at a social function was hardly the kind of behavior he should be encouraging, let alone instigating. But by God, this woman drove him to increasingly desperate measures. If she—

"Silas, what are you do—"

Before she could even finish the question, he pulled her to him for a searing kiss. She sank against him with a quiet moan that had him wishing they had a few more palms to hide behind.

They finally stopped to come up for air and stood, chests heaving, staring at each other.

"You know, my dear, I think I'm feeling rather poorly. Perhaps we should cut the evening short."

"Oh, you poor darling," Arabella said, already wrapping her hand through the crook of his arm and all but dragging him from the room. "We should get you home immediately."

They nodded their goodbyes to the startled people they passed in their haste to depart and all but ran to their carriage.

"Tell your driver to take his time," she said, gathering her skirts with a delightful flash of ankle and climbing inside without waiting for assistance.

He chuckled in delight and followed her up.

This woman…what was he ever going to do without her?

# Chapter Sixteen

Arabella put on the pearl earrings Silas had given her that morning and sighed. The man seemed determined to shower her with gifts, though she had told him repeatedly it wasn't necessary. He seemed to be trying hard to please her, but she didn't understand why. And he kept giving her the oddest things. Last Saturday was a telescope, which she found fascinating but wasn't particularly interested in. Perhaps once she'd retired to the country she'd find more use for it. At the moment, it held her favorite hat, so at least it was somewhat useful.

And she had appreciated the gold chain he'd given her to hold her spectacles. It was quite useful to have them around her neck rather than in her pocket. But she did wish he'd stop giving her jewelry. Especially once she noticed that he tended to gift her with the more extravagant pieces on Thursdays. The day after the Wednesdays when he'd disappear on his mysterious errands. All that did was make her more curious, and suspicious, about what he was doing on those days she'd promised not to ask about.

And she really had no use for such baubles. Once Anne was wed, Arabella didn't have any intention of continuing with the relentless balls and soirees. All of the lovely things he kept giving her would just be hidden away in her jewelry box. Oh well. Perhaps someday her daughter could—

She stopped short and stared at her pale reflection. She most likely wouldn't have a daughter. Unless she gave birth to one first and had to try again for a son. And suddenly she wasn't sure what she wished for more. When she'd entered into this agreement, she'd prayed every day God would see fit to grant her a son so their agreement could be fulfilled, and she could move on with her life. Now…

She placed a hand on her belly. Well, now she wasn't sure what she wanted. A little boy, as handsome as his father, to be the next Duke of Whittsley, certainly. But if the child she carried was a boy, she'd never have a little girl. One with her father's jovial nature and a dimple just like his that appeared when she laughed.

Arabella shook her head. It was all too easy to imagine a brood of laughing children playing on the lawns at Fallcreek Abbey. And it frightened her how much the thought appealed to her. That wasn't part of the agreement she'd made.

Speaking of the agreement…she needed to tell Silas. But if she did…

She bit her lip, her hand straying to her belly again. Her sister had more suitors than she knew what to do with and seemed quite taken with Jean-Pierre. Enough so that Arabella expected an announcement any day now. Which meant Silas's part of their bargain would be fulfilled. And if she were truly pregnant, as she was now certain she was, then her part was fulfilled as well. Rule number one. Her sister's marriage and an heir. And then they would part.

And she wasn't ready for that just yet. Wasn't ready to say goodbye.

She closed her eyes and took a deep breath. Becoming attached to a man who had never agreed to be hers would not be wise. She would tell him. But…not just yet. There was time. He would notice eventually, of course. But after all, she hadn't even seen the doctor yet. She only had her own suspicions, no matter how firm they might be. She could wait a few more weeks.

For now, she had a soiree to attend, preceded by a dinner with Silas's grandfather. And those were always an ordeal to get through. The men obviously loved each other but both seemed determined to keep that to themselves, resorting to bickering and nagging at the slightest provocation. Unexpectedly entertaining though it might be, it could also be exhausting trying to keep the peace between them. But they might as well get it over with.

Once they arrived at Lord Mosley's residence, however, they were kept waiting long enough that Silas finally decided to go searching for his grandfather himself. Arabella just smiled and shook her head at Silas's grumblings and made herself comfortable in an overstuffed chair by the fireplace with a book she'd found lying on the side table.

Lord Mosley entered the room not three minutes later, looking about with a growing crease between his brows until his eyes settled on her. He pursed his lips, his eyes narrowed, an expression that probably sent terror running through most people. But it was so reminiscent of Silas when he was in a mood that Arabella couldn't help smiling. Which seemed to surprise Lord Mosley enough that he stopped scowling and gave her a faint smile in return.

"Well, I am pleased to find you here, Your Grace, but where is that indolent grandson of mine?" he said.

"He went looking for you, I believe."

Lord Mosley snorted. "That boy never did have any patience."

Arabella resisted pointing out that *that boy* was now a thirty-year-old man who was used to getting his own way, due in large part no doubt to his grandfather.

"Grandfather," Silas said, his sudden appearance making Arabella jump. "Where have you been?"

Lord Mosley chuckled a bit at her reaction before turning his attention to Silas. "I don't know what you mean, you insolent pup. I've been right here having a word with your lovely wife since you saw fit to leave her all alone in a strange house."

"To be fair," Arabella said, "I quite enjoy being on my own."

"Hmm, I don't find that an acceptable excuse at all."

Arabella smiled, and Silas looked back and forth between them, his eyes narrowing until Lord Mosley shooed him away. "Stop glaring at me so suspiciously. Anyone would think I'm trying to run away with your wife. I will, however, claim the honor of escorting her into dinner."

"I don't think—" Silas began, but Arabella cut him off.

"That would be delightful, my lord."

Leaving Silas standing there staring at her, eyes wide with surprise, was worth every bit of the discomfort she'd feel taking the arm of the grandfather-in-law she barely knew. Anything that riled Silas was a plus in her book.

For all her trepidation, dinner went surprisingly well. Both men behaved themselves admirably enough. For the most part. Toward the end of the meal, Lord Mosley turned a critical eye toward his grandson, looking him over with a deepening frown.

"You look tired, Whittsley. Too much gallivanting about, I'd wager. I know it's not from overwork."

Silas gave him a tight smile, but before he could respond Arabella interrupted. "Actually, it's probably my fault."

Silas and his grandfather both turned to her with twin expressions of utter shock, and she belatedly realized how her statement could be construed. Especially because their activities upon returning home from each evening's festivities *were* likely what had put the faint shadows beneath Silas's eyes. And her own as well, no doubt.

"Oh, no, I...that's not what I...I only meant that on top of his regular work keeping the estates in order, I've had him escorting me and my sister from one event to the other. My sister, Anne, is having quite the season and is determined to make a brilliant match. So, of course, she must attend all the best events, and Silas has been so gracious in chaperoning."

Lord Mosley harrumphed. "Not much of a hardship, I still say, as he'd be attending the parties regardless."

"That may be. But even you have to admit that doing so on the arms of demanding women is enough to exhaust any man."

Arabella worried she had laid it on a bit thick with that remark, but Lord Mosley merely nodded.

"You are not wrong, my dear."

She turned a pointed look to Silas, who nearly choked on his wine.

"Yes," he said, patting his mouth with his napkin. "I'm a veritable saint."

"And so humble," Arabella murmured, grinning into her wine when Silas laughed.

Lord Mosley glanced between the two of them with a confused look. He finally shook his head and stood.

"Well, I am honored that you took the time from your busy schedule to dine with an old man," he said.

Arabella and Silas stood as well, and she leaned over to give the old man a peck on the cheek. "We will always take the time for you, Lord Mosley," she said, choosing to ignore the sarcastic tone with which he'd spoken.

"Oh, well," he stammered, patting her hand where it lay on his arm. "That's quite all right, my dear. Yes. Well…" He cleared his throat, gave Arabella a little bow, and sent a scowl in Silas's direction before excusing himself.

"What did you say to get my grandfather to take his leave like that? It would be handy to know for my future reference," Silas said, frowning after his grandfather.

"I was sweet and kind and made him feel loved," she said, with a teasing smile.

Silas grimaced. "Never mind. I think I'd rather deal with his company."

Arabella laughed and took Silas's arm so he could escort her out to their carriage. "I don't know, Your Grace. I don't think a little sweetness would hurt you."

"Hmm," he said, handing her into the carriage and climbing in after her. "I think you're sweet enough for the both of us." He nuzzled at her neck, and she shivered, putting a hand on his chest, though she didn't push him away.

She shouldn't encourage him, but with his lips trailing over her neck and throat, she couldn't help herself. Didn't want to help herself. She leaned into him, turning her head to give him better access, and his happy growl against her skin sent another delicious shiver through her.

"We don't have to attend the soiree, if you'd rather return home," she said, rubbing her cheek against his. "Since you're so tired, as your grandfather pointed out. You could probably use the rest."

He chuckled and nipped at her earlobe. "And your sister?"

"She'll be fine. Aunt Adelaide is an adequate chaperone. We can take one night off from match-making duty."

"You don't have to convince me, love." He pressed another kiss to her neck and then hung his head out the window to tell the driver their new destination.

Thankfully, they weren't too far away. She pulled Silas's necktie off, and he laughed.

"I'm not sure what's gotten into you this evening, wife. But I'm enjoying it immensely."

She wasn't sure what had gotten into her either. She didn't want to examine it too closely. All she knew was she wanted Silas, and she was damn tired of trying to fight it.

# Chapter Seventeen

They somehow managed to make it to their bedroom with most of their clothing still intact. Barely. They stumbled into the room, lips locked, hands frantically tearing at each other's clothes. The fire was out, and the candles and gaslights had yet to be lit. With the drapes drawn in their room, it was almost completely dark.

They broke apart just long enough to work at the buttons that held her elaborate dress together.

"I'll light the lamps," Arabella said, moving toward the wall. But Silas caught her arm and pulled her back to him.

"Leave them off," he murmured, drawing her into his arms.

"But…" She stopped, letting him push her bodice from her shoulders. Her skirts and under-trappings followed until she stood before him totally bare. A moment of rustling fabric and his own clothes joined hers on the floor.

He took her hands and guided her to the bed, pressing her back and following her down to the mattress. His hands skimmed over her body, and she trembled under his touch, unable to see much more than his outline. She couldn't do anything but lie there and feel. Feel his hands, his lips. The tender care with which they worshipped every inch of her.

"Silas," she breathed.

"I've got you, love," he said between kisses. "I've got you."

And in the dark, without the sight of him to distract her, that endearment suddenly sounded a lot less like a flirtatious throw-away. Without his laughing eyes and wicked grin, with only his gruff voice and the sensations he was creating with his touch, it felt...real. All of it. This wasn't an attempt at procreation. It wasn't even a tumble just for the fun of it. He was making love to her. The sheer sensuality of it overwhelmed her. It didn't feel pretend anymore. Every touch, every brush of his lips shattered her just a little bit more. Lying there in the dark, she couldn't do anything but feel every emotion he evoked with every touch of his body.

And it was too much.

Too much when this would never last. Too much when as soon as she told him she was pregnant, this would be over. She couldn't keep him. What they had between them couldn't continue. They had multiple contracts and a set of ironclad rules to ensure that. The parties, the flirtations, even their heir-making attempts...all of that she might have been able to walk away from and still keep her heart intact.

But this? This absolute symphony of sensation and emotion? She'd never walk away whole. He'd own a piece of her forever.

"Silas," she said, pushing on his shoulders to stop him. "Silas, wait."

"What is it, love?" he asked, his thumb brushing across her cheek.

She reached up and ran her own thumb over his bottom lip, her hand cupping his cheek.

He turned his face into her hand and kissed her palm, and her heart fractured.

"Can we…please, can we light the lamps?"

He froze against her. "You want the lamps lit?"

"Yes. Rule number two, remember," she said, forcing a laugh to try and keep the moment light, though she knew the attempt failed miserably.

"I…of course," he said, getting up from the bed.

He didn't argue, didn't even ask why, he just did as she asked.

But she could tell just in those two words that she'd surprised him. Hurt him. And her bruised heart cracked a little bit more.

It was for the best. For both of them. She just hoped he'd understand.

• • •

Silas rejoined Arabella on the bed, pulling her into

his arms again. She snuggled into him with a sigh of relief. Had she been afraid he'd be angry?

He kissed her again, showing her just how much he still wanted her. Her request stung a bit. Their damn rules. He'd loved the idea when they'd come up with them. A set of rules they both agreed to live by? Rules that would keep their relationship in its place? Keep things from getting real, from getting messy? Genius. So he'd thought. At this moment, he hated the rules. Cursed the day he'd set them to paper. Even while he knew that she'd been right to ask for the lights, insist they follow the rules. Because he obviously wasn't the only one who had felt the difference in their lovemaking.

Without those damn lights blazing, everything was heightened. He hadn't even realized how well he knew her body until he could no longer see it. He knew every dip and swell. Every spot that would ring another sigh from her. Every inch of her was immortalized in his memory. And without their sight, there was nothing there to distract from the sensations, the emotions wrought from every touch.

Moving together in the dark made everything more intense. The sounds she made when his fingers brushed across her skin, the way her body arched against him…the way her breath caught in her throat when he told her how beautiful she was, how much he wanted her, needed her. Everything had been so much *more*.

Too much.

She'd been right to ask for the lights. It was safer. Yet it still felt like they'd lost something precious.

He breathed in, savoring the soft floral scent of her as their limbs tangled together. They were better off sticking to the rules. Focusing on accomplishing their goals. He was definitely getting too attached to his wife. His reaction both to touching her with the lights off and his hurt feelings when she asked him to stop were proof of that.

She writhed under him, her movements growing more frantic. His eyes locked with hers as he moved over her, inside her. He entwined their fingers together, his gaze never leaving hers. And when that building tidal wave finally crashed, carrying them both over the edge, they held on to each other, their hearts pounding in time, their breath mingling.

He rested his forehead against hers, the realization finally hitting him. The lights hadn't made a damn bit of difference. At least for him. It was *her*. His growing feelings for her. He sighed, cradling her to him.

What kind of fool fell in love with his wife?

# Chapter Eighteen

Arabella took a last look in the mirror and made sure everything about her appearance was suitable before grabbing her gloves and hat, then opening the door from her chamber to the connecting sitting room. Her stomach roiled with another bout of the nausea that was becoming more of a frequent occurrence, and she paused to breathe through it. Though this time she didn't think it was entirely the baby's fault. Or not directly, in any case.

She was going to tell Silas about the baby today. And see how he might feel about her putting off her country retirement for a while. Maybe forever. That wasn't part of their agreement. He was supposed to get his life back the moment she found out she was pregnant. But they'd been so happy together lately. She couldn't help but hope that he'd want that to continue. Maybe she shouldn't tell him just yet. Though surely he'd become suspicious soon. He'd known about her courses just after the wedding, of course, though she was now doubting they had been a true cycle at all. But he must be expecting them to begin again soon.

She took a deep breath and slowly let it out. No. She needed to tell him, now, before she lost her nerve. If she could find him. While she spent every night with him, most often in his room, her dressing room and clothing were all kept in her own room. And he'd already been gone when she'd awoken that morning.

She'd meant to talk to Silas before now, tell him about the baby and…everything. But they always seemed to get distracted when they were alone in each other's company for more than three minutes. The thought filled her with a now familiar heat and brought a smile to her lips. Surely, he'd want such nights to continue. What she was feeling couldn't be completely one-sided.

He'd be thrilled about the baby, of course. And maybe, hopefully, *surely*, he'd be happy that she wanted to stay with him, be his wife permanently in more than name only.

Just the thought of his face when she told him that she'd fulfilled her part of their first rule brought a huge smile to her lips. She hurried from the room, excitement replacing her trepidation.

She finally found Silas in the foyer, donning his hat and gloves. "Oh, there you are," she said, hurrying down the last few stairs. The footman already held the front door open, and his groom held his horse ready in front of the house. "Are you going somewhere?"

"It's Wednesday," he said, his face tight.

"Oh. Yes, of course," she said, her voice fainter than she'd intended. She couldn't believe she'd forgotten what day it was. "I…wanted to speak with you for a moment."

He gave her a tight smile. "Can it wait until this evening? I really should be going."

She swallowed hard past the sudden lump in her throat. Silly of her to get worked up, but she couldn't seem to help herself. She forced a nod. "Of course."

"Are you going to your father's today?"

She nodded. "Charlotte is picking me up soon. I thought perhaps you might like to go with us and inspect Anne's suitors."

"Another day perhaps. Besides, I'd wager all of her other suitors pale in comparison to the Duc D'Auvergne."

She forced a smile, trying to keep her tone light. "Yes, but then you aren't the one who must marry him."

He grinned, though it was not his usual carefree smile. "This is true. I've already found my ideal wife."

He leaned down and kissed her forehead before clapping on his hat. "I may be home late," he said over his shoulder. "Don't bother waiting up if you are tired."

And with that, he was out the door.

Charlotte arrived in her carriage just as he rode away, and Arabella quickly affixed her hat, pulling on her gloves as she went outside.

"Was that your husband leaving as I arrived?" she asked when Arabella climbed in to sit beside her.

She shoved all her hurt and disappointment to a back corner in her mind and swallowed hard before answering. She was determined not to make a fool of herself in front of her friend. "Yes."

Charlotte, alerted by her tone no doubt, glanced at her with a raised brow. "And where was he off to this fine morning?"

Arabella sighed. "It's Wednesday." At her friend's frown, she elaborated. "Rule number ten. Wednesdays are set aside for his mysterious errands, no questions asked."

"And you've managed to keep that agreement I take it?"

"Of course. I haven't asked one of the dozens of questions tumbling about in my head. Though it's entirely possible it's something quite boring. Perhaps he enjoys watching the baker bake bread or some other such nonsense."

Charlotte snorted. "Unlikely, I think. And as for your list of rules, you agreed not to ask questions. You didn't agree not to find out on your own." Arabella looked at her in surprise and Charlotte gave her a mischievous smile. "If that's what you want to do, of course."

Did she really want to know where he disappeared to every Wednesday that was so secretive he couldn't tell his wife? And apparently enough of a disgrace that his grandfather berated him for it?

Yes. Yes, she did. Oh, the guilt would no doubt eat at her mercilessly. But she couldn't help it. She had to know what, or more likely who, commanded his attention so. For the sake of their child, if no one else.

She gave a sharp nod. "All right, then."

Charlotte grinned and leaned forward to have a word with her driver. Then she sat back. "He has a few minutes' head start on us, of course, but with the streets this busy he won't be able to travel too quickly. And we at least know which direction he was headed."

Arabella spared a thought for her sister and aunt, but the sight of no less than five carriages parked in front of Bromley Hall when they passed by eased her guilt. Her sister was very happily occupied, no doubt, and her aunt would be just as delighted. Her father, on the other hand, was probably hiding miserably in his study, but that couldn't be helped. He'd be happy enough that Anne was happy. So long as he needn't join in the fun.

They followed the path Silas most likely had taken and were lucky enough to catch sight of him far ahead of them a few blocks down. Charlotte instructed her driver to discreetly follow that horse, and they sat back to see where he'd take them. They didn't have to wait too long.

The city blocks began to thin out, leading to the less populated areas of the city, until he finally reined in his horse in front of an elegant, but modest, by the duke's standards surely, two-story brick home. What was he doing here?

The house was surrounded by a wrought-iron fence that enclosed a neatly landscaped garden. Ivy crept up the front facade of the house, and flowers bloomed from every available nook and cranny of the yard. It was certainly well cared for. Similar homes dotted the street on either side. It seemed the type of neighborhood a respectable barrister or doctor might live in. Did Silas perhaps have some problem with the law? Or his health? Though even if that were the case, surely anyone he needed to see would come to him.

Charlotte instructed her driver to park up the lane, close enough they could still see the house, but far enough away they wouldn't be immediately seen or identified should Silas catch them unawares.

After several minutes, he reappeared in the rear garden of the house. He stood near the steps, looking around as though searching for someone. A faint cry rose from the back corner of the garden, and a woman ran at Silas, launching herself at him. Arabella was too far away to see her clearly. But she looked like she was a little shorter than Arabella's own height and had magnificent swathes of rich golden hair flowing down her back in a shocking display. With her long skirts and the impressive profile her corset highlighted, she was certainly old enough to be putting her hair up. Which meant this was no child he was visiting.

Silas caught her and spun her around, holding her close before setting her back on her feet. He cradled her face in his hands for a moment and said something to her. Arabella couldn't hear what, obviously. But it was equally obvious that he was pleased to see the woman. Especially when he leaned down to kiss her forehead before taking her hand to lead her back into the house.

Arabella sat in the carriage in stunned silence, trying to ignore the sharp pain radiating through her chest. She took several shallow breaths, pushing past the emotions clogging her throat, and shoved everything down into the recesses of her heart where it belonged. He wasn't hers to weep over and she needed to remember it.

"Ari, I'm sorry…" Charlotte said, but Arabella shook her head.

"It's all right, Charlotte."

Her friend didn't look like she believed that

for a moment, so Arabella forced a smile. "Truly. It is. Our marriage was not a love match, remember? In fact, I told him in no uncertain terms he could continue living his life as he saw fit. He's obviously being discreet."

Charlotte watched her with pity-filled eyes. "But the two of you have seemed so happy. I thought—"

"Just because we get along well doesn't mean we are in love, Charlotte. And I'll be leaving him to his own devices soon anyway. It's better that he maintains the...connections he had before we wed. It will make it all the easier for us both when I leave."

Charlotte nodded, though she didn't look like she believed her. It didn't matter. Every word of what Arabella had said was true. And if she kept repeating them to herself, maybe the truth of them would soothe the pain that she'd felt the moment that woman had jumped into Silas's arms. Pain she had no right to feel. That she was foolish to feel. She had no claim to Silas's affections. He'd certainly never treated her with anything less than the honor and courtesy she deserved as his wife. In fact, he treated her a good deal better than many husbands she'd heard of, better than their agreement required. And he'd done everything he'd promised and more to keep up his end of their bargain. Even if they intended their marriage to be a true one, she'd have little cause for complaint.

"Can you ask your driver to take me home, please?" she asked. "I think we've seen all we need to see here."

Charlotte nodded and spoke to the driver, and then sat back and patted Arabella's hand. Arabella said nothing. She appreciated Charlotte's concern, but it was misplaced. And unwanted. The last thing Arabella desired was to be the object of Charlotte's pity. Of *anyone's* pity.

When they arrived at Whittsley House, Arabella climbed down without waiting for the driver to help her. Charlotte still watched her, worry etching her brow.

"I'm fine, Charlotte. I promise. Just a little tired. It's been a very long week."

"If you insist," she said, sitting back. Though she didn't look entirely convinced. "Will you still be attending the Weatherbys' ball this evening?"

Arabella was about to answer no. After all, her husband wouldn't be there to attend with her. It didn't occur to her to go without him. Until now. She could attend with her family and at least see how things were progressing with Anne and Jean-Pierre. Why should she sit at home all evening, moping about a man she shouldn't be thinking about in the first place?

"Of course," she said, her smile coming much

easier. "Anne has been speaking of nothing else for days."

Charlotte's concerned expression faded a bit. "Wonderful. I'll see you there, then."

Arabella waved her off and hurried into the house. She had a ball to get ready for.

. . .

Silas entered his silent house and handed his hat and gloves to his butler. It wasn't unusual for the house to be quiet. After all, his wife's favorite pastime was curling up in a corner to read. But the house just felt empty.

"Would you like some supper, Your Grace? I believe Cook has kept something warm for you."

"Yes, thank you." He started up the stairs, eager to remove his boots and get comfortable. And see Arabella. "Just send a tray up to my sitting room. Has my wife retired for the night?"

"No, Your Grace. I'm afraid the duchess is not at home."

That stopped Silas in his tracks. "Where is she?"

"She is attending the Weatherbys' ball this evening, Your Grace."

Silas clenched his jaw to keep it from dropping open. She went to a ball? On purpose? Without him?

"Forget the food," Silas instructed, turning

to hurry up the stairs. "Have the carriage made ready—" He stopped again. "Or did my wife take it?"

"Yes, I'm sorry, Your Grace. Shall I have your horse brought back around?"

Silas shook his head. The Weatherbys' house wasn't too far. "I'll walk."

"Very well, Your Grace. I'll have your valet attend you."

Silas nodded his thanks and hurried to his room, where he prepared for the ball in record time.

Less than half an hour later, he arrived at the Weatherbys', eyes searching for Arabella before he'd cleared the threshold.

"Whittsley!"

Silas acknowledged Charles but went back to scanning the room immediately.

"Looking for someone?" Charles asked, the amusement in his voice betraying he already knew the answer to that.

"My errant wife," he ground out.

Charles's eyebrows raised. "She attended without you? The cheek of the woman!"

"I know. I..." Silas broke off with a growl when he caught sight of his friend's laughing face.

Perhaps he was overreacting. After all, it was perfectly acceptable for her to attend, especially in the company of her own family. There were no rules against it. In fact, attending more parties would go a long way in keeping the fact that Anne was now closely related to the duke foremost in people's minds. It would only help their cause. So, he should be glad of it, even. Happy that Arabella was content to amuse herself while he was otherwise occupied. But the thought of her dressing up and dancing the night away without him rubbed him the wrong way.

The notes of a waltz struck up and he relaxed a fraction. At least he knew she wouldn't be dancing now. Rule number seven. Waltzes were *his*. So he could keep his search to the outer edges of the ballroom. Perhaps she was over at the refreshment table, since she hadn't eaten anything at home before leaving. Or she could be—

Silas stopped short, his jaw dropping open.

"What is it?" Charles asked, glancing at his friend and then looking out at the floor to see what had astounded him so.

"My wife," he muttered through gritted teeth.

Charles frowned and followed his gaze to where the duchess danced with Viscount Brathwaite. The soon-to-be *late* Viscount Brathwaite.

"She's a lovely dancer," Charles said. "It's good to see her coming out of her shell a bit, eh?"

The grin his friend aimed at him grew bigger the more Silas scowled. Charles finally laughed and jerked his head toward a less populated corner. "Let's wait for your wayward wife over there.

Maybe I can find my own as well," he said with a snort, looking around with a slight frown. "That woman is always wandering off somewhere."

Silas would have preferred marching onto the dance floor and reclaiming his wife. But as that would cause more of a scene than anyone would care for, he followed Charles to his corner.

He caught Arabella's eye when he walked past and held her gaze until she was twirled away. He was somewhat gratified at her wide-eyed surprise to see him. They were going to have a discussion about the consequences for breaking the rules.

She danced by again, her eyes flashing this time when she caught his gaze. He smiled, rather looking forward to the conversation.

And speaking of conversations... The mamas had stopped pushing their daughters on Silas since his marriage, naturally, but that didn't mean there was a shortage of people wanting his attention. Married or not, having the Duke of Whittsley attend your ball or soiree assured you an excellent turnout, so there was a good number who wanted to get his assurance he'd attend some event or other. Along with more mind-numbing chatter that a few weeks ago he would have found amusing.

Now, the only person he wanted to speak with was his wife.

He held his patience until she'd danced no less than three more dances and was in imminent danger of being approached for a fourth. Another waltz. It was time to intervene.

Before the poor chap could ask her if she'd honor him with a dance (and Silas didn't bother to look at the man long enough to identify him), he stepped in, cutting the man short. Unforgivably rude, but he no longer cared.

"Would you do me the honor of dancing with me, Your Grace," he said, holding out his hand to his surprised wife.

She looked at it, then at him, then back at his hand, and for a long moment he thought she might deny him.

"Of course." She took his hand with a strained smile and let him lead her onto the floor.

She said nothing until the music started and they took their first steps. "That was unforgivably rude, Silas. It is odd enough for you to insist upon dancing with your own wife, but to step in when another man is about to ask... I don't know what to think. Poor Lord Chapton seems most put out."

Silas scoffed. "Lord Chapton will soon find another, more available young woman to drool over. Dancing is for finding a husband, after all, and you already have one."

"A fact I'm not likely to forget. And it was still rude," she muttered.

Silas ignored that. "I'm surprised to find you here."

Arabella raised her brows. "Are you?" She shrugged. "You said you would be home late. I didn't see any reason why I should sit around the house while you were gone all night doing... whatever it is that requires your attention every Wednesday."

Silas searched her face, and his eyes narrowed to catch any hint of what was really going on in that head of hers. But her expression was one of bland disinterest, betraying nothing. "Rule ten, my dear. You agreed to it readily enough. Are you regretting our arrangement so soon?"

"Of course not," she said with that same bland tone, though something flashed in her eyes. "I agreed you could have your Wednesdays and that I'd not ask you any questions. Well, it's Wednesday. And I have not asked you a single thing about your whereabouts or activities. I did not, however, agree to sit around the house on my own while you were away, nor did you ask it of me. So, I'm sorry, but I don't understand your seeming disappointment to find me having a lovely evening surrounded by my family and friends."

"You broke rule number seven," he muttered.

"Hmm, yes I did. Unavoidable, I'm afraid. Turning down a request to dance would have been unforgivably rude."

He couldn't argue with that, though he'd like to, as she wasn't wrong. Still he frowned, unable, or at least unwilling, to examine his reaction to finding her at the ball dancing with a string of other men. But she was right. Even if they'd arrived at the ball together, it would not only be odd but rude to spend the evening in each other's company. They'd raised more than a few eyebrows already the times he claimed his waltzes previously.

She also correctly pointed out that he'd made no stipulations on what she could do with her time. Not just when he was otherwise engaged but during any day. He had no right to feel the cascade of conflicting emotions that crashed about within his chest. Nor should he indulge in them. Keeping a rein on them was easier said than done, though.

"I'm not disappointed," he said.

She raised a brow, her mouth quirking into a half smile.

"I'm surprised. There's a difference."

"Hmm." The music drew to a close, and she bobbed her head in a slight bow. "If you'll excuse me, Your Grace, I think I will go check on my aunt."

He should have escorted her back to her aunt, but they'd already raised enough eyebrows. Allowing her to walk the few feet to her kinswoman unaccompanied was far less likely to cause a scandal than if she decided to pummel him about the head with the fan she'd pulled from her bustle pocket. The short, sharp flicks of that lace-trimmed tool of womanly virtue said clearly, without her actually having to say the words, that she did not wish to be bothered.

Handy things, fans. Had she fluttered it provocatively near her breasts or blinked up at him shyly from behind its gilded edges, he'd happily take her up on her flirtation and find a nice secluded alcove or garden pathway to take her. But the way she was whipping it about now, no reasonable man would get within six feet of her for fear of being slapped with it.

At least she hadn't asked him more about where he'd gone that day. He found, to his surprise, he didn't like keeping secrets from her. But then it wasn't his secret to give away. So keep it he must. And some things were better left unknown, for all involved.

He took a deep breath and let it out slowly, but before he could decide whether he wanted to leave or try to get his wife in a better mood, Jean-Pierre approached him.

"Whittsley, I wonder if I might have a word?"

"Of course, D'Auvergne. Shall we?" He gestured to the quiet corner he'd abandoned in favor of his wife, who was now whispering excitedly with her sister.

"Things are going well?" he asked, nodding toward Anne.

"Very well. In fact, that is what I wished to speak to you about." Jean-Pierre glanced toward

Anne and beamed. "I have asked the beautiful Anne to be my wife and she has accepted."

Silas flashed his biggest smile and clapped Jean-Pierre on the back. "That is excellent news, my friend. I'm very glad to hear it." His friend had no idea exactly how glad. Jean-Pierre was a duke. A French duke, but a duke nonetheless. Which meant not only would Anne be very shortly betrothed, but to a man who, by all appearances, made her very happy *and* was an excellent match. Which meant Arabella owed him a concession of his choosing. Oh, and he could think of so very many things he'd like. The choices were staggering. And intriguing.

"But surely you should be speaking with her father, not me," Silas said with a chuckle.

Jean-Pierre laughed. "Yes, well, that is just it. I've never asked a father for his daughter's hand before. I thought, since you had experience with this particular father, you might…"

"Ah. You wish for some advice in dealing with Lord Durborough?"

"Exactly," Jean-Pierre said with relief.

"You needn't worry, my friend. As long as Anne is happy, Lord Durborough will be as well."

Silas imparted what words of wisdom he could, though he didn't think it was much. A few months ago, he wouldn't have worried about it. He'd have spouted some nonsense and gone about his day. He did truly wish his friend and sister-in-law happiness, though, and sincerely hoped he could be some small measure of help. Jean-Pierre seemed much relieved by their discussion, at least. However, by the time they'd finished, Arabella had disappeared again. She was making a disturbing habit of it.

He searched throughout the main rooms and courtyard and ended up back in the reception hall where guests milled about, though in smaller numbers than in the crowded ballroom. Silas was about to go back and search the dance floor for his errant wife when a flash of emerald silk from behind a curtained alcove caught his eye.

He marched over, but instead of barreling in, he quietly pulled back the curtain. She hadn't noticed him yet, so he leaned against the wall and folded his arms, smiling down at his wife. She'd kicked off her slippers and had tucked her feet beneath her on the bench where she was curled up with a book.

He rubbed a finger over his lips, and she finally looked up, then sat bolt upright when she realized she was caught.

"Breaking another rule?" he asked, shaking his head and making a tsking noise. "That's two this evening."

She snapped the book shut and set it beside her on the bench. "I didn't realize you were keeping count."

He gave her a slow, sensual grin that had her cheeks heating as he took a step inside the alcove, filling the space.

"Whatever shall I do with such a wayward wife?"

She tried to glare up at him but failed. He took her hand and drew her up. She kept her gaze on the floor, but her lips tugged into a small smile. He pulled her closer, wrapping an arm around her waist, and she glanced up at him from beneath her lashes.

"You could let me go back to my book," she suggested, her lips twitching.

"That would only be a punishment for me."

She gave him a delicate shrug. "I wouldn't object to that."

He chuckled. "I'm sure you wouldn't." He pulled her even closer, until she was flush against him and had to crane her neck to look up at him.

"Dance with me," he said.

"Here?"

"Why not?"

"There's not much room. And they aren't playing a waltz."

He leaned down to brush his nose along her jawline. "I don't care," he murmured in her ear.

A fine tremor ran through her, but she didn't pull out of his arms, and when he began to sway, she followed his lead.

They didn't speak again, just clung to each other while gently turning to the music. He didn't know what he was doing. This was never part of the plan. He was breaking all his own rules and he didn't care anymore. As much as he needed an heir—no…wanted a child, with her—he didn't want to lose her. She hadn't said anything about altering their arrangement. Then again, neither had he. Yet.

But the way she held on to him as they moved…surely she felt something for him too. Surely it wasn't one-sided. Maybe this thing between them didn't need to be temporary. Maybe they could have a life together, whether they ever had a child or no—though he would love a whole parcel of children with their mother's beautiful eyes and sharp wit.

He'd never been afraid to take what he wanted before. But he didn't want to go too fast, push her too hard. But he also knew he could never stand by and watch her walk away. Not anymore. Which meant they needed to have a conversation.

His lips found hers, and she sank into him with a whimper that tore at his heart.

No. He couldn't lose this woman. So he was going to have to figure out a way to keep her. Rules or no.

# Chapter Nineteen

Arabella felt a perverse sort of satisfaction to leave Silas alone in his bed, as he'd left her the previous morning. Still, she groaned with frustration at herself. He'd lived up to every single promise he'd made her, had broken none of their rules. Well…he'd stretched a few. Her cheeks burned and a bolt of pure desire streaked through her at the memory of his idea of public affection.

Still. He'd done what he'd promised. Married her. Restored her family's reputation. Even made their heir-making attempts a pleasure that she looked forward to, craved even, instead of a chore to accomplish as she'd expected. And now, in almost no time at all, he had found her sister not only a respectable husband, but a duke! Even if he was French.

Arabella had no cause for complaint.

And after the way he acted at the ball the night before, and afterward when they'd returned home, she harbored even more hope that he would not only be thrilled over the prospect of their child but might not object to her staying on. Of course, she'd never know if she didn't tell him. Which she would. Soon. Just not right that moment because she was expected at her father's.

Jean-Pierre would be declaring his intentions today. Once he had, and their father had put his stamp of approval on the matter, there would be much to do.

Their wedding wouldn't need to be rushed as her own had been. They'd have time for a proper engagement. Aunt Adelaide was already talking about a ball to celebrate their betrothal. And, of course, there would be the wedding and following celebration to plan. Jean-Pierre was descended from royalty. Very minor royalty, dethroned, defrocked, and exiled, for the most part. But royalty nonetheless. Which meant everything would need to be perfect. And extravagant. Arabella had already promised to help in every way she could, and the contracts weren't even discussed yet, let alone signed.

That step didn't take long, as luck would have it. Their father had no such qualms with Anne as he had with Arabella. Anne had been counting the days until her wedding since she was a little girl. And it was obvious to anyone who saw them that Jean-Pierre and Anne were madly in love. Her father agreed to the match without hesitation, and the women left the men alone to negotiate the marriage contract details while they got down to the really important business of planning the engagement ball.

When they were halfway through their first pot of tea, and somewhere between the discussion of the floral arrangements and whether they should serve lemonade along with punch and champagne, Silas burst into the room, followed by a flustered footman who tried in vain to announce him before he entered.

"His Grace the Duke of Whittsley," the poor man wheezed, executing a wobbly bow before leaving the duke alone with them.

Anne and Aunt Adelaide stared at Silas in open-mouthed astonishment, but Silas ignored everyone but Arabella.

"Where did you go?" he asked.

She smiled up at him serenely. "Here, obviously. Would you like a cup of tea?" she asked with the sweetest and most innocent expression she could muster.

"Tea?"

He seemed so confused Arabella had to bite her cheek to keep from laughing.

"Anne, why don't we go see if your father and new fiancé would like some refreshments," Aunt Adelaide tactfully suggested.

Anne glanced back and forth between Arabella and Silas with a slight frown, but she nodded.

As soon as they were gone, Silas slumped into

the chair across from Arabella and she looked him over, her forehead furrowed.

"Is something troubling you, Silas?"

He raised a brow. She very rarely called him by his given name outside of their bedroom. But she was growing more used to it. Either that or the luster had come off the coin a bit, as they said.

"Yes. I'm cross with you."

She raised her own brow at that. "And that troubles you?"

"Yes."

Her lips twitched again. "Seems you'd be used to it by now. Are you really troubled or just troubled that you are troubled?"

He frowned again. "Both?"

At that, she gave up and laughed. She sat back, shaking her head. "That makes two of us."

He cocked an eyebrow. "Oh?"

She took a deep breath and plucked at her skirts. Then realized what she was doing and tried clasping her hands in her lap. But that seemed too formal, so she fidgeted with the edge of the lace tablecloth that hung—

"Ari. Is there something wrong?" Silas asked, leaning forward to take her hands in his.

"Wrong? No," she said with a nervous laugh. "I've been waiting for the right moment…but there never seems to be one…but I've wanted to tell you…"

He raised a brow and she smiled, happiness and sheer terror warring inside her until she laughed again.

"I am with child," she said, squeezing his hands, her eyes desperately searching his face for any sign of how he might feel at the news.

"You… You're what?" he asked, blinking at her like her words weren't quite sinking in.

"The doctor hasn't yet confirmed it, but my courses are a week late. At least. Those that occurred after the wedding were odd to say the least, so it's possible I am quite dreadfully late, and I am never late. Ever. Charlotte explained what else to look for and I've been feeling ill and tired…" She broke off when she realized she was rambling. About her courses no less.

"That could just be my company," he said with a faint grin.

She laughed, unable to keep the smile from her face. "Could be. But I don't think so. I'm no expert on the matter, of course, however, I think we are safe in assuming our contract has been fulfilled. Though I'm not sure if we can declare a winner in our little race, with Anne's engagement happening on the same day I'm telling you about the child. Though the child was conceived before Anne's engagement, so…"

She finally noticed that he hadn't said anything. Or done anything. Or…really even breathed since she'd told him. Let alone smiled or acted like the news was in any way welcome. Her smile fell from her lips, and she pressed a hand to her middle, trying to keep her belly from sinking to her feet. Her skin suddenly felt too tight across her face, her lips numb.

"Silas?"

. . .

Silas watched her, his eyes searching her face, flickering every few seconds to the belly that even now cradled his growing child. His heart thundered in his chest, his whole being screaming at him to say something, do something, to stop her from walking out of that room and make her stay with him.

Because he had no doubt she was about to destroy his world. She was so happy. It shone from her. He was happy as well, of course. The news of a child was most welcome. What he'd wanted. The reason he'd entered into this whole scheme. That she could give him this gift... His throat grew tight at the thought. *Their* child. A miracle and a blessing both.

And a curse.

No. Not a curse. Never that. He already cherished it. How could he not? It was a part of her. But...its presence, abstract though it might be at the moment, also meant that their happy little bubble of marital bliss was over. And Arabella was apparently thrilled that it was so. No doubt she couldn't wait to leave. Claim her prize of retirement to Fallcreek and go back to her quiet life amongst her books. She'd made no secret of the fact that she was counting the moments until she could make her escape.

So be it.

Though letting her walk away would feel like tearing his own heart from his chest, he wouldn't say a word to diminish her joy in her hard-won freedom. He could only thank his maker that he'd kept his mouth shut and not burdened her with his foolish notions of a true marriage.

"Silas?" she asked again, her brow creased in concern. "Are you not pleased? I thought—"

"Of course I'm pleased," he said, forcing a smile. "And my grandfather will be doubly so, no doubt. A bit surprised, perhaps, that it happened so quickly. But I'm thrilled with the news, naturally."

She gave him a hesitant smile. "I'm glad." She looked down at her clasped hands in her lap, her sudden timidity not boding well. It could only mean she meant to broach a subject that made her nervous.

"I wanted to discuss our future arrangements with you..." she started, but he interrupted her before she could continue. He knew all too well what she was about to say. And he didn't want to hear it.

"I have news of my own, as a matter of fact."

"Oh?" she asked, startled.

"I must leave immediately for a trip. I have been putting off a few business matters over the last several months that can no longer be ignored."

"You're leaving?" she asked, her eyes wide. "For how long?"

He couldn't meet her gaze, so he busied himself with straightening his clothing, brushing bits of invisible lint from the cloth. It was true that he'd been ignoring several business matters, but then he always did. Or at least had, in the past. Lately, he'd been making an attempt to stay more on top of things. But he could take care of what needed doing from home. He had managers to do the traveling for him. However, with her news, it seemed a good time to make himself scarce. He didn't think he could bear watching her leave. So, a trip it was. The longer, the better.

"I'm not sure. A few weeks at least, though it could be much longer. So I suppose your news is impeccably timed."

She frowned. "How so?"

"Well, now that our little agreement has reached its desired conclusion, you can retire to Fallcreek, as you wished."

"Fallcreek?" Her frown deepened.

"Or any of my other estates, if that one is no longer where you wish to go. My family has enough properties that we should be able to avoid each other nicely. Just as you wished."

"I see."

"Yes. Well…" He made to stand up, but Arabella's quiet voice froze him in place.

"I saw her."

Silas froze with the ice that suddenly ran down his veins. "What?"

Arabella couldn't quite hold his gaze, but she straightened her back and stuck her chin in the air. "I followed you on your last visit. I saw *her*."

Silas stood and raked a hand through his hair. He worked very hard to keep Eliza's existence a secret. Only his grandfather had been aware of her, and Silas would vastly prefer that was not the case. But his grandfather, at least, he could trust to keep silent. He couldn't trust anyone else with this. He'd been careless if Arabella had not only found out about her but had actually seen her after just a few short weeks.

"I don't know what you think you saw, but I can promise you—"

Arabella blew out an exasperated breath and stood, waving her hand at him. "Don't do that. Don't try to tell me I didn't see what I know I saw. I was there. I *saw*." She took a deep breath and turned back to him, making a great effort to meet his gaze.

"The woman you saw…it's not what you think. But I can't tell you more than that. I know you don't understand. But she is my responsibility. I cannot abandon her. Will not. I wish you could just trust—"

"Trust is earned, Silas. Not given." She sighed and rubbed her hand across her temple. "I'm sorry. Perhaps I am being unfair. I know I agreed…and maybe it wouldn't have mattered if I…if we…" She sighed again and looked at him with a faint smile. "Well. It is what it is, I suppose."

He wanted to tell her everything. Explain. But he truly didn't know what to say. He'd protected Eliza for so long. She had no one else. She was the one rule he could not bend. And the one on which Arabella, as well, would not compromise. He had no choice.

"You agreed," he said quietly. "Rule ten…you promised—"

"Damn the rules," she said, the words all the more gutting because she said them quietly, brokenly, as she watched him, the last spark of hope dying from her eyes as he remained silent. But what could he say?

Finally, her gaze dropped, and the sigh that escaped her lips speared him right through the heart, shredding it to ribbons. "I'm sorry, you're right." She stood and walked to the door. "We agreed upon the rules. There's no changing them now."

She spared him one last glance before she opened the door.

"Goodbye, Your Grace."

# Chapter Twenty

Arabella's heart swelled with happiness as she watched a glowing Anne stand beside Jean-Pierre accepting their guests' congratulations on their engagement. It wasn't their formal engagement ball yet, of course. That would take several more weeks of intense planning that had Aunt Adelaide in her element. But they were all too happy for Anne not to celebrate, so her aunt had quickly organized a small dinner and dance for fifty or so of their closest friends.

Arabella had dreaded it. The last thing she wanted to do after that dreadful scene with Silas was attend a party, even one for her beloved sister. But watching how happy Anne was went a long way to soothing Ari's soul.

Silas had been right, damn him. Jean-Pierre was perfect for Anne.

And Silas was perfect for her.

She couldn't stop the thought from invading her mind, though she'd been trying to do nothing but that since she'd left him standing in her father's salon two weeks prior. But nothing had changed since that morning.

Well, that wasn't true. Everything had changed. She no longer went to Silas's room at night but slept alone in her giant bed in her own chamber. Not that it mattered, as he'd left two days after their disastrous talk. He'd come to her bedroom door before he'd left. She'd heard him standing outside. Could see the shadow of his feet. Hear his breathing. And his muttered curse as he'd turned from the door and gone back to his own room.

And then he'd gone. And Arabella had thrown herself into whatever she could to keep her mind off him and what he might be doing while he was away. She'd spent most of her waking hours at her family home helping with arrangements for Anne's engagement ball. And in the evenings, as Silas was no longer around to drag her to every party and soiree in the city, she stayed home with Bub and tried to keep her mind on her books. Which had proven near impossible.

So, she continued with her plans to leave London. She wanted to be gone before Silas returned, and since he'd given her no indication how long he'd be gone and she hadn't heard from him since he left, she decided she should leave as soon as possible. Now that Anne's party had taken place, she could go. Though, of course, she'd return for the engagement ball. But until then, she'd bide her time in the country. Though the excitement of the famed Fallcreek library had dimmed somewhat for her. Still. She knew she'd be content there. Eventually. Maybe once her child was born.

She brushed a hand across her belly, still in awe of the fact that she was truly with child. She prayed it was a boy. She'd agreed to give Silas a second child if the first was a girl. But she wasn't sure her heart would survive that. Being with him like that again. In his bed. In his arms. Not if she could never be in his heart.

She'd barely had the strength to walk away the first time. She'd never manage it a second.

"You're not dancing this evening?" a gruff voice said as a man sat down beside her.

She looked over and gave Lord Mosley a tight smile. "Not tonight, no. I'm afraid I'm feeling a bit poorly."

"Ah. Well, being married to my grandson would sour anyone's stomach."

"Oh, he's really not so bad," she said, before she could think why she felt the need to defend him. "He's a good man underneath all the jokes and self-deprecation. I think he just prefers others don't see it."

Lord Mosley looked at her in surprise. She was a bit surprised herself. Normally she agreed with Lord Mosley's opinions of his grandson.

He harrumphed. "He's far too gregarious for my liking. Always has been." He stared down at her with interest. "Though lately, I'll admit, he seems to have become a bit more serious. That's your doing, I expect."

"Mine?"

Lord Mosley nodded. "He seems to finally be taking an interest in his responsibilities. Maybe realizing there's more to life than parties and frivolity."

Arabella smiled, though she again felt the overwhelming urge to defend her husband. "He could be a bit more serious about some matters, I agree. But I quite like the frivolous side of him."

Lord Mosley snorted. "That makes one of us. Still, things seem to be going well between you and my grandson."

It was not a question.

"Everything is going as I expected, yes," she answered, not at all comfortable with where this conversation was heading, but not comfortable with lying either.

"Then why are you retiring to Fallcreek so early in the season?"

She glanced up at him in surprise.

"Oh, come now, my dear. There is very little that is truly a secret in this city. The servants know everything. And they do tend to talk to one another. And Silas is my grandson, after all. The Duchess of Whittsley retiring to the country halfway through the season, without her husband, is the most gossip-worthy news of the week."

Arabella's mouth dropped open in dismay. The last thing she wanted to do was cause a scandal. In fact, she hoped removing herself would help prevent one. The thought of her marriage problems affecting Anne was also of the utmost concern.

She forced what she hoped was a bland expression onto her face and lightly shrugged. "I haven't been feeling very well. We hope the fresh country air will do me some good."

Lord Mosley nodded. "Quite right. Best thing for you. I hoped the situation was something along those lines. Glad to hear it isn't due to any…other issues."

Arabella refocused her attention on him. "Such as?"

The old man visibly clenched his jaw. "Nothing that is any of your concern."

His tone brooked no argument. And under normal circumstances, she'd listen to the feeling of dread settling in her gut and let it alone, but she couldn't anymore.

"You know where he goes on Wednesdays, don't you?" she asked.

"Obviously my grandson has not seen fit to share his activities with you. For a very good reason. And for once I agree with him." He stood and bowed. "Good night, Your Grace."

She stared after him in astonishment. Then she sighed deeply, suddenly so tired she could barely move, and went to make her excuses to Anne and Jean-Pierre.

Despite her exhaustion, she couldn't sleep that night. Her mind was on Silas. As it always was. For all the good it did her. They were just too different. They wanted different things. It was best to just follow the plan and move on with their lives now that they'd fulfilled their goals. She'd have to have some contact with him, true, because of their child. But hopefully it would be limited. And avoidable for a while at least.

The last couple months had been a whirlwind. She was ready to get back to her quiet, solitary life. She'd already packed her trunks and had them ready to go. Her father's carriage would take her to Fallcreek at dawn. She wouldn't need to bother Silas again.

A slight meow was her only warning before a slight ball of fluff launched itself at her as she climbed into bed. She grinned and gathered Bub to her, burying her face in his fur.

"You'll like the country much better than the city, Bub," she said, curling up with the now purring cat. "Maybe we'll both find some peace there."

Though she doubted it.

• • •

Silas didn't look up when his grandfather entered

the study but kept staring into the flames dancing in the fireplace.

"You're a fool, you know," Lord Mosley said, dropping into the seat beside Silas.

"I'm very well aware of that. Though I'm curious what you think I've done this time."

"You disappeared for a week and then you showed up on my doorstep and have been skulking about my house for days now. What you should have done was gone to that party tonight."

Silas sighed. They'd already had this conversation. "Why?"

"She was looking for you. Though she tried to hide it."

"Who?" he asked, though he knew damn well who.

His grandfather gave him the look that nonsense question deserved. "Who indeed. That poor woman you somehow coerced into marrying you."

Silas snorted. "She coerced *me* I'll have you know. And I thought you barely approved of her."

Lord Mosley harrumphed. "A man can change his mind. If she was the one who coerced you, then why does she seem to be abandoning you?"

Silas gritted his teeth until his jaw ached. "I'm the one who left."

"Oh? Then why are you sitting in my study? Leaving for a week before coming back home with your tail between your legs doesn't count. Go back to your own house."

Silas let his head drop on the back of his chair. He should. He knew that. But what would he say to her? If she'd even let him in the door. He wouldn't if he were her.

"And what's this about her retiring to the country in the middle of the season?"

Silas scowled. His grandfather always seemed to know everything. "She hasn't been feeling well. The country air will do her good."

"Hmm, yes. Almost exactly what she said."

"Then perhaps you should believe her."

Lord Mosley shrugged. "It's of no consequence whether I believe her or not. I simply find it odd a young woman would find the company of dusty books in the country more appealing than that of her new husband."

Silas chuckled at that, though there was little humor in it. "As that man is me, considering your poor opinion of me, I'm surprised you find it so odd."

"You might have a point there."

This time Silas's laugh did have humor behind it. "Glad to hear you admit it."

His grandfather didn't say anything for a minute, and Silas hoped that he'd be on his way. But of course he had no such luck.

"She asked me about your…trips."

This time he gritted his teeth so hard his jaw popped. "And did you enlighten her?"

His grandfather glowered. "Absolutely not. You know how I feel about that. And now that you've lost your wife over it, I hope you'll finally listen to me."

"I have not lost my wife over this or anything else," he snapped.

His grandfather pursed his lips, and Silas blurted out the information he'd meant to keep quiet. "She's with child."

Lord Mosley's eyebrows hit his hairline. "Congratulations. Didn't think you had it in you."

"Neither did I," Silas said, surprised that his grandfather didn't seem happier, since getting Silas to sire an heir had been his main purpose in maintaining contact for so long.

"You'll be a father now. With all the responsibilities that entails. All the more reason for you to abandon—"

"She's already been abandoned by everyone else in her life," Silas said, finally losing a grip on his temper. "I will not be the next to desert her."

"Even if it means losing your wife?" Lord Mosley asked.

Silas gritted his teeth again and looked back into the fire. It was an impossible decision. One he couldn't make even if he wished to. He could only hope that he'd have time to fix what had gone wrong with Arabella. They would be connected by their child now. She wouldn't leave him completely. He hoped.

"I know how you feel," Lord Mosley said, his words laced with a sadness Silas had never heard. He sighed deeply. "But she's not—"

"She is my sister!" Silas ground out. "And your granddaughter, though you do your best to forget that fact. I'm not the one in the wrong here. You are! She cannot help the circumstances of her birth."

Lord Mosley pursed his lips together. "It doesn't matter. There would be talk…"

"Ah yes," Silas said, sitting back against the cushions. "That was the real reason you sent her away. You couldn't bear that any hint of a scandal touched our family. And there would be no hiding that Eliza was a bast—"

"Do you really think she'd be happier out in society?"

Silas looked away, unable to hold his grandfather's gaze, unable to argue with him over that point. People were cruel, hateful. He released a long sigh. Perhaps his grandfather had done the best he could with Eliza. When his daughter, Silas's mother, had died giving birth to Eliza, he'd set the child up with a family in the country and had sent her to a series of boarding schools in Switzerland when she reached school age. As far as Silas could tell, she'd been well looked after. And, truly, her life hadn't been much different than that of many other wellborn girls.

But she hadn't been happy. Hadn't been loved. No one from her family had visited her, and she'd spent her holidays at the school until Silas had discovered her whereabouts and had moved her to the house in the city so he could visit her every week. He'd kept her a secret as his grandfather wished. For her sake, though. Not the family's as was his grandfather's intention. Though Silas, of course, didn't wish for his mother's reputation to be besmirched. But neither did he want Eliza to suffer for the rest of her life because of their mother's indiscretion.

He wished he could do more for her. But he would do what he could. And he would never abandon her to her fate alone. Even if it meant losing the woman who had come to mean more to him than anything.

"Perhaps I should tell her," he said, his gaze fixed on the blazing logs.

His grandfather scowled and shook his head. "Tell her what? That now that she's finally gotten her family's reputation repaired, you're going to ruin it all over again with a fresh scandal that will never go away?"

While Silas didn't agree that anyone's well-being was served by Eliza being hidden away, he nodded. "Yes."

"You're a greater fool than I realized."

Silas shrugged. "Perhaps."

Maybe he was a fool. But he was certainly a hypocrite. He'd asked, no, *expected* Arabella to trust him. To trust that his Wednesday visits were not a betrayal of her. Yet he hadn't trusted her enough to tell her the reason for those visits. Hadn't trusted her not to betray Eliza. Hadn't trusted her enough to accept Eliza.

What right did he have to ask for what he himself hadn't been willing to give?

He stood and marched to the door. His grandfather twisted in his chair. "Where are you going?"

"To have a discussion with my wife."

"Silas, I forbid—"

Silas rounded on him. "You are in no position to forbid me anything. I have listened to your advice and your warnings of disaster for years. I'm done. I will not give up either of them over a secret that should never have existed in the first place. Arabella is strong, and kind, and I trust her with my life. And with my sister's. You're either going to have to learn to accept them both or leave us to live our lives in peace."

He turned on his heel, ignoring his grandfather calling his name behind him. It was long past time he told Arabella the deepest, darkest secret of his life. He only prayed she'd forgive him for not telling her sooner.

Only by the time he made it back to their house, it was to discover he was already too late.

Arabella was gone.

# Chapter Twenty-One

Arabella stood in the center of the room that she had dreamed of for so long. Fallcreek's library was…everything she'd imagined. More even.

The mammoth space should have felt cold, cavernous. But freestanding bookshelves were spread almost haphazardly around the room, creating smaller seating spaces that felt homey and inviting. Thick rugs covered large sections of the wood floor.

And the books… Arabella slowly turned, taking them all in. Mahogany bookcases stretched from floor to ceiling along every wall. And each and every one was crammed full of books. So many she'd never be able to read them all. Though she'd be thrilled to give it a try.

On two walls, some blank space had been left every few bookshelves on which hung tapestries and paintings that she would happily spend hours staring at. The outer wall showcased three floor-to-ceiling mullioned windows framed by heavy draperies between the bookshelves. And the wall on the far side of the library was taken up almost entirely by a massive fireplace with the most ornate mantel she'd ever seen.

A corkscrew staircase led the way to a second-floor gallery walkway so one could reach the upper shelves, and plush furniture was spread throughout the room, luring her to get lost in their cushiony depths. Crystal knickknacks and figurines sat upon the higher shelves, and her lips twitched, picturing Bub on the loose. Her heart ached at the thought of him...more accurately, at the thought of his master, who liked to pretend he wasn't totally enamored of the little beast.

The library was everything she'd ever wanted. And a few months ago, she could have walked into that room, locked the door, and died a blissful woman. Now...now, she wanted Silas by her side. She wanted to drag him from shelf to shelf while she explored every nook and cranny. She wanted him there to share every moment.

How had she ever thought she could come to this place, *his* home, even if he'd spent little time here recently, and *not* think of him? There were touches of him everywhere. The library was decorated in the same deep shades he favored. Her hand trailed over a throw blanket on one of the overstuffed chairs. She picked it up and crushed it to her nose, inhaling the faint mint scent that was so familiar. Then one of the paintings caught her eye and she sank onto the sofa, her heart thumping painfully as a little sob caught in her throat.

A beautiful woman sat with a chubby-cheeked little boy on her lap while a litter of kittens played at their feet. The set of the nose, the slant of his eyes…the artist had even caught the mischievous twinkle that still shone from them. The boy had to be Silas when he was young.

She placed her hand on her belly, imagining that their son would look quite a bit like that little boy in the painting.

Exhaustion pulled at her, and she slowly stood and took a deep breath. Expecting Fallcreek to be a haven to hide from Silas and her feelings for him had been laughably foolish. There was no escape from her own heart. There was also nothing she could do about it right that second. Perhaps she was just tired. A good night's rest would set her right.

Only the next day brought no relief from her unrelenting thoughts. Nor did the day after that. Even buried under mountains of books and soft blankets, with the staff pampering her like a spoiled princess, she couldn't think of anything but Silas. After three days of her own torturous thoughts plaguing her, she gave up and had her trunks repacked.

She would go home, to Vinethorpe, as she should have from the start.

Vinethorpe was no better. She was no longer surrounded by mementos of Silas's past but somehow that made it worse. Instead of imagining him curled up in front of the library's fireplace or thinking of the fact that she was sleeping in his bed, she was at home in her old room, thinking of her life before she'd met him and how much she'd changed. Because of him. Because of her feelings for him. She spent two days comparing and contrasting her life before and after Silas, and she ended up thinking of nothing but how much she missed him and how long the years ahead of her seemed without him.

She couldn't stay here, alone with her thoughts. But she couldn't go back to Fallcreek. And she certainly couldn't return to London. Trying to learn to live without him when he wasn't there was difficult enough. She'd never manage if she actually had to see him. Besides…she'd agreed to retire to the country. She'd promised, in writing, to disappear from his life. And he'd made no move to stop her when she'd made good on her promise. So, she'd go to the only place she had left where someone might welcome her. Hopefully.

Alice. It had been far too long since she'd seen her eldest sister.

Arabella's carriage pulled up in front of Oak

Tree Lodge, the small country house that once belonged to her grandparents and that her sister now called home. Alice came out, her small son on her hip and a slight frown creasing her forehead until she saw who had arrived.

"Arabella!" she cried, throwing her arms around her the moment Arabella stepped foot on the ground. "What are you doing here? Oh, never mind that yet. Let's go inside."

Arabella laughed, hugging her sister again and taking a moment to admire her nephew. John came out and smiled at her rather shyly. "Hello, Miss Arabella. Or I suppose that would be Your Grace now."

"You are family now, John. Just call me Arabella."

He smiled and nodded at her bags. "Why don't you two go in," he said to Alice. "I'll bring your bags in."

Arabella smiled her thanks and followed her sister into the house.

The inside was clean, cozy, and perfect. Arabella took the first deep breath she'd been able to take in weeks and released it slowly, letting the tension drain from her.

"Come to the kitchen," Alice said. "I've got the kettle on. I hope you don't mind if we dispense with the ceremony. I think I could rummage up a proper tea service to serve to Her Grace in the parlor if that would be more fitting." She laughed and was turning toward the kitchen before Arabella answered. There was no need for an answer, of course. Arabella would have been mortified if her sister had started dropping curtsies and fawning over her.

"A nice cup of tea in the kitchen sounds wonderful, thank you."

She settled into a chair near the fireplace, and her sister plunked the baby on her lap. "Mind him for me while I get the tea."

Arabella laughed, surprised, but held out a finger for the baby to grasp. He grabbed onto her with startling strength.

"He's strong," she said.

Alice nodded proudly. "Just like his father."

"Who's just like his father?" John said, coming up behind his wife to kiss her on the cheek.

"Your growing son," she said with a laugh, leaning back against him.

Arabella's heart filled with warmth at the sight of her sister's obvious happiness. Her actions had caused the family quite a bit of trouble, no doubt about it. And she was ashamed for how harshly she'd judged her sister. But, in the face of such obvious love…what other choice had there been? Arabella would sacrifice much for such a love now.

John kissed his wife tenderly before heading back out the door to see to Arabella's driver and horse before they returned to Vinethorpe.

Her throat contracted with unshed tears, and she turned her attention to her nephew to try to keep her mind from Silas and everything she had just left behind. The baby drowsed sleepily against her chest, and after Alice had laid out the tea essentials, she took him and placed him in a basket near the table that was obviously kept there for that reason.

"You look very happy," Arabella said when her sister took a seat beside her.

"I am." She smiled, her contentment shining from her eyes. "I am sorry for the trouble it's caused the family. But…" She shrugged with a smile tinged with sadness. "I don't regret it."

Arabella took her sister's hand. "Nor should you. The two of you are obviously very happy."

Her sister patted her hand. "And what of you? Not that I'm not thrilled to see you, but you are newly married yourself and there is Anne's wedding to plan."

Arabella glanced at her in surprise, and she nodded at a stack of letters in a box on the table. "Anne writes me every week."

"Ah," Arabella said, filled with shame that she'd only managed a handful of her own letters.

"What is wrong, Ari?"

Arabella slumped in her chair and let the whole story spill out, from the moment she'd thought of her scheme to propose to Silas to the moment she'd gotten in that carriage and left the city.

"I went to Fallcreek Abbey, like we'd always planned. And it was...incredible. So beautiful. And the library!" She grabbed her sister's hand. "Oh, Alice, you can't imagine such a wonderful place. There are so many books there it would take me until I was old and gray to read them all and maybe not even then."

"Then why are you sitting in my kitchen instead of basking in your books at Fallcreek?"

Arabella fiddled with her teacup, staring at the leaves that stuck to the bottom and sides until they blurred. "I don't know." She finally glanced up at her sister with half a smile. "Without him there..." She looked back at her cup. "It just felt wrong. I only stayed a few days. And then I went home, to Vinethorpe. But...that didn't feel like home anymore either. I didn't know where else to go."

"I'm glad you came here," Alice said, taking her hand again. "But did it occur to you that these places don't feel like home to you because *he* is your home?"

Arabella blinked up at her, startled. "No. I mean...he and I...we...it's not like with you and John."

Her sister raised an eyebrow. "Isn't it?"

Arabella gave a humorless laugh. "Of course

not. You and John married for love. You defied everything to be together. Silas and I…it was just an arrangement. To help Anne." She glanced at Alice apologetically but continued on. "He needed an heir, I needed to restore our family's reputation for Anne's sake. That…that's all there was to it."

Alice scoffed and sat back. "You don't believe that any more than I do."

Arabella stared open-mouthed at her and then slumped back against her seat with a soft snort. "I'd forgotten how well you see through me."

Her sister just smiled and waited, and Arabella eventually sighed.

"That's all it started out to be. But somewhere along the way…"

"It became more."

She nodded and Alice smiled. "Then why are you sitting in my kitchen?"

"Because it's what he wants."

Alice raised a brow. "Are you certain of that?"

"Yes."

Alice didn't look convinced. "And what about the baby?"

She looked pointedly at Arabella's stomach, and Arabella looked up in surprise. "How did you know?"

Alice laughed. "It hasn't been so long since I was with child myself. I know the signs. How far gone are you?"

"Only a few weeks. The doctor said he won't be able to confirm just yet, but my courses are never late, and I've been so tired and ill lately. Charlotte seemed sure of my condition."

Alice nodded her head knowingly. "As am I. Congratulations."

"Thank you," Arabella said with a sad smile. "I was so happy about the baby and thought he would be also, but when I told him he seemed…I don't know. Pleased, but dismayed as well, I think. Or perhaps it was shock." She sighed. "I don't know."

Alice laughed. "That is a fairly typical male reaction, I think."

"Is it?" Ari asked, a small spark of hope flickering in her chest.

"Absolutely. Think about it. They'll now have this tiny offspring for whom they are responsible. And for someone like your husband, who had a well-known reputation for irresponsibility and often juvenile behavior—sorry—"

Ari waved her off, unable to argue against the description too much. Though, Silas was no longer quite the unthoughtful rascal he'd been when they'd wed. He'd changed. At least she'd thought he had.

Alice continued. "Becoming a father can be rather terrifying for someone who isn't used to having to think far beyond his own wants and needs."

Ari frowned. "I suppose. Still, if he'd wanted me to stay, all he'd had to do was ask. And he didn't."

"Did you tell him you wanted to?"

Ari bit her lip. "No."

Alice just stared at her, her look clearly saying what she was thinking, and Ari groaned.

"It's not that simple, Alice."

"Isn't it? Sounds to me like the two of you just need to have a good, honest conversation."

"I tried. But I still don't trust him. He's keeping something from me. And even that I might be able to live with. But this…" She shook her head and then told her sister what she'd seen when she followed him.

Alice frowned and chewed on her lip. "Did you tell him what you'd seen?"

"Yes. And he still wouldn't tell me who she was. And he wouldn't agree to stop seeing her."

Alice sighed. "I'll admit, it does seem suspicious. But you don't have any idea who this woman is. Perhaps she's a kinswoman?"

Arabella shook her head. "As far as I know, he doesn't have any other kin nearby. And if that was the case, why wouldn't he just tell me?" She frowned. "I do get the sense that there's something not quite right…it's more than just another woman. His grandfather is aware of her and disapproves of him seeing her. But, as much as I hate to say it, plenty of men have mistresses. I wouldn't expect them to be flaunted so openly, but such situations are typically open secrets. Not of the importance Silas and his grandfather seem to be placing on it. I just…I can't fathom what might be going on. If I can't trust him to be honest with me…and if he can't trust me enough to share his secrets… then what hope do we have?"

"I don't know," Alice said, taking her hand. "But you haven't known each other long. Only a couple months. Trust isn't always so easily given. Perhaps it will come in time, the more you get to know one another."

"Perhaps."

"Isn't it worth trying? For your little one?"

"I…I'm not sure. I've made such a mess of things. I don't know if he'd even want me to come back at this point, regardless of the child."

"I'm a bit surprised, considering you are carrying his heir, that he allowed you to go gallivanting about the countryside unaccompanied in the first place. I would think he'd welcome you home."

Arabella chewed her bottom lip and then sighed deeply. "I…left without telling him."

Alice's mouth dropped open at that. "He doesn't know where you are?"

"No. Though he probably assumes I'm at Fallcreek Abbey."

"Ari…"

"I'm sure he has no complaint. He's off on a trip of his own. Most likely with whoever that woman is." Actually, she wasn't sure of either of those things, but she didn't want to admit that to her sister. "We had an agreement. Once Anne was taken care of and I was with child, we'd go back to our own lives. I'd retire to Fallcreek and he could go back to living his life as he saw fit. I may not have told him the exact moment I was leaving, but he knew this moment would come."

"Yet you are not at Fallcreek."

Arabella frowned. "I know. I will let him know where I am. And I will return to Fallcreek. I just… need some time. I needed a place to gather my thoughts. The last few months, from the moment we met, have been…" She waved her hands, at a loss for words.

"I can imagine," Alice said. "And you are welcome to stay here as long as you need. But I would advise that you at least let your husband know you are safe. Even if you think he doesn't care for you, and I am not convinced of that, you are carrying his child."

Arabella nodded. "I know. You're right." She sighed deeply. "I will write him in the morning. For now, I would just like to rest."

Alice smiled and stood, drawing Arabella in for a hug. "Of course. I'll show you up to your room."

Arabella followed her gratefully, her mind still spinning. She knew she needed to let Silas know where she was. Eventually. But she would love a few days where she didn't have to think about him or their situation or what the future would hold.

Though she knew that would prove impossible.

# Chapter Twenty-Two

"What do you mean she isn't here?" Silas said, startling his housekeeper so much she blanched white and took a step back.

He took a deep breath and forced himself to calm down. Shouting at his staff wouldn't get him answers any faster, though they had better answer fast before the panic that was clawing its way through his gut grew worse.

"Hawley," he said, looking at his butler. "The duchess sent word to ready the house for her arrival. She left London weeks ago. Do you mean to tell me she isn't here? And no one thought to send word?"

"My apologies, Your Grace. She did arrive as expected. But she stayed only a few days and then departed for her family home. I'm afraid we didn't think to send word to you in London as we assumed you were aware of her plans. And as she was traveling to her father's estate, it did not seem odd…"

Silas nodded, keeping his outward calm, though inside he was roaring with frustration. And fear.

"She said nothing, gave no reason why she wanted to leave?"

"No, Your Grace. I'm sorry."

He turned and started up the stairs, taking them two at a time and forcing poor Hawley to run to keep up. "Did she stay in my chambers?"

"No, Your Grace. We readied your rooms for her, but when she found out she asked us to move her belongings to the Blue Bedroom."

Silas scowled again but headed for the Blue Bedroom, throwing the door open when he got there.

There were definite signs she'd been there. A small stack of books on the bedside table. A shawl he'd seen her wear draped over a chair.

"We weren't sure when she'd be returning, Your Grace. We felt it best to leave the books she'd chosen."

"Yes, yes, that's fine. You can go. Thank you."

He waited until the door closed and then walked to the stack of books. The top book sat askew, as if she'd just put it down. He ran his hand over the cover before picking it up and flipping through the pages, not seeing a word.

He had no such confidence that she'd return. Ever. Else why did she leave in the first place? And why didn't she take the books with her? His damn library was the only thing she wanted out of this marriage. She'd been so excited to come revel in it that she hadn't even waited for her sister's engagement ball but had left almost immediately after telling him about their child. Yet she didn't even take these few books that she'd personally chosen? Why?

He sank to the edge of the bed and rubbed a hand over his face.

Perhaps because she had no intention of ever returning and didn't wish to take anything with her that she didn't feel belonged to her.

Damn her and her ever-sacrificing nobleness.

She was wrong. He'd happily give her anything she wanted. It had all been hers since the moment she'd fallen into his arms. Everything. Everything belonged to her. Everything he had. This house. The library.

Him.

But she didn't want…any of it. And he wasn't going to force it, or himself, upon her. She never wanted this marriage in the first place. If she wanted to be left in peace, then that was what he would do. The last thing he wanted was to cause her more pain. He'd caused her enough already. So.

He sighed and ran his hand over his face again. For a man who had everything he'd ever wanted— freedom from marriage-seeking mamas, an heir on the way, and a wife who didn't want him—he was certainly miserable.

He snorted. He should have been more careful what he wished for. He took a deep breath and stood, looking down at the book he still held and making a sudden decision. If she didn't want him anymore, so be it. But she could at least have something that she actually *did* want.

"Hawley!" he called, marching out of the room. The man couldn't have gotten too far. "Hawley!"

"Yes, Your Grace?"

He spun around to look at the man who materialized behind him. "There you are. Find me a trunk or a couple of crates and bring them to the library."

Hawley's eyes widened slightly, but he didn't question the order, merely nodded and set off to make it happen.

Silas went to the library and spent the next several hours combing through his collection and choosing dozens of books he thought she might like. Books on poetry, animals, art. Every novel he could find. And finally the stack that she'd chosen for herself. It would do for a start. She could have them all if she wanted. He'd build her a library wherever she chose to live.

He just had to find her first.

A task that ended up being more difficult than he'd anticipated.

Two days later, he stood in the receiving room of Vinethorpe and stared at the butler who'd received him.

"What do you mean, she's not here?" he asked, fairly certain he'd just had this exact conversation. "She told the staff at Fallcreek that she would be traveling here and the coachman at the abbey drove her here himself."

"Yes, Your Grace. She *was* here, but only for a couple days."

He opened his mouth to say something and then snapped it closed again. While he doubted she'd purposely decided to send him on a wild chase around the English countryside, that was exactly what it felt like. Then again, maybe she *had* done it on purpose. She did enjoy riling him. And he undoubtedly deserved the aggravation.

"Where is she now?"

"She's gone to stay with her sister, Your Grace."

"Anne? Back in London?" Now that would be just his luck.

"No, Your Grace. With Mistress Alice. She lives at Oak Tree Lodge, just a few miles from here."

Finally. Progress!

He instructed his footman to unload the crates of books and the present he'd bought for her during his travels and set out on horseback for Oak Tree Lodge.

He didn't know what he'd say to her when he

got there. What could he say? He needed to tell her about Eliza. Ironically, that would be the easiest thing he had to tell her. Much easier than finding words for all the emotions tearing him up inside.

But when he arrived within sight of the house, he stopped short. Arabella stood in the backyard, laughing as she twirled a baby around before bringing him down for a cuddle. She looked so… carefree. Happy.

He clenched his jaw, that ache in his chest that had been there since he'd found her missing growing until it felt as though his heart would cleave right in two.

What sort of a fool was he? Running and hiding from his wife for weeks on end because he couldn't bear to hear her tell him she didn't want him, and then chasing her about the countryside so she could do just that while he begged her to take him back? And what good would that do? It would only distress her. Ruin the happiness she'd obviously finally found.

Riding away from her might destroy him. But better that than cause her a single moment of misery. What right did he have to take this happiness from her now?

They would see each other again. Soon. They must, for their child's sake. But he could give her the time she obviously needed. He would not intrude on her peace when she'd made it clear she didn't want him there.

He turned his horse and left, his heart breaking more and more with every beat of his horse's hooves.

But he had no one to blame but himself.

• • •

When Arabella finally returned to Vinethorpe, it was with a renewed sense of purpose. She'd stayed at Alice's much longer than she'd intended. But it had done her good. She hadn't realized how much she'd needed the respite. She still didn't know what she was going to do about her situation. But she couldn't leave things as they were. For her child's sake if not for her own. So, when she got back to London, she and Silas were going to have to figure things out.

She also had her sister in tow. Much to Alice's chagrin. She had done nothing but worry since the moment Arabella insisted she and John attend the engagement ball with her. Arabella still had doubts she'd get them to the actual party, but she'd gotten them as far as Vinethorpe, so there was hope.

She went straight to her room to pack the belongings she'd left there, Alice fast on her heels.

"I'm still not certain of this, Ari," Alice said for the dozenth time. "You know we won't be well received."

"Nonsense," Arabella said, though her sister spoke nothing but the truth. Until Silas had agreed to her scheme, even she and Anne weren't received, and they had done nothing wrong. Still, she was finally in a position to do something about the unfair treatment, and she wasn't going to allow her sister to be snubbed.

"You will be attending as the guests of the Duke and Duchess of Whittsley and the Duc D'Auvergne and his soon-to-be duchesse. No one will dare say a word."

Alice frowned, but even she couldn't argue against that.

"Now," Arabella said. "Anne's ball is in a few short days, and there is so much to do. I'm sure Aunt Adelaide has everything well in hand but having to deal with all the preparations on her own is more than we should have asked of her."

Alice laughed. "First of all, she is more than capable of running a full-scale military campaign. I'm sure a mere engagement ball, let alone the wedding, is proving no challenge. Besides, you know how she loves being in charge. She is probably in her element right now."

Arabella smiled fondly. "True. Still, an undertaking of this magnitude is a lot of work, and I didn't intend to leave her alone for as long as I did. Which is why we are heading back to London first thing in the morning."

She stopped with a gasp at the threshold of her room. Several crates were stacked at the foot of her bed, and a large flat package lay on the bed.

"What's all this?" Alice asked, peering around her shoulder.

"I don't know. I didn't leave them here."

"They must have been delivered after you left. Who are they from?"

There was only one person they could be from.

She picked up the letter on the top crate and opened it. It said simply, "These were always meant to be yours."

"What are they?" Alice asked.

Arabella lifted the lid from the first box with a shaking hand, her breath leaving her in a rush when she saw the books nestled inside. Each one she picked up made her heart beat faster. They were all on topics that interested her. In fact, quite a few were books she'd nearly chosen for her first reads but had put back for later.

They were too personally suited for her for the choices to be random. Silas must have hand-picked them. Which meant all those times she'd been chattering away about some topic she knew bored him to tears, he'd actually been listening. Arabella sank onto the edge of her bed, not know-ing what to think. This wasn't the act of a man who didn't want her. Who didn't know her. These books were chosen by someone who knew her deeply.

Someone who loved her?

"What is that?" Alice said, pointing at the wrapped object on the bed.

"I...I'm not sure." Arabella stood and pulled it toward her, carefully removing the wrapping.

By the time the entire painting was revealed, she could no longer hold back her tears.

"I take it this painting means something to you?" Alice asked gently.

Arabella looked up at her and smiled. "We saw it in the gallery one night." A pang of pure desire rushed straight to her core when she remembered what else had happened at the gallery that night.

Alice tilted her head with a knowing smile. "Obviously a good memory for you."

Arabella blushed but didn't elaborate. She ran a finger over the frame of the painting. "He asked me which of all the paintings there was my favorite. I chose this one. He didn't understand why I liked it."

"But he bought it for you anyway."

Arabella's breath left her in a rush. "It appears so. I..." She shook her head, truly at a loss for words.

"Perhaps he cares for you more than you think."

Did he? Her heart skipped and she pressed a hand to the small round bump of her belly. Perhaps there was a chance for them after all.

Though…there was still the matter of the glaring secret he refused to share…

"I wonder when these arrived," Alice said, making Arabella's stomach drop to her toes.

She'd been gone for over a month. If he'd brought these to her just after she'd left, hoping maybe for them to come to an understanding, he might assume after not hearing from her for so long that she had no interest in reconciling. And nothing could be further from the truth. Perhaps. There were still matters to clear up but…she was at least open to discussion…but if he thought she wasn't…

She jumped up and hurried down the stairs, looking for the housekeeper or butler or anyone who could tell her when Silas had been here. If he had even come himself. More likely he'd just had the boxes shipped. But still…

"Ah," she said, upon finding the housekeeper in the salon with John, overseeing the tea service. "Mrs. Berth, the crates in my room…when did they arrive?"

"Oh, several weeks ago now, Your Grace. Did the duke not find you?"

"What?" she asked, her stomach clenching with dread.

"The duke, Your Grace. He brought the crates and the painting, and when he was told where you were, he set out for Oak Tree Lodge. He didn't return, so we assumed he'd found you."

Arabella dropped to the sofa, the sudden on-slaught of emotions roiling within her threatening to choke her. "Thank you," she managed to whisper.

"Perhaps a nice pot of tea would help," Alice said, and the housekeeper nodded, sending the maid off for two more cups before following after her.

"He must think…" Arabella trailed off.

"It doesn't matter," Alice said. "If he cared enough to bring everything here himself, then he cares enough to wait for your response."

"Does he?"

"There's only one way to find out," Alice said with a twinkle in her eye. "There's still enough time to make it to London before nightfall."

For a moment, excitement rushed through Arabella, and she nearly jumped up to order the carriage to be readied straight away. Until she remembered what day it was.

She sat back with a laugh that sounded more like a sob. "He won't be there. It's Wednesday."

Alice sighed and sat beside her. "You'll never know what is going on or who that woman is until you ask him."

"I have asked him, Alice. Repeatedly."

"Perhaps now he's ready to tell you."

"What woman?" John said with a frown.

Arabella couldn't bear to tell him something so shameful, so Alice quickly filled him in. John's frown grew deeper though he seemed more confused than upset. He rubbed a finger over his upper lip.

"I wonder if she could be his sister."

Alice and Arabella looked at him in stunned silence and he looked between them, surprised and a bit amused. "It was the talk of the town for months," he said. "Well, at least among the servants. The Whittsleys did do an admirable job keeping everything quiet."

"Keeping what quiet," Alice said.

"The duke isn't an only child, or at least that's the rumor. My mother's cousin was a maid in the household and was there the night his sister was born. It was a difficult birth and the duchess died shortly after. The duke wanted nothing to do with the child. Some assumed it was because he was mad with grief over losing his wife and blamed the baby. But there were whispers that the duchess had had a lover and the child belonged to the other man. So the duke sent her away."

"The poor child," Alice said, and Arabella's hand strayed to her belly, protectively cradling her own baby. "What happened to her?"

John lifted a shoulder. "No one knows. The family never mentioned the child again, and anyone who knew of her probably assumed she'd died with her mother. And with the duke following not long after his wife, the gossip died down soon enough."

Arabella rubbed at the ache in her chest, feeling like the pieces of the puzzle that made up Silas were finally falling into place. If this were true, it would make sense why he couldn't tell her such a horrible secret. Why his grandfather, a man so determined to maintain the reputation of their family, and apparently his daughter, would so disapprove of Silas having any contact with his sister for fear the secret would get out. Such a tale would be the talk of the town for years. It was a miracle the Whittsleys had managed to keep it all a secret for so long. No wonder Silas was so protective of her. Wouldn't she do anything to protect her sisters?

Just the thought of Silas caused the crack in her heart to open wider. What a terrible burden for him to bear all these years. And she had only made it worse.

"I…I must go," she said, jumping to her feet.

Alice and John didn't even question her. John merely stood and nodded. "I'll have them ready the carriage."

Arabella smiled at him gratefully.

Alice took her hand. "We'll go with you. Our belongings haven't been unpacked yet and we were all going to London anyway. You shouldn't be alone in this."

Arabella hugged her sister. "What have I done?"

Alice held her and rubbed her back like her mother used to do when they were little. "You've done nothing wrong. You didn't know the situation." She pulled away enough so she could look at Arabella's face. "And remember, we aren't sure that is who the woman really is."

No. But it made the most sense. It explained his absences, his secrecy. And how he could be so tender and loving with her, seem to care for her so much, after just coming from the arms of another woman. If that woman were his sister and not his mistress…then perhaps he did care for her. Maybe even loved her. As much as she loved him.

Unfortunately, the moment they arrived in London, Aunt Adelaide descended in full hysterics, panicking over the next day's ball. By the time they calmed her down and got everything sorted, the hour was late, and Arabella could barely keep her eyes open.

Tomorrow then. Surely he'd come to the ball. He was still family. Jean-Pierre was still his friend, and he'd been instrumental in matching the couple. She would find him at the ball.

Her last thought before her exhausted eyes closed was a quick prayer that the man she'd promised to leave forever would be there. And be happy to see her.

# Chapter Twenty-Three

Silas stood at the window in his study, watching the moon peek through the branches of the trees in the garden. He'd hoped looking at a peaceful setting would impart some of that peace to his soul. But it was no use. He would never find peace without Arabella by his side. And he'd long since stopped hoping she would return to him. He'd had no word, from her or about her, in weeks. He'd hoped once she saw his gifts, she'd realize how he felt about her. But perhaps it wasn't enough. Or maybe it was just too late.

His hand clenched at his side, and he scowled at his reflection in the glass. Or maybe he should try speaking to her in person instead of waiting for her to decipher his feelings from a box of dusty old books and a depressing painting.

He growled in frustration and spun around, marching for the door. He never should have ridden away from her that day. He should have gone to her, told her how he felt, told her about Eliza, and explained why he hadn't told her before. Begged her to forgive him. To give them another chance. To come home with him.

Instead, like a coward, he'd left. Too afraid of hurting her to tell her the truth. Or perhaps he needed to start admitting he was too afraid of her rejecting him to tell her the truth.

Well, no more. She might very well throw him out on his ear, but he would tell her everything that was in his heart. And pray she felt even an inkling of what he felt for her.

Because he couldn't live without her anymore.

He shoved his arms into his jacket and jammed his fingers into his gloves. Anne's engagement ball had already begun. And no matter where his wife might be spending her days now, she wouldn't miss her sister's ball. She hadn't responded to his other overtures, but he'd bribed Aunt Adelaide to let him add a few things to the ballroom. If that didn't get his wife's attention, well…he'd have to resort to dropping to his knees in front of her and begging.

He was tempted to walk to the Bromleys'. The fresh air would do him good, calm his nerves a bit. But the carriage would come in handy if he was able to talk some sense into his wife.

The ride was excruciatingly brief, and thankfully the ball was in full swing when he arrived. He tried to blend in with the crowd as much as he was able, being unforgivably rude to his friends and acquaintances when they tried to greet him. His mind was not on pleasantries and for once in his life, he found it impossible to pretend. Glancing around the room, he saw that Aunt Adelaide had acquiesced to his request after all, and he breathed a sigh of relief. And anticipation. Now he waited.

"Whittsley," Charles said, looking him up and down as he came to stand beside him. "You look… positively constipated. Is something amiss?"

Silas snorted. "Everything is amiss. But I'm hoping to remedy that shortly."

"Really? I look forward to watching."

Silas shot him a glare and Charles laughed, stopping abruptly when Silas held up a hand to silence him.

"What is it?" Charles asked when Silas tilted his head and frowned.

"They are playing a waltz," he said.

Charles's eyes widened a fraction. "Yes. They often do that at balls, I've heard."

Silas ignored that. "Didn't they just play one?"

"Did they?" Charles asked with a shrug.

Silas clapped his friend on the back. "If you'll excuse me a moment, I…"

Charles just smiled. "I saw her a few minutes ago near the back doors."

Silas flashed him a grateful grin and made his way through the crowd again, barely hearing those who tried to pull him into a conversation. He needed to see her. Even if she wouldn't speak with him. He could come up with a foolproof kidnapping plot later; he just wanted to reassure himself that she was well. That she—

He stopped short, the breath leaving his body in a rush. She stood near a large potted plant at the corner of the dance floor, her gaze fixed on a stack of books that had been arranged on a small table.

Her fingers glided lovingly over the volumes, and he knew she'd love nothing more than to sweep the whole stack up and go hide away in the corner. Though at the same time, she'd want to stay and make sure her sister's party was flawless. Because that's just who she was. No matter what the cost to herself, she'd ensure her loved ones were taken care of, happy. And she'd be unwavering in her pursuit of their happiness. His tenacious little spitfire.

He'd known from the first moment she'd tumbled into his arms that she'd be more than a handful. The hurt ankle had been a painfully obvious ploy, though the fall, he'd bet his dinner, had been real. He couldn't imagine what it had cost her to go to his house that day. Flout convention. Risk further ostracism. She'd gone to the home of the most eligible bachelor in London and offered to bear his child. His mind still reeled from the shock. But he couldn't resist her then. And he still couldn't.

He was hers. Forever. To do with as she

pleased. To order through whatever outrageous schemes crossed her mind. He'd do whatever she asked. Even agree to however many new rules she wanted to impose.

As long as she agreed to stay with him, always.

He watched her, his heart pounding in his chest, as she wandered to another table adorned with a selection of books and shook her head. A small smile played on her lips, and when she glanced up, her eyes looked suspiciously bright.

He took a step forward and stopped again when the notes of the next piece floated through the ballroom. A waltz. Again. The third in a row. Or was it the fourth?

His breath punched out of him in a silent laugh and happiness washed through him.

That diabolically wonderful creature.

• • •

Arabella stared down at the books, swallowing hard past the sudden lump in her throat. When she'd seen the first stack, she hadn't thought much of it. A random stack of books on the foyer table was odd, of course, especially on this particular night. Aunt Adelaide had Bromley House running like clockwork, and Arabella pitied the servant who had left the books there.

But then she'd entered the refreshment room.

There had been a stack of books on a table near the door. And two books left on the chaise in the corner. And another on the chair beside the alcove in the hall.

In the ballroom, she'd found three more stacks scattered strategically throughout the room. Always near an out-of-the-way corner or placed on a comfortable seat. A place she might want to curl up and escape for a moment should the festivities prove too taxing.

Had she not agreed to rule number five, that is.

She'd always prefer hiding in a corner with her books to socializing with…well, just about anyone. But with Silas at her side, she didn't mind it quite so much. In fact, everything was easier when she was with him.

Oh, the man drove her to distraction and would probably turn every one of her hairs gray before she was thirty. But the moment he'd caught her in his arms, she'd known that was the only place she wanted to be. These weeks without him had been nothing short of miserable. Never in a hundred years would she have thought she'd prefer the company of a rule-breaking, flippant, hedonistic libertine to the pleasures of solitude and a magnificent library, but…here she was. Pining over the man.

If he could ever forgive her for stubbornly insisting on following those damn rules.

The band struck up the chords of a new waltz and she glanced around. She'd had a word with them before the guests had arrived. No waltzes until the Duke of Whittsley had appeared. And afterward…

Her gaze met his and she sucked in a breath. And then promptly forgot how to breathe until he took a step in her direction. And another. His eyes never leaving hers until he stood before her.

"Arabella," he murmured, standing so close there was barely a breath of air between them. But he still hadn't touched her. Instead, he watched her with a hint of trepidation, as if he weren't sure how he'd be received. Or, more likely, was afraid that if he made any sudden moves, she'd bolt.

"Was this you?" she asked, her fingers trailing over the books, though she still hadn't torn her gaze from his.

He gave her a slow smile that had her heart leaping from her chest. "I thought you might want to escape from your guests for a few moments."

"But that's against the rules."

"Hmm. So it is," he said, holding out a hand. "I believe they are playing a waltz, wife. For the fourth, or is it the fifth, time now?"

She took his hand, giving him a smile that had his fingers tightening around hers. "So they are."

"Planning on obliterating rule number seven?" he asked, drawing her into his arms.

She shook her head. "From now on, all my dances are yours, Your Grace. If you want them."

He pulled her with him into the alcove and then crushed her to his chest, wrapping his arms about her with a groan. He buried his face in her neck, and she wrapped her arms about him, taking her first real breath in a long time.

"I hope you meant that, because I'm never letting you go again," he murmured, and she let out a sob and sank against him.

She didn't know how long they just stood there holding each other. She could have remained there in that moment forever, clinging to him like ivy to a trellis.

He finally pulled away, just enough to press a kiss to her forehead before drawing her down to the sofa with him. His fingers brushed across her cheeks and then his gaze strayed to where her hands cradled the small bump of her belly. He reached out, then hesitated.

"May I?" he asked, and her heart swelled so much she thought it might burst.

She nodded and smiled up at him, and some of the ice that had settled in her chest over the past several weeks shattered, filling her with warmth.

His hand cupped her belly, and she placed her hands over the top of his. He released a shuddering breath.

"Our child," he said, with such awed reverence

in his voice that she couldn't speak past the lump in her throat.

He pressed a kiss to her temple and rested his forehead against hers for a brief moment before drawing in a breath. "Arabella, I owe you an apology. And an explanation," he said, sitting back. "I should have told you long ago. I thought I was doing the right thing. But I should have trusted you with the truth. The woman you saw me with that day was my sister, Eliza. She…" He trailed off, obviously not quite sure how to explain the whole complicated history of his family.

She took his hand. "It's all right. I know enough."

His eyes flashed to hers. "You do?"

"Yes. I'll explain later. For now…thank you for telling me. For trusting me."

"Are you…did you only return for Anne's ball or…"

His eyes searched hers and then he flashed that grin that never failed to make her heart sing.

"It was the books, wasn't it? You came back for the books."

She laughed. He always fell back on that humor of his when he was uneasy. God, she loved him. "Yes. I was afraid you'd empty that beautiful library of yours and bury Vinethorpe in a mountain of crated volumes."

"Whatever will make you stay," he said,

his eyes dancing. "Charles has a rather robust library. I'm sure I could abscond with a few dozen volumes, and he'd never notice."

She laughed again and put her hand up to cup his cheek. "I appreciate the thought, but it's unnecessary."

"Is it?"

"I came back for you, Silas. Just you. I want to stay. To have a true marriage. To be with you. If…if you want me."

"If?" he said, his breath leaving him with a laugh. Or a sob. She couldn't tell which and it didn't matter.

He pulled her to him again and kissed her. Over and over again. "I think it's the only thing I've ever truly wanted in my life."

"That can't be true," she said, partly joking. Partly not. It was still nearly impossible to believe this man who'd stolen her heart could want her as much as she wanted him.

He pulled away just far enough so he could gaze down at her. "I don't think you understand what you've done to me. You've changed me, Ari. Changed my life. I couldn't go back to the way things were even if I wanted to. I probably should have run when I had the chance," he said, chuckling, and she laughed, a fine tremor running through her. "But despite my worst intentions, you've made me want to be a better man. One who is still not worthy to claim you. But who will spend the rest of his life endeavoring to be so."

"Silas," she breathed, trailing her fingers along his jawline. "You give yourself far too little credit."

He chuckled again. "Now that is something of which no one has ever accused me, madam. If nothing else, I give myself far too much credit on a regular basis."

"No, you don't," she said, giving him a gentle smile. She shook her head, her heart bubbling over with love for the man in front of her. The man who'd lost his parents too young, who'd had too much responsibility thrust on him far too early. Who craved love and acceptance probably more than he'd ever realize. But she saw him. Saw all of him. And loved every part.

"You tease and make jokes at your own expense and yes, perhaps occasionally there is a slight delusion of grandeur." He barked out a laugh and she grinned and then cupped his cheek. "But you are a good man, Silas. Better than most. A man I am very honored to call mine."

His eyes flashed before closing for the briefest of seconds. "Yours," he murmured. "For now and always."

He rubbed his thumb under her bottom lip, his other hand coming up to cup her face. "I love you, my wife." He rested his forehead against hers, and she sucked in a breath, trying, and failing, to contain the ecstatic joy that filled her. "I love you so much I may burst with it."

She laughed again and smiled up at him. "I love you, too, my husband. So very, very much."

He brushed a thumb across her cheek and looked intently into her eyes. "I know I should dissuade you from this as I am quite possibly the worst man you could choose to be your husband. But I'm selfish and greedy and would commit any number of unspeakable sins to keep you by my side for the rest of my days. So, I will very happily beg you to stay with me. Always."

Her laughter spilled over again. "While I don't agree with your assessment of yourself, there is nowhere I'd rather be than at your side. So yes. I shall stay."

He kissed her again, his lips moving over hers, obliterating all the weeks of longing and heartache. She could feel every ounce of love and passion that he fed into that kiss, and she gave it back to him, pouring her heart and soul into every brush of her lips against his. All the waiting, the unknowing, the doubt and confusion…all of it evaporated. Gone. Replaced with an outpouring of love that she wasn't sure her heart could contain.

She finally pulled away, breathless and beaming, but he kept his arms about her, like he was unwilling to let her go just yet. Which was just fine by her.

"You know," he murmured against her skin as he pressed a kiss to her neck, "I think we're going to need a new set of rules. Especially since I burned the other one."

Her eyes widened and she lifted her head so she could meet his gaze. "You did?"

"I can be a bit destructive, I'm afraid," he said with a shrug.

She laughed, her happiness overflowing and filling her with a glowing warmth. "I guess I'll have to keep a better eye on you."

"Dance with me," he said, drawing her to her feet.

"I suppose they *are* playing a waltz."

Silas chuckled. "We should probably tell the musicians they may play something else before the guests think this is the oddest ball they have ever attended."

Arabella delicately snorted. "I'd wager it's a bit late for that." She glanced up at him from under her lashes. "So, if you burned our agreement, does that mean I may waltz with other partners?"

"Absolutely not. Waltzes still belong to me."

She pursed her lips together. "Not very charitable of you."

"Thank you for noticing." He spun them out from the alcove and held her tight when her steps faltered.

"Silas, everyone can see us now."

"Good." He leaned down and kissed her, a bare brush across her lips that somehow still managed to send her blood racing through her veins.

"I do not believe that would count as an appropriate display of affection."

Silas's smile had her breath catching in her throat. "I think that part of our agreement should be modified."

"Do you now?"

He nodded sagely. "Public displays of affection should now be encouraged, appropriate or not." Then he leaned down to murmur in her ear, his warm breath sending shivers across her skin. "Private displays of affection will be varied and plentiful and will be rewarded by more such displays." He pressed a quick kiss to her neck and straightened. "Though gifts of other sorts will be happily received as well."

She laughed. "Is that all?"

Silas frowned suddenly and Arabella followed his gaze to where his grandfather stood chatting with the happily engaged couple.

"I wouldn't mind if you would kindly continue to sing my praises to my grandfather."

She laughed again. "It would be my pleasure. Especially as such praises seem to have improved familial relations considerably."

"That they have." He smiled down at her.

"Anything else?"

"I think we can worry about the rest later. We have our whole lives to get them right."

He laughed and gathered her close. "I look forward to the negotiation."

# Epilogue

Arabella stood at the window in her wedding finery, watching the heartwarming scene taking place in the garden while she waited for Silas to finish getting ready. And he needed to hurry, or they'd be late for Anne's wedding.

She finally heard his footsteps come up behind her, but she didn't turn, and he slid his arms around her from behind. She leaned back against him with a contented sigh.

"We're going to be late," she admonished. "Can you never be on time for anything?"

He chuckled. "My audience expects perfection. Perfection takes time."

She laughed but rolled her eyes. "I think the audience will be there for Anne and Jean-Pierre."

He shrugged. "We may have to disagree on that point, my dear."

She laughed again. "You're ridiculous."

"I know. But don't tell anyone."

"It'll be our secret," she said with a soft snort.

He hugged her close and watched out the window with her for a few moments. "I never thanked you," he said quietly, all humor gone from his voice.

"For what?"

"For bringing Eliza here. She's been so happy."

Arabella entwined her fingers with his and gently squeezed. "We're her family. She belongs with us."

He kissed her cheek and rested his chin on her shoulder as they watched Eliza on the back lawn, playing with four-month-old Arthur under the watchful eye of his nurse. Arthur had recently discovered the delights of the peek-a-boo game and giggled and kicked his chubby little legs at Eliza, who would happily play with him for hours.

Arabella had stayed at Fallcreek the majority of the year with Arthur and Eliza, preferring the quiet of the country to the bustling city. Silas traveled back and forth, though he'd been taking to staying longer and longer at Fallcreek. They would likely still come to the city for the season every year, though mostly to visit Anne and Jean-Pierre who would spend most of their time there after they were wed. And for Eliza's first season, of course, though Silas grew adorably cross whenever the subject was broached. He was frightfully protective of his little sister. Arabella was determined to find her a husband who would make her as happy as Arabella was herself. Silas would just have to grow used to the idea.

Their grandfather…he had been a surprise. Lord Mosley, once it became obvious Silas had no intention of keeping Eliza hidden away, had, for the most part, kept his opinions to himself. While he hadn't welcomed Eliza with open arms the moment she'd stepped through the door, he'd been civil to her. Kind even, when he thought no one was watching. Arabella had caught him staring at Eliza with a look of wonderment a few times.

And no wonder…she was the image of her mother. And was often the only one who could get Lord Mosley in an agreeable mood. Miracles *did* happen. The crueler members of society had spread their gossip, as they were wont to do. But a new scandal soon took its place. There was always a newer, juicier scandal waiting around the corner.

As for Alice and John, they were happy where they were, though Arabella was thrilled they had taken to visiting Fallcreek more.

Silas nuzzled at her neck. "I know we never agreed upon a second heir, but if you are willing to negotiate…"

Arabella laughed and turned in his arms to kiss him properly. "We can discuss that later. We have a wedding to attend."

Silas scowled and Arabella laughed again. "Until Anne is duly wed, your part of our agreement is technically unfulfilled. Whereas, if you'll notice," she said, gesturing to their fat, happy baby on the lawn, "I've fulfilled my part quite admirably, if I do say so myself."

Silas followed her into the entry hall. "I would like to point out that it is not my fault your sister and her patient fiancé decided to have a fashionably long engagement. How was I to know they wouldn't want to cause more gossip by rushing into a hasty marriage like her reckless elder sisters?"

"Yes, well, Anne has always been the odd one in the family."

"I don't know about that…"

"Oh," she said, playfully hitting his arm.

Silas put a hand to his chest. "I would also like to point out that not only did I find your sister a husband, but I found no less than a duke and therefore you owe me a favor which I have yet to claim."

Arabella raised a brow and wrapped her arms around her husband's waist. "Oh? But that was part of our old agreement. Which you told me you'd burned."

"Well, yes, but I'm sure I have a copy lying around here somewhere."

She chuckled and squeezed him tighter. "And what favor would you claim?"

"Hmm," he said, pulling her in for a quick kiss. "I haven't quite decided, but I'm leaning toward a puppy."

She closed her eyes and shook her head.

"Heaven help me."

Silas kissed the tip of her nose. "I'm sorry, my love, but I'm afraid it's too late for divine intervention. You're stuck with me. Although I think I might want to put that in writing, just in case you decide to bolt again."

Arabella sighed and looked to the ceiling. "Lord give me strength."

Silas snorted and clapped his hat on his head. "I'm pretty sure the Lord washed his hands of me long ago. I'm your problem now."

She laughed, her happiness bubbling through her. "You're absurd. Now, let's go hurry this wedding along."

He caught Arabella around the waist and hauled her to him for a very thorough kiss. "And when we return home, we'll get started on heir number two. I need at least four more."

"You want five children?" she exclaimed.

"At least. Though should it come to that, we can add an addendum granting you a day to yourself every month. Actually, you should have that in any case as I—and I'm sure my offspring will be likely to follow—am no doubt exhausting."

"Truer words have never been spoken."

"Wonderful! Well, since you concur, I propose our heir-making attempts should occur as often as possible. Where's Charlotte?" he said, looking around. "She needs to write that down."

"You're incorrigible!" Arabella said with mock outrage. "But even still, I will happily agree."

"I'm glad to hear it," he said, drawing her in for a kiss that left her breathless. "In fact, we can add that to the new agreement."

"What?" she asked, still a bit dazed. He should not be allowed to kiss her like that when they were having a discussion. Trying to concentrate on anything but him was near impossible.

"That I shall make every effort to ensure you are happy. I don't even mind accompanying you on more of your odd little excursions."

"Really?"

He shrugged. "They haven't been nearly as bad as I'd feared. Though I reserve the right to object to these occasions. Just in case."

She laughed. "Very well then. And you have already made me very happy, Silas," she said, rising onto her toes to wrap her arms about his neck.

"As you have made me, my love."

"Then that is all we need."

He smiled and then lifted her and gave her a kiss that had her toes curling.

When he finally pulled away and set her down, he kept her hand in his. "There is only one more stipulation I'd insist upon."

She raised a brow. "And what is that?"

"I think we can agree to live our lives where we see fit, so long as we agree with the unavoidable necessity that we must remain together. Because I love you too damn much to ever be apart."

She sighed happily. "With that rule, I whole-heartedly approve."

"Excellent."

"Although," she said with a slight frown, "what fun are rules if we don't wish to break them?"

Silas pulled her to him with a laugh and kissed her again. "I've created a monster," he said, smiling against her lips. "Never fear. We can always throw in a few that are made to be broken."

She beamed up at him. "Deal."

# The Revised Rules

1. ~~Both parties will happily make every effort to achieve the other's happiness.~~

2. ~~They will keep trying for babies for as long as it takes. Heir-making attempts will occur as often as possible.~~

3. ~~Public displays of affection are encouraged, appropriate or not. Private displays of affection will be varied and plentiful and will be rewarded by more such displays. Though gifts of other sorts will be happily received as well.~~

4. ~~The duke and duchess will discuss which events they wish to attend together and will stay for as long as mutually decided upon.~~

5. ~~The duchess gets a day to herself every month because the duke (and likely his offspring) is exhausting.~~

6. ~~The duchess may still waltz only with the duke.~~

7. ~~The duke will accompany the duchess to~~

whichever odd and non-societal excursions that she wishes. They haven't been nearly as bad as he'd feared. He reserves the right to object, however, in the event such suggested occasion be too far from interest or propriety.

8. The duchess will kindly continue to sing the duke's praises to his grandfather. Such praises have improved familial relations considerably.

9. As the duchess's sister is now married to a foreign duke of extreme wealth and is deliriously happy, the duke reserves the right to claim his favor from the duchess. He's leaning toward a puppy.

10. The duke and duchess agree to live their lives as they see fit, spending their time in both town and country, so long as they comply with the unavoidable necessity that they must remain together. For each loves the other too much to remain apart.

The Only Rule: The duke and duchess will endeavor to live happily ever after.

# Acknowledgments

Thank you to Liz Pelletier, my fabulous editor and publisher—you always make me feel like I'm capable of accomplishing anything, and I can't tell you how wonderful it is to have you in my corner. I love that you are always just as excited as I am by these stories, and I can't wait to create more of them with you! Lydia Sharp, you are amazing and wonderful and I am so grateful I get to work with you. Thank you so much for everything you do for me! And to the dream team at Entangled—Jessica, Riki, Debbie, Curtis, Meredith, Heather, Katie, and all the amazing people behind the scenes—thank you so much for your hard work and support from start to finish and in between. To Bree, Elizabeth, and Toni—thank you for making this book gorgeous inside and out! And Toni, you have been there with me since the very beginning. The better part of two decades at this point! Thank you for always being there for me. Having a friend like you is truly priceless.

Thank you to my agent extraordinaire, Janna Bonikowski, for all your support, guidance, and hard work on my behalf. You always have my back and always have time to spitball ideas and geek out with me over them, and you help make a tough job a little more fun.

To my historical gals—Lexi Post, Sapna Bhog, and Heather McCollum—I love our chats so much! It's been wonderful having your support and friendship. Thank you all! And to Lisa Rayne, I have so loved getting to know you. You have kept me sane, kept me writing, and kept me loving what I do, even when I hate it, and I can't thank you enough! You arc always there when I need to brainstorm, vent, or just relax and chat with a friend, and I am grateful to have you in my life.

To my sweet husband, Tom, I know I drive you nuts, but you hang in there with me anyway. Thank you for always being there to help me find the glasses that are on my head, make sure my clothing is on the right way, and go above and beyond to calm my anxiety. I couldn't do this without you. You are my rock and I love you forever. To Connor and Ryanna, you are my world. Always. I'm glad you aren't too embarrassed by your eccentric old mother, because I'm afraid to tell you it's probably just going to get worse! I love you both to the moon and back. To my parents, siblings, and family who have loved and supported me from day one—you'll never know how much it means. Thank you all!

And to all my readers out there—you guys are why I get to do what I do. Thank you for all the love and support!